Works by S.M. Perlow

Vampires and the Life of Erin Rose

Novels
Choosing a Master
Alone
Lion
Hope
War

Short Stories
Alice Stood Up

—

The Grand Crucible

Novels
Golden Dragons, Gilded Age

—

Other Works

Short Stories
The Girl Who Was Always Single

WAR

VAMPIRES AND THE LIFE OF ERIN ROSE

S.M. Perlow

Bealion Publishing

A Bealion Publishing Book

Editor: Lynn O'Dell, Red Adept Editing Services
Cover design: Streetlight Graphics
Formatting: Polgarus Studio

smperlow.com—updates, social media links, and more
information about the story

ISBN: 978-0-9992858-4-8

1.0.4-p1

1

Beneath a starry Virginia sky, a simple wooden casket rested on a metal frame, ready to be lowered into a hole in the earth. Zhilan stood closest, with her hundred-nine-year-old fledgling, Renshu. They faced gray-haired, leather-skinned Father DeFrancesco. Grant and Max bracketed me, a little farther back. Behind the priest, across the long cemetery field, a gust of wind pushed bright flickers of flame up the hill.

The wide blaze approached, rolling over gravestones large and small. The expanding, heightening wall of yellow and orange flared from a glowing red base.

Notes of the flavor of Ariane's ancient blood crawled through my mind. The inferno bore down on my immortal friends, me, and the very mortal priest saying words over the drained body we had all gathered to say goodbye to. Five rows until flame devoured Father DeFrancesco.

The raging fire consumed a line of gravestones, then another. Markers adorned with crosses or with angels and flowers carved into them, and those with long epitaphs burned the same as the plain stones, just like the dry, manicured grass between them.

Four rows.

The fire grew twice as tall and wider, filling my field of vision—a massive tidal wave of destruction. Three rows until Zhilan's human friend's coffin. I could outrun the blaze. At the last second—the last instant—I could dart away. All the vampires could. Two rows. The old priest wouldn't get far at all.

No sound accompanied the wave. One row. No heat from it warmed my immortal skin.

Mid-sentence, furious flames reduced Father DeFrancesco to ash. Lithe Zhilan and solid Renshu fared no better. Nor did I. The fire seared my short chestnut hair and tore through my black clothes, the light skin of my long legs and toned arms, and my defenseless emerald eyes.

I blinked, and the inferno vanished. Lush green grass filled the grid between unburned gravestones. Father DeFrancesco, still speaking, was fine, as were Zhilan and all my friends. I was unhurt. Tao's lifeless body lay untouched inside the casket.

On a few occasions, I had awakened to vivid recollections of the hellfire I had glimpsed in Ariane's blood months before, and I let that vision play out at the funeral because it felt especially appropriate. While the fires of Hell had not risen from their divine depths, a blanket of fresh darkness was descending upon everyone, everywhere. The harsh world was getting harsher.

––––––––––––––––

The red rain changed everything.

Victoria had no definitive answer as to why it had

happened or what it meant. She had been disappointed after seeing the beam of flame rise from the chapel in Blatten, Switzerland, ending in a terrible ball of raging fire. "Shaken" might even have been a fair description of her reaction, but nothing more dramatic or longer lasting. The roots of Victoria's faith had grown deep over eight hundred years.

She had estimated that the Spectavi would run out of synthetic blood two months after that rain had fallen all over the world. During the seven weeks since, she had honed in on the specific date. The line from the Spectavi vampires to their human government allies—offered via their global corporation, Eure—refuted the existence of any serious problems. Modifications to the synthetic had been necessary, but were easily implemented. The truth was that, while Eure's factories continued to churn out the company's pharmaceutical, defense, and consumer products, along with all the rest, synthetic blood remained impossible to create. National governments had a clearer picture about that, though they were being fed baseless assurances of an imminent solution, when in fact, the Spectavi had made no progress at all.

The red rain had rendered nearly every mortal man and woman's blood useless to all Sanguan vampires, including me. Like flavorless water, nothing came with my drinks— no feelings, taste, or fire to feed my thirst.

Blood banks had been ransacked and run dry of nourishing drinks for vampires, but I had Luke and Caleb. And while I had a hunch as to why their blood remained hot, succulent, and as full of thoughts, memories, and emotions as before, it was only a hunch. More certain, and dangerous to them, based on reports worldwide, their blood would still feed *any* vampire.

Amid the guesses and speculation about the cause of the red rain, the idea that the end could be near for Sanguans had gained traction. The Spectavi would be fine, people and pundits in the dark about their production problems reasoned, paying no heed to the increasingly perilous nighttime or the existence of those like Luke and Caleb.

When Spectavi responded to Sanguan attacks alongside the police, sometimes the synthetic drinkers won. Other times, the drinkers of human blood prevailed, and almost always, men and women ended up broken, drained, or both. Enterprising Sanguans with a sense of restraint found a reliable source of replenishing blood in kidnappings. I hadn't heard from Blaine, my goofy club-going friend, in two weeks, but if he'd met a sad fate, it had likely been murder and not abduction, considering his blood would not quench a vampire's thirst.

Far fewer people went out after sundown, and Sanguan clubs had become significantly less crowded as rules preventing attacks in the establishments stopped being consistently enforced. However, the night of Tao's funeral, on the balcony level of a big club in Arlington, with my knife—a thin seven-inch blade that folded into a black aluminum handle—strapped to the outside of my leg, I watched a packed dance floor of ebullient humans.

Music pounded. Darkness pervaded. The lack of space meant most men and women danced in the small range from intense to passionate. Like other clubs around the world, the place had filled because of a Sanguan call for humans to rise up and "show the world that the time had come for the Spectavi to fall, not the Sanguans."

Caterine and Ariane—the first vampires the world had ever known—initially had their names invoked to endorse the rallying cry by Sanguans in Perth, Australia and then by others all over. The message had gone viral online and received extensive coverage on television and in print. Humans found a variety of reasons to be excited. A lot of people had grown tired of the gloomy nights since the red rain and simply wanted to get out. Others enthusiastically supported the Sanguans and opposed the Spectavi—either in general or specifically because they believed the stories of Spectavi leadership using synthetic blood to control the minds of their vampires. Some people merely hoped to catch a glimpse of the famous French identical twins.

While Caterine and Ariane kept silent, rumors of which clubs they would attend were driving capacity crowds in cities everywhere into frenzied states. I had my doubts, but local whispers pointed to the twins appearing in Arlington, amid the same scene I watched from the balcony.

"Call your friends!" a ragged Sanguan near the DJ shouted over the music. "We'll open the rooftop if enough show up!"

The crowd cheered.

The Sanguan raised his fist. "We'll make the government, the police, and those Spectavi bastards hear us!"

The roaring response faded as the pulsing beats and dancing picked up. Blood drinking was an infrequent sight, and considering how the world had changed, it made sense, but nevertheless struck me as a big difference from every other time I had been to a club.

In the far corner of the room, two Sanguans spoke into each other's ears to keep their conversation private. A vampire with noticeably gray skin stumbled in. The tint of his flesh almost certainly meant he was starving. As his eyes grew wide, another Sanguan rushed to him and pulled him to the side of the room.

I grabbed my knife from its scabbard.

A large group of men pushing their way out to the middle of the dance floor met considerable resistance from those already occupying the space. A guy punched someone. Another guy punched back. Flying fists and angry shoving spread out from the epicenter in a ring. A vampire darted into the commotion, biting people as he went.

"Not yet!" a Sanguan called. "Not yet!"

Another rushed into the crowd—then a third, and then a dozen more. Thirsty vampires streamed in, sinking their fangs into one neck, arm, or body after another. Men and women screamed and shoved their way toward the entrance below me, under the balcony.

The vampire near the DJ shook his head. "Do it! Do it now!"

The fleeing crowd bounced back from the entrance, then kept pushing in that direction in vain.

"It's locked!" a guy yelled.

"They locked us in!" a girl screamed.

When a wide-eyed immortal carried a man out a rear

door guarded by two vampires, everything became clear. Caterine and Ariane had no intention of showing up— anywhere. They hadn't called on the masses to rise in demonstrative protest. Other Sanguans had orchestrated the whole thing to draw out humans with fruitful blood and kidnap them.

A woman kicked and screamed while being dragged out the back. I jumped down and headed across the club for that exit.

One of the guards at the door asked, "Not taking anyone with you?"

I put away my knife. "No." I pushed the door open and left.

I called the police first. Then I called to double-check that Caleb was at home and Luke was tending his bar—both were fine. I tried Blaine, and when he didn't answer, I headed for his favorite club, just in case.

A similar, chaotic scene was playing out when I got there, but I didn't find my friend. The Spectavi had already arrived at the second and third clubs I tried. Blaine was at neither.

With so many clubs, by the time the Spectavi and the police showed up, there wasn't much to be done. A lot of people died, and many others went missing, likely imprisoned by Sanguans to be fed on nightly.

Most of the vampire bars and clubs didn't reopen after the following sunset, and I assumed the rest would shutter up before long. Already, the attacks, the closures, and Caterine and Ariane's absence and silence had rendered most of the twins' would-be human army disillusioned, but I figured the conniving sisters knew what they were doing.

The coming night in a week and a half when the Spectavi would run out of synthetic blood loomed large in the minds of those privy to the production issues. Failing a solution, people like Luke and Caleb were both the hope that vampire kind could survive and the catalyst that might lead immortals to tear apart the mortal world.

It was the hell on Earth prophesized in the book *Figli del Diavolo*, brought about in part by Caleb's brother, David Sartori, who had murdered entire families to locate a fragment of the True Cross and perhaps to wash the world clean of vampires. It was the hell Caterine and Ariane had spoken gleefully of while slowing my pursuit of David in Switzerland. And it was the hell that was taking a form unlike any I had ever imagined.

2

With eleven days of Spectavi synthetic supply remaining, I snuck into Zack and June's apartment near George Washington University from the rooftop stairwell entrance, via the top of the tall office building next door. Sitting in their living room on a tattered recliner with my knife hanging off my belt, I wore black pants, my leather coat over a gray shirt, and my calf-length boots with three-inch heels.

My friends were taking summer classes before their senior year. I was only two years older than they were—one, if the count stopped at twenty-two, when I became a vampire—but the gap felt larger, especially recently.

Cute, thoughtful Zack, and petite, blond-haired June sat in the middle of the ugly couch that her mother had insisted she take from her family's basement. Zack's roommate had retreated to his bedroom and shut the door upon my arrival. I was thirsty, but didn't think I had let it show.

"What happened to Tao?" Zack asked.

"He went to buy beer for a guest," I said. "In the parking lot at the grocery store, he couldn't get away when the vampire attacked."

"I'm sorry," Zack said. "That's awful."

Outside, a police siren grew louder, then quieted as it got farther away.

June asked, "Did they catch the killer?"

"Yes."

"That's good, at least," she offered.

"Yeah." I took a slow breath. "How are things around here?"

Zack responded, "They canceled all the evening classes." A blaring ambulance horn came and went. "And we never go out at night. Ever."

"Good." I wished I had more to say. They both looked scared, and it crushed me not to be able to drink their blood and taste their fear, along with the young couple's budding love. Sadness and bleakness would have dominated those sips, but *courage* would have flickered from their darkness. Maybe. I couldn't know. I had tried again two weeks before, and their blood remained useless to me.

And would that drink have helped me calm their fears? Not really. I had watched the same news and read the same stories online. I heard the sirens in D.C., out near my house in Virginia, and wherever I went. True, I understood better than they the demonic hunger that drove Sanguans to attack with such blatant disregard for the law, but Zack and June got the point.

Those vampires craved blood, because like mine, their existence depended on it. When we couldn't drink, our bodies cried out for the life-giving liquid. An aching emptiness hit us softly at first, not unlike the initial pangs of mortal hunger. But as those pangs grew, crept deeper, and screamed louder, our lips might dry, our eyes burn, and from the top of our bodies to the bottom, our aching ravaged us. It was the inverse of the pure pleasure and utter fulfillment that came from satisfying our thirst, and unlike me, most Sanguans didn't have two people eager to offer such salvation.

An unexpected tear slid down June's cheek. "One of my friends was probably kidnapped. She's been missing for two days."

"I'm sorry," I said. "There's a guard here all night?"

"Yes, one," Zack answered.

Spectavi guards patrolled the city and were stationed at apartments and college campuses. One would likely be able to keep out a stray Sanguan or two, but that assumed the intruders used the front door. Regardless, more than that would be trouble, as it already had been once in D.C. On that occasion, the three blood drinkers didn't make it out of the apartment alive, but fifty of the residents didn't, either. Similar, increasingly frequent attacks were occurring in cities worldwide.

June wiped her face dry. "Have the Spectavi had any luck making new synthetic blood?"

I had told them the truth about their issues. "No. Nothing's working."

"What'll happen when they're finally out?" she asked.

"I don't know, but more thirsty immortals can't be good at this point."

"They could drink from other vampires, couldn't they?" June asked.

"They could," I said. "But that blood would not replenish like your kidnapped friend's would, so it's only a short-term solution. And if a vampire drank from another, the one who had been drunk from would die, or at least be left weak and in need of blood themselves. So far, Sanguans have turned against those who have attacked our own kind."

"Do you think this is the end?" Zack asked. "That the world as we knew it will finish crumbling away, and those of us who manage to survive will be left with… with some kind of uncivilized hell to live in?"

"There's hope," I said. "There has to be hope."

Bright light shone through one window, then moved to the other. The whooshing of helicopter rotors followed.

I stood. "They know I'm here."

"How?" Zack asked.

"They must have spotted me on the cameras," I said. "On the way in."

"But you didn't do anything!" June went to the window, pulled it all the way up, and leaned her head through the opening. "She didn't do anything!"

I darted over, grabbed her wrist, and yanked her away from the window. Looking out, I decided I didn't want anything to do with the pair of rotary cannons mounted on the Spectavi attack helicopter pointed at us. While I stared at the pilot in his standard gray fatigues, contemplating how the silver in those guns' explosive rounds would hurt, how excruciatingly slowly the holy metal would make my wounds heal, or if a direct hit would rip me apart, rendering pain and rate of recovery moot points, my fingers ran along June's smooth skin. The soft flesh protected the delicate veins and arteries underneath, but did little to dull the pulsing of blood inside them. What I would have given for one fruitful, fiery sip…

The pilot smiled.

"No, June." I should have fed before going over there. "There's a window in your bedroom, right?"

"Yes," Zack said.

I marched across the living room, past the tiny recessed kitchen, and into the bedroom. I lifted the window, pushed out the screen, and spotted choppers hovering on each side. I jumped down seven floors, then raced around the corner, far faster than the Spectavi could fly.

While the helicopters pursued, assault rifle bullets whizzed past me from the opposite side of the street, where two Spectavi rattled off shots. I darted right to avoid their fire, pulled my knife off my belt, and flipped open the blade. I dodged left, weaving side to side to close in on them.

Should I let them live? A bullet nicked my ear. I could merely maim them, so they wouldn't be able to pursue me. I ducked under the stream of bullets and launched myself at them. In one motion—*fshwt!*—I sliced apart the pair of midsections.

The four pieces of Spectavi hit the ground. They would not be able to pursue me.

The helicopters had caught up, but grew quiet while I raced north five blocks, then east three. I couldn't hear them at all when I stopped in front of the dive bar where Luke worked, knowing full well the citywide camera system had tracked my route from Zack and June's. I figured I had a minute before the Spectavi arrived.

I went in, ignoring the Sanguan who enjoyed being known as the Big Bulgarian Bouncer. At the far end of the side bar, Luke poured a light beer for the lone customer, who might once have been quite tasty, but probably wasn't any longer. The place was dark, as usual, and the hard rock music blasted as loudly as always. Between vacant stools, I leaned against the bar.

Luke, wearing a tight t-shit and faded jeans, came over to me. "Hey, baby. How's it goin'?"

"Fine." I gazed up slightly at the six-foot-two, twenty-eight-year-old, whose dirty-blond hair was long enough to hide a bite mark near the back of his neck. "Just sliced a couple Spectavi in two."

"Really?"

"Yeah. How 'bout you? How's everything here?"

"Desislav's out front," he said. "We're good here."

"*Desislav?*"

Luke leaned close. "Who are you afraid of?"

"Sanguans." I could practically taste the blood oozing out of Luke's muscular arms. "I'm afraid of any Sanguan desperately craving a few drops of blood, drops they *need* to keep themselves alive or drops they *want* to stave off the agony of their thirst."

Luke shook his head. "Whatever." He turned away.

I grabbed his shoulder and turned him back. "No show tonight?"

"Not yet." The lead singer smiled smugly. His band,

Shattered Nights, had made headlines playing free impromptu shows with some other groups around D.C. over the last few weeks. The media played up the raucous late-night concerts as successful acts of defiance against lawless Sanguans. Shattered Nights had been enjoying a steady rise in popularity for months, and those shows helped continue the trend.

The song in the bar ended, and I heard a faint siren outside.

I pulled Luke closer. *Oh, that scent!* I glanced at the other customer.

Luke took a look. "He's cool."

I leaned in through Luke's hair and chomped into his neck. *Blood! Beautiful, blood.*

I saw Luke onstage at his last show. He loved the attention—from both the crowd and the media—but defiance? Not him and his band.

Luke's sweet blood.

I pulled more into me.

My Luke.

Drums beat, guitars whined, and Luke's voice soared above it all—above the darkness, above the depths, he soared!

My rock star.

I withdrew my fangs. Luke had told the truth. His blood confirmed that they had no show planned for that night.

I squeezed his shoulder. "Call me if you're going to play." I left and raced to Virginia.

———————

The next night, Caleb and I sat in swiveling, aluminum-framed chairs on his apartment's rooftop balcony, four stories above the desolate D.C. streets. Unlike at Zack and June's, it appeared I had succeeded in arriving unnoticed by the Spectavi. My knee-length black skirt concealed the knife strapped to the outside of my left thigh.

Caleb had on his favorite loose white dress shirt, he had recently gotten his dark hair trimmed, and a rare break from shaving had left him with a bit of stubble. The fit twenty-seven-year-old, who wasn't quite as tall as Luke, took his glass of red wine from the table between us. "I still can't believe about Tao."

"Me neither," I said. "He was as prepared to be attacked as anyone, and he didn't stand a chance."

"And he just went out to buy some beer?"

"Yeah." I shook my head. "He shouldn't have been out, but Zhilan was meeting with this Army general later that evening, General Sharpe. A week ago, his teenage son, out when *he* shouldn't have been, was attacked by a Sanguan. Renshu happened to hear a scream, saved the boy, and for his trouble, General Sharpe said he'd meet with Zhilan. She planned to explain that some Sanguans, like us, never kill when they drink."

"How high up the chain is Sharpe?"

"He's a major general. He works for the director of the Joint Chiefs of Staff. That director—"

"Works for the chairman of the Joint Chiefs," Caleb interrupted. "*The chairman* is on the National Security Council advising the president. Don't forget, I work in defense."

"Considering how little you care about your job, I figured you might need the reminder."

"Ha ha. What about the assistant to the president for Vampire Policy? He's on the Security Council. Any chance General Sharpe has his ear?"

"Maybe," I said. "But I doubt it, since Zhilan didn't mention it."

"Well, Sharpe's not *too* far from the president. Talking to him is better than nothing."

"I guess. So anyway, he was coming over, and Zhilan has plenty of rare old wine, but Tao got word that the general preferred beer. Tao was trying to be a good host, as always."

"Damn."

"I've spent an irrational amount of time wondering if the general would have even drunk a beer. He surely wouldn't have had more than two."

"Did Zhilan go after the vampire?" Caleb asked.

"As soon as she found out. She said she took her time with him."

"That doesn't sound like her."

"No. She hides it, but she has to be crushed at losing Tao."

"I'm sure." Caleb sipped his wine. "How's everything else?" He held his glass to his nose.

"I chopped apart a couple Spectavi yesterday."

He stopped sniffing. "In the city?"

"Yes."

"You sure that was a good idea?"

I shrugged. "*They* came after *me*."

"Why?"

"I think just because I was in an apartment building."

"They might target you now," Caleb said.

"I doubt it. This is war. There are casualties. And they know who I am—their leaders, certainly. I'm sure they've known exactly where I live and haven't tried anything."

Caleb put down his glass. "I'm nervous without Victoria around." She had been sent up to New York City to help keep the peace.

A car drove by. I wondered how our war would change in ten days, when the Spectavi ran out of synthetic. While I believed hope for the world had not flickered out, I feared Satan was winning, high above. Because why would God alter nature so drastically that *Hell* appeared so inevitable? David Sartori's crimes were indisputable. The Spectavi's use of their synthetic to control their vampires seemed clearly wrong, and humanity's acceptance of the Spectavi's ways was either worse or just more frustrating. If the red rain had come as a judgment upon the world for those things, at least its cause was known. But what kind of Creator would damn His entire creation over such crimes? Or anything?

I had returned to Riggs Library at Georgetown and carefully examined each page of the old book that depicted Nicolas Duchart's failings in the Dark Ages, which resulted in his sisters, Caterine and Ariane, being transformed into vampires. I scoured the Italian book that foretold the hell that would follow the red rain. I found no other prophesies or veiled hints about changing things back. I had once thought my life's big test was finding the True Cross before the twins and David Sartori did, but in retrospect, considered the odds of succeeding in that quest so remote that my real task remained before me. I was contemplating making the long trip to Ahmose's hidden Pacific island, Seorsum, for the ancient historian's council.

Caleb asked, "How's Luke?"

"Uh, fine." In reality, while he hadn't played a show the night before, constantly worrying that Luke would play was driving me crazy. Caleb, in contrast, lay low and openly shared his plans with me.

Caleb's blood told me he often wondered if I loved Luke. Caleb wrestled with the question, just as Luke worried about my feelings for Caleb. But Caleb had never asked about Luke that directly, and answering in detail would have been complicated... and awkward.

Caleb changed the subject. "Still no sign of the twins?"

"No."

"I'm worried what they're up to *this* time."

"Yeah," I agreed. "We figured it out too late last time."

"Yup. And to be honest, I'm afraid they'll turn their attention to you."

I had glimpsed that fear in his blood and deemed it wholly unnecessary. While my immense, superhuman strength and tremendous speed couldn't match Caterine and Ariane's, I was quite powerful. The blood that had made me a vampire, that of the former Spectavi leader, Edmond Duchart, gave me those gifts and others, like improved sight and hearing and the ability to heal from most wounds. I would grow more powerful with age, and already, I didn't fear Edmond's fifteen-hundred-year-old sisters.

But Caleb's concern was sweet, so I smiled. "The twins do not like me."

He matched my expression. "No, they do not. Would you ever try to 'heal' them—to turn them back into humans, or at least calm them down—like you tried to when you were Vera?"

"How could I? I'm not a scientist anymore, and they're not about to crawl back into their steel coffins at Eure."

"Right. But theoretically, do you think there's any chance it could work?"

I pictured my younger self working side by side with William, the Spectavi's chief scientist. "Honestly? No. I mean, who knows? But if I spent years trying before, with Edmond and William's help and all the resources of the Spectavi, and failed then, I really don't see it at this point."

"Yeah."

I recalled my curious dreams of the twins before I went to work at Eure, the painful ones that came while I was there, and Edmond's tale of how they attacked my mind as Vera. "Plus, they sure don't seem to have any interest in being 'healed.'"

"True." Caleb shook his head. "With them sick, weak, and on the brink of death for three years instead of being married as planned, I understand why they were furious—at everyone—at the start."

"They killed their fiancés once they were vampires," I reminded him.

"Exactly. And then, a thousand years later, pile hundreds

of years of imprisonment on top. If there had ever been a chance they might change their ways, I wonder if it died in those coffins."

"It may have," I said. "I'm just so mad at myself for setting them free."

"But you didn't know what they were really like. Edmond wiped your whole life away and, presumably, could have done it again. He left you no choice."

"I know, but… if I had found another way. If I had made different decisions earlier, they could still be locked in Edmond's basement."

"Edmond would probably be alive. Would that be better?"

"No," I said, recalling his sisters climbing from their coffins and ripping his head from his body. "I guess not." By the time I let his sisters loose, what else could I have done? Edmond had been a monster.

Caleb glanced down at the street. A mostly empty city bus passed by. "Quiet night."

"So far."

"What if it weren't?" he asked.

"Hm?"

"What if it weren't so quiet, and you weren't here?"

I knew what he was driving at. I reminded myself to focus on dealing with the twins instead of dwelling on past choices and took Caleb's hand. "I *am* here."

He pulled his hand away. "I'm not asking you to pick me instead of Luke. You could keep seeing him."

"I won't make you a vampire," I said. "Either of you."

He muttered something I didn't catch.

"What?" I asked.

He appeared so sad, but that wouldn't let him off the hook.

"What did you say?" I prodded.

"It's selfish."

The subject had come up with both Luke and Caleb before, and I had seen it in them time and again when drinking their blood, but the topic had never made Caleb so outwardly upset.

I had pictured it with each of them. I would hold Luke or Caleb and drink from him until draining him just short of the point of death. Then I'd bite my wrist, *he* would feed on *my* blood, and then he would be a vampire, immortal and with the strength to not have to fear other vampires in the grim world.

But to do that, I *would* have to pick one. It would be years after I made my first fledgling before a second wouldn't turn out weak and most likely defenseless in our war with the Spectavi. I had asked Zhilan and Renshu if either would turn Luke or Caleb into an immortal. They both politely said no, and Zhilan reminded me what a personal thing making a fledgling was. Max had made a vampire two years before, I couldn't ask Grant, and when I broached the subject to others, they echoed the same sentiment as Zhilan.

While the problem of having to pick one was very real, another issue troubled me. Maybe I could have picked one. Maybe not. But in my heart, I felt wholly unprepared to be responsible for a young blood drinker. I could protect the two of them as humans. That meant fighting, which I loved.

But vivid memories of my infancy as a vampire remained fresh. My demonic thirst had driven me to drain most I drank from, before Zhilan showed up. Even then, when she let me out of her sight, I sucked blood from my victims until traces of cool in the liquid quickly became a chill that meant I had sucked them to their deaths.

Only imprisonment and torture by the old Greek Sanguan, Alexander, had taught me my lesson. If Zhilan, who had made three fledglings and had two hundred seventy years of experience to draw on, couldn't tame me, how could *I* teach Luke or Caleb?

Caleb's eyes glistened. It *was* about me choosing him over Luke.

I asked, "Aren't you scared the world will run out of blood for vampires?"

He leaned toward me. "If that happens and I remain mortal, it means I'm dead. The world's always been hard for humans, and now it's even harder, especially for those like me. I'd rather take my chances as a powerful vampire than as a frail human."

"You wouldn't be so powerful as a *starving* vampire," I said.

"I don't think it'll come to that, and neither do you."

"But I can't be sure."

"I am." Caleb inched closer. "I dream of forever with you, Erin."

His visions of an endless life with me and with a world of fascinating mortals were ones I had seen in his blood over and over. "I can't," I said, thinking of Luke left all alone. "I'm sorry."

He opened his mouth, seemingly ready to protest, before leaning back and asking, "What about how the twins got captured?"

He wanted to know how they had become Edmond's prisoners. Like me, Caleb found tales of my kind from long past nothing short of captivating—the more consequential, the more world changing, the better. I had been saving the story of the twins' imprisonment.

I asked, "What time is it?"

He checked his phone. "Twelve seventeen."

While I wouldn't turn Luke or Caleb into vampires, from the bottom of my heart, I wished for them to be happy. "All right. Here's what Victoria told me."

In the seventh century, the Byzantines developed a technologically advanced flame weapon that accounts say burned on water. Late that century and early the next, the weapon was vital to the European power's naval defense of its capital, Constantinople, during two Arab sieges. For hundreds of years after that, it facilitated Byzantine imperial expansion and helped quell civil wars. The weapon went by many names, including "sea fire," "war fire," and recently, "Greek fire."

The Byzantines kept the details of Greek fire, including its ingredients and how to deploy it in battle, as closely guarded state secrets. Individuals only knew how to create a specific portion of the weapon or use a certain part in a long chain of parts required for the weapon to function correctly.

As a result, when those who worked with Greek fire were captured, their interrogation and torture could not reveal enough information to be useful. And on occasions when the completed substance was stolen, thieves never discovered how to manufacture it on their own. The secret nature of Greek fire proved either perfect, or perfectly flawed, because since the twelfth century, the powerful weapon had not been seen. Its formula lost, Greek fire had disappeared from the world.

In 1698, near Basingstoke, England, Charles Paulet, second Duke of Bolton, held a reception at Hackwood House, his palatial mansion. The event was winding down. Soft string and woodwind notes had grown calmer and quieter since the evening's lively start. Candles of the chandeliers in the stately room had gone out, while others burned low. The crowd of noblemen and noblewomen had thinned considerably.

Only two immortals were in attendance—Victoria, an imposing five-hundred-year-old German warrior with light skin and a perfectly toned physique, and Edmond, her maker, the fourth vampire ever to be. He was tall and powerfully built, with broad shoulders and a full head of black hair. Time had turned his skin even lighter than hers, and while he often appeared far kinder and warmer than his fledgling, at that moment, his intense focus on her in his arms left little room for such softness. Victoria, her long raven-black hair worn straight, rested her cheek on Edmond's shoulder while they danced.

He ran his fingertips over the laces of her black corset. "A magnificent gown, for a magnificent creature."

Victoria kept her head to Edmond's ornate blue doublet. "I knew you would like it."

"My queen is as beautiful as she is strong, as breathtaking as she is fierce."

"My king is as cunning as he is powerful." Victoria opened her mouth to bite.

"Edmond," the thirty-seven-year-old duke interrupted, with his teenage wife, Henrietta, at his side.

Victoria lifted her head.

"My Lady," the duke said. "Mr. Duchart, thank you again for your help these last few months. My lands are again safe."

The duchess blushed at Victoria's steely stare.

"Charles, you are most welcome," Edmond said. "Your father was ever kind to my friends and me, as you have been. My assistance is my thank you for that."

"My father was a touch... odd."

"Yes, he was," Edmond agreed. "But we all enjoyed the peculiarities of his company immensely."

The duke smiled.

"Thank you for your hospitality," Edmond said. "I sincerely hope this serene evening ends pleasantly enough for you and your guests."

The duke and duchess gave confused looks while Edmond led Victoria away. Around the corner, not far into an empty hallway, Edmond guided Victoria to the wall. He leaned his powerful body into hers and, above her black chain necklace, sank his fangs into her pristine white neck.

She ran her hands through Edmond's hair while he sucked her blood. Her bosom, already squeezed over the top of her corset, heaved with deeper breaths, but her steady expression persisted. She kissed his forehead.

Her mouth sprang open. She chomped into his neck's tough skin, and abandoning her stoic countenance, Victoria pulled blood from her maker with vigor. Edmond sucked down her blood. Harder and faster, his fledgling sucked back.

He finished and savored a gulp. "My queen."

Victoria stretched out a long sip and then sucked once more. "My king."

"Come." Edmond took her hand.

Their fang marks healed before they exited the hallway to rejoin the few remaining couples at the reception. Victoria returned her cheek to Edmond's shoulder.

"My Lord!" Two Spectavi burst into the room—youthful Tristan and hardy Bennett, straight swords at their sides.

The music and dancing stopped.

Tristan pulled a clump of folded papers from his inside jacket pocket. "My Lord, we have it."

Edmond reached for the papers, and Victoria disappeared into the hallway.

Two katanas slashed through the Duke's guards at the entrance. Tall, lean, ghostly pale Ariane dressed in red and her twin, Caterine, in black, both had their blond hair up in tight braids. Two Sanguans with longswords caught up with the pair—the one-time medieval knight, Erec le Roux, and Alexander, who had not yet been crippled by the loss of his feet and arm.

Edmond pushed the papers back to Tristan, who shoved them into his jacket pocket. Victoria returned, a longsword in each hand. She threw Edmond his battle-tested blade.

Caterine smiled. "Edmond, you should have invited us to your little party."

Edmond called to the humans, "Go, please."

The duke and duchess stepped toward the side of the room.

"No!" Ariane yelled. "Stay, all of you!"

"Fight me." Edmond nodded to Tristan and Bennett. "Or fight them. But let these people go."

Caterine rolled her red eyes. "Fine. It matters not. Run along, sweet mortals. When we have finished here, we'll find you."

After a few cautious steps, the humans hurried from the room.

"Thank you," Edmond said to his sisters.

"Now give us the papers," Ariane demanded.

Victoria raised her sword. "No."

"Silence, wench!" Caterine yelled. "I did not ask *you*."

Ariane called, "What good is a little fire to you and your devoted flock? You do not require such a thing to keep your precious *peace*."

"You will not have this weapon." Edmond readied his blade. "Its secret should have remained undiscovered, but at least it has come to us."

Tristan and Bennett drew their swords.

Caterine looked at Erec and then Alexander with his dark-tinted sword. "Bring us that paper." The ancient twin raced at her brother while her sister engaged Victoria.

Erec clashed blades with Bennett, Alexander attacked Tristan, and the battle began. Victoria fought nearly as quickly back then, and as precisely, but her strength could not match her opponent's. Her longsword's reach beyond Ariane's katana offered a crucial advantage as Victoria moved swiftly around the room, aiming to slow, wound, or if absolutely necessary, maim her foe.

Edmond, who had steadfastly commanded that his sisters not be killed, had no trouble matching Caterine's abilities.

"Rragh!" Alexander roared. The vicious vampire's blade met Tristan's, who fought back to back with Bennett, who blocked Erec.

Ariane leapt to avoid Victoria's swing—and her next. The Sanguan darted forward, and—*tyn*—her strong strike pushed Victoria backward. *Tyn!* Victoria retreated farther.

"Weakling. Why my brother drags you around with him is beyond me." Ariane smiled. "Pretty dress, though."

Victoria swung her mighty sword in response. Ariane met the attack with ease.

Bennett yelled as Alexander's blade sliced open his arm, and blood poured. Tristan came to his companion's aid, repelling blow after blow while Bennett collected himself.

Caterine swung at Edmond—*tyn!* "We are creatures born of Hell, brother—Ariane and I more truly than any other. Such potent flame is meant to be ours."

Edmond swung—*tyn!* "You are a daughter of Eve, like your sister. You always have been, and you always will be." *Tyn!* "In God's name, I swear you will not have this weapon."

Caterine swung hard—*tyn—tyn—fsht*. Blood streamed down Edmond's cheek from the healing gash. She said, "In Satan's name, *my* creator's name, I swear we will."

Fshwt! A deep cut across Tristan's thighs sent him to his knees.

Alexander chided, "You fall short of your reputation, young one. This disappoints me."

Tristan, aided by Bennett, limped for the corner. Sofie entered the room and darted toward them.

"Gah!" Ariane noticed the smaller warrior first.

Sofie's longsword met Alexander's.

Caterine stepped back from Edmond. "The wench's miserable whelp. How many of you are there?"

Four fresh Spectavi arrived. Tristan and Bennett fled the mansion, with Sofie blocking Alexander's way.

Edmond answered his sister, "An eternal army who believe that you two should give men and women a chance to write their own history."

"No!" Ariane screamed. "They are weak! All of them."

"They will suffer," Caterine joined in. "*We* suffered, and before we allow humanity to kneel before us, to accept their true place as mortal cuisine for their immortal masters, *they* will suffer."

"Never," Edmond responded. "I have opposed you for a thousand years, and I will *always* oppose you while such is your aim. I will not see the Lord's magnificent creations shackled and servile."

"My dear Edmond," Ariane said, "*you* may not be around to see our glorious world of pain and despair, but it *will* come to pass." She glanced at her sister, who nodded. They raced out of the room, followed by Alexander and Erec. The Spectavi made no effort to stop them.

———————————

Crrcrack! Caleb and I turned, and beyond his sliding glass door, his locked apartment door swung open, pushed by a thin white arm. Leather pants hugged the long legs of both Caterine and Ariane. The one-minute-younger twin had opted for a loud, hot-pink leather top while Caterine had chosen charcoal. A strap cut across each diagonally, holding their katanas to their backs. Ponytails kept their long hair out of their faces.

I peered over the roof's edge—four stories to the quiet street. Caterine had been interrupted when drinking from Caleb in Switzerland, and I refused to give her another shot at finishing him. The twins darted toward us.

I grabbed Caleb, ran across the roof, and spun to see the twins breaking through the glass door. Shards and fragments burst out, and others crumbled to the roof.

I took hold of my knife and flicked open the blade. "What do you want?"

Caterine pulled a large piece of glass from her arm and walked toward us. "Pain, anguish, despair. How many times are you going to ask us that?"

Ariane drew her katana. "To be fair, sister, the most complete answer is not that simple."

"True, true," Caterine agreed. "The world falling apart, delightful as it has already been and glorious as it *will be*, is

31

not sufficient for you, Vera. You must taste something far worse."

"I've tasted enough pain." I lifted Caleb, held him high so I'd hit the ground first, and leapt off the roof.

We landed on the sidewalk, and I let him go. "I should have brought my sword."

"What do we do?" he asked.

No one was on the street or inside the scattering of parked vehicles lining it. I grabbed my phone off my other thigh and handed it to Caleb. "Text Zhilan. Tell her where we are and that it's the twins."

He typed while I kept watch.

"Sent." Caleb held out the phone for me.

"Keep it." Since he couldn't fight them, he stood a better chance of being useful with the phone. "Is your car in the garage?"

"Yes."

"Do you have your keys?"

"Yes."

The garage was on the opposite side of the building, around two blocks. We hurried beside the brick wall, and at the corner—*swoosh!*—a sword sliced thin air in front of me.

I shoved Caleb back and—*tyn*—met Caterine's next heavy strike with my knife. Step after step, I blocked and retreated. *Tyn*—I blocked and kicked—*smack!*—into Caterine's midsection, sending her flying.

"Erin!" Caleb called.

I spun to a grinning Ariane, who held Caleb's wrist—my Caleb!

I slashed at the fiend's arm, and she let him go. *Tyn-tyn-tyn!*—I drove her back.

"My, my, Vera," Ariane said. *Tyn-tyn-tyn!* "You do like this one."

She swung harder, and my block was weak against her might. *Tyn!*—I hit more firmly.

"You love him!" Ariane retreated around the corner we had been heading for.

Police sirens sounded not far off. For a change, the damn hidden-camera system had come in handy, but knowing Victoria wouldn't be among the respondents disappointed me.

"Come on." I took Caleb's hand, and we jogged down the street. Stopping at the corner, I motioned for him to stay behind. I darted around and found no one to fight. "Let's go."

Laughter cackled over the approaching sirens.

"Keep moving," I said.

Caleb and I headed for the underground garage's entrance, scanning high and low for the voice.

"He, he, he." It sounded farther ahead, or above. The garage was close.

"He was delicious last time," the voice said.

From across the street, Ariane shot at us. *Tyn!*—I blocked her strike. Caleb moved against the wall. *Tyn!*

Streaking into the fight, Zhilan met Caterine's katana with her straight black sword. My friend's short red dress indicated she had been out, which the appearance of Renshu in a tuxedo virtually confirmed.

Caleb crept against the wall while I fought Ariane with Renshu.

"You again," Caterine said, battling Zhilan, whom she had last seen in Alexander's compound.

Caleb disappeared into the garage.

"I assure you." Zhilan swung her blade. "I am quite tired of you."

Ariane elbowed Renshu across the face. I blocked her cut at him.

"Ah!" She sliced into my side.

Caleb's black Mercedes raced out of the garage and veered toward us.

Renshu blocked Ariane. *Fshwt!*—she sliced open his shoulder, and his sword arm fell limp.

"Renshu!" Zhilan called. She rushed to protect her fledgling while I got between her and Caterine.

Caleb lowered the car window. "Get in!"

Renshu grimaced.

"Go," Zhilan told him. "You can no longer help us."

He got in the front seat, and the engine roared as they sped off.

A rocket flew by and—*boom!*—hit the brick wall, leaving a small crater. A Spectavi tossed the launcher to the ground and raised an assault rifle.

Zhilan and I raced after Caleb's car and caught up to it a block away. Caterine, Ariane, and four Spectavi followed. Zhilan and I clashed blades with the twins yards behind the car. Bullets whizzed by. Caleb swerved to avoid a man stepping into the intersection. We swerved, and so did the Spectavi.

The twins darted to our pursuers, cut down a pair, then effortlessly caught up with us. I took another wound to my side, and Zhilan her leg, but we were keeping the twins away from Caleb's car. Two silver SUVs joined the pursuit.

Caleb crossed to the wrong side of the road to speed past a bus. He weaved in between cars at an intersection. Running and fighting simultaneously proved difficult and, combined with the disadvantage of my short weapon, led me to play more defense than I would have liked. Nevertheless, after all our hours practicing *against* each other, I enjoyed fighting alongside Zhilan.

The twins dropped back and flipped an SUV. It burst into flames. In front of us, another SUV raced around the corner, headed our way. Reinald, the twelve-hundred-year-old Spectavi leader who had succeeded Edmond, scowled at us from the front passenger seat as he passed.

Zhilan and I stopped. She said, "So they're after the twins."

"And the twins"—I took a few quick breaths—"seem to be after Caleb. Where should we go?"

"Alexandria… Grant's."

Boom! The blaze behind us intensified. I had no doubt Caterine and Ariane had avoided the fire and were relishing all the destruction and death. They appeared content to battle Reinald and not follow us, however, which was most important.

Zhilan and I caught up to Caleb's car again.

I pulled open the door. "We need to get Luke. He's working at the bar."

Caleb glanced at me.

Zhilan said, "Grant and Alice are fetching him."

3

Caleb parked in the alley behind Grant's narrow brick row house. Getting out of the car, Renshu rotated his arm, which seemed improved, but not a hundred percent. I shut my door and followed him, Caleb, and Zhilan through Grant's small backyard.

Light filled the alley. I grabbed my knife. A taxi pulled up with Luke in the backseat. Grant, wearing jeans and his brown bomber jacket, and Alice in a tank top and leather pants followed on Grant's motorcycle. Neither wore a helmet, and it became clear why—she was a vampire. Grant had mentioned he was considering asking her if she wanted him to make her an immortal. Apparently, she had. They parked next to Caleb.

I put away my knife and called to Grant, "Thanks."

He nodded and got off his bike after Alice did. Luke stepped out of the cab.

"You all right?" I asked.

"I'm fine," Luke said. "You?"

"Yeah."

"Let's get inside," Zhilan ordered.

Single file, we marched in and through Grant's sparse kitchen, which was too small for us all to fit in at once. In his living room, a long brown leather couch, a loveseat, and a recliner surrounded the flat-screen TV. I stood behind the smaller sofa with Caleb on one side and Luke on my other.

Alice was—or had been—an American University law school student in her mid-twenties. Coming out of the kitchen, she stayed close to Grant like a child afraid of parting from her protector. Big, broad-chested, and muscular, Grant looked the part, though he was far more than just a brute.

I had seen him drinking from her on that same long couch in his old house in D.C. months earlier. Before that, before I became a vampire, Grant had met me at the club Fire and Ice and revealed that he had picked Alice to drink from because she reminded him of me—tall, thin, green eyes, and chestnut hair, long like mine had been. The resemblance was undeniable. That her new fangs matched mine, as well, made everything more awkward—but not between me and her or Grant. Luke and Caleb would no doubt be jealous of what Grant had done for Alice.

"What happened?" Grant asked.

"The twins," I said. "I was with Caleb." Luke's face fell. "We were outside talking, and they broke open his front door. We jumped from the roof and called Zhilan." I turned to her. "Thank you. And I'm sorry to ruin your night out."

"Please." She waved her hand. "Perhaps it was overly ambitious to steal a last bit of civilized fun before such things grow impossible. I am glad you contacted me." Her confidence seemed unshaken, her nineteen-year-old Chinese face no older, but her brightness subtly dimmer than normal.

"What did they want?" Grant asked.

"Caleb." In an effort to reassure Luke of his importance to me and convince him of the danger, I added, "And Luke."

"They really don't like you, Erin," Grant remarked.

I smirked. "Yes, thank you."

"What do we do?" Luke asked.

Zhilan answered, "For now, you two need to stay with us after nightfall. We will see if the twins try anything later or tomorrow and then decide what to do."

It would be difficult with both of them around, but I'd be unable to do anything except worry about Luke and Caleb if they weren't with me.

"What about work?" Luke asked. "I'm supposed to be behind the bar tomorrow night."

"Cancel." I shook my head. "I'm sorry." Money was no issue for Caleb, despite the fact that he hardly went into the office. And I had millions of dollars, but Luke refused to take any of it so he could quit bartending.

Grant said, "There's a bed upstairs if one of you wants to sleep until sunrise. The other can take the couch. I'll share my coffin in the basement with Alice." She slid her hand across his back. "And I have an extra for Zhilan and Renshu. Erin, you take Alice's."

———

Caleb and Luke sat on opposite ends of the couch, watching TV when I ascended from the unfinished basement the following night. Out front, an ambulance sped by, its horn blaring and lights flashing. Either the timing was a coincidence, or a Sanguan hadn't waited long after nightfall to attack. I had texted June the night before, and then when I awoke. She and Zack were fine and hadn't had any trouble related to the twins or otherwise. I emailed Blaine, again imploring him to respond and let me know he was safe.

Zhilan announced, "I'm going to do some reconnaissance, especially to try to see if the twins followed us and are close by. Renshu will stay here."

"If you're near Arlington, will you get my sword from my house?" I asked.

"Certainly."

I was surprised she would part with her fledgling. And while I had never been overly impressed with his skill in battle, her rationale was clear. The twins were two, so Renshu would come in handy if we needed to flee from Grant's on foot.

Alice, who had strapped a long knife to the outside of her right thigh over her pants, again rested her hand on Grant's back as they headed out through the kitchen. They were going for drinks. Grant knew a few Sanguans willing to share the mortals that continued to feed them. I had a strong suspicion that Grant and Alice would also share each other's blood, and perhaps even some other immortals'.

"Be careful," Zhilan said to the rest of us, then gave Renshu a quick look before going out the front door.

He asked me, "What do you think?"

I glanced at the guys on the couch. My thirst intensified, but drinking just wouldn't have worked with them both around. "I don't like doing nothing, but here's not a bad place to stay and see if the twins try anything." I sat on the loveseat.

"I concur." Renshu settled into the recliner. "Erin, I have never asked you about the black cross you have tattooed on your neck."

"What do you want to know?"

"When did you have it done?"

"When I woke up as Erin, with no memory, and God was the only one I had to talk to," I explained.

"Do you ever wonder, in the face of all that's happened, about the all-knowing, all-powerful being the cross is for?"

"Of course," I said.

Despite the conversation being nothing new to Luke, he paid close attention. Caleb *always* perked up for such topics.

Renshu asked, "Knowing all you do, after experiencing all you have, would you have the same mark branded on your skin?"

"I think so," I said. "I don't regret it, and I like it."

"Why do you like it?"

I looked out the window and answered, "There's so much evil, everywhere. And maybe evil's winning. But whatever God's plan or if His fate in His battle has left Him not doing the planning, the cross reminds me that there's good out there, too."

Renshu nodded. "Did you hear what happened in the Philippines today?"

I turned back to him. "No."

"The mass suicide," Caleb said. "A thousand people were

convinced that God sent the red rain and what's come after as a punishment."

"Maybe it was," I said, "but even if so, what does killing themselves accomplish?"

Caleb shrugged. "I agree, but to them, their suicides were a penance."

Renshu asked, "Has Victoria offered any news concerning the synthetic blood recently?"

"Sort of," I said. "Though is it actually news if it's all the same? They can't make any more. They'll be out in nine days."

Luke crossed his strong arms. Caleb brought his hand to his chin—a set of recent fang marks adorned his wrist. Luke and Caleb *could* make an endless supply, and they sat *right next to me*.

"I worry about when they run out," Renshu said. "That the newly thirsty Spectavi will not be as obedient as they are at present. With less of them focused on keeping the peace and additional mouths out in search of drinks, things will grow worse."

I said, "I wish there was something we could do to change things back. I hate being so powerless."

Renshu motioned to the couch where Luke and Caleb sat. "Why do you think their blood continues to be… satisfying?"

He was really asking *that*? My body screamed at me for that blood. And I could have had it. I could have drunk from one, the other, or both in a matter of seconds. "I don't know."

"According to Grant," Renshu said, "Alice's blood also survived the red rain unchanged. But he decided she would be safer as one of us."

I glared at him.

"*I* think we'd be safer," Caleb said.

"Me, too," Luke agreed.

"You could starve," I reminded them. "Blood could eventually run out, and *I* might starve."

"You won't," Luke said.

"We wouldn't," Caleb added.

"How can you be so sure?" I asked.

"I just am," Caleb said. "You told me you think there *has* to be hope, that this can't be the end for humans *or* vampires. I agree with you."

"What if you're wrong?" Renshu asked. "And blood for vampires does run out?"

"I've told Erin this," Caleb said. "There's a big difference between getting really scarce and running out. Once blood's really scarce, I'd rather take my chances as a vampire with Erin than stay one of the hunted humans."

Caleb looked so upset, Luke disappointed, and both incredibly vulnerable and delicious. I had to change the subject. "I was telling Caleb about the twins' capture. Mind if I continue?"

Renshu folded his hands in his lap. "Please."

I filled the newcomers in on the beginning and picked up the story late the night after the Duke of Bolton's reception.

At Bodiam Castle, southeast of London, Tristan and Bennett flew through the moonless sky, over the moat and high sandstone walls. They landed in the torch-lit square courtyard, crashing into a wheelbarrow, a bale of hay, and a trough of dirty water. Ten Spectavi with muskets and swords, wearing chainmail, rushed down from their posts on the wall and out of the long row of barracks and offices.

Tristan got up. "They follow close."

"Who?" a guard asked.

Bennett stood and brushed himself off. "Who do you think?"

A guard atop the high outer wall peered out and reported, "All's quiet. No twins. No one approaches."

"They're out there," Tristan insisted. He pulled folded papers from inside his jacket. "The secret of Greek fire. With it, the twins could cause unthinkable destruction."

Bennett added, "We must get it to Niaux, France."

"So go," a nearby Spectavi said.

Two splashes sounded from the moat outside the castle. Others rushed to see where the guards had fallen. Tristan ran into the high tower at the rear of the stronghold on the east side. The more seasoned warrior, Bennett, drew his sword and stood at the ready outside the wooden door at the tower's entrance.

On the castle wall, guards readied their weapons and scanned for the enemy. The moat water settled, and except for links of Spectavi chainmail rustling and leather gloves and boots creaking, the night was still.

From the front east tower came a yell. "Ahh!"

Guards aimed their muskets, but Bennett saw nothing except a pair of boot bottoms on their way over the wall. A few seconds later, perhaps after the twins had sucked their victim dry, he heard a splash.

A grunt sounded from the west tower. The twins might have split up, Bennett reasoned. All turned to face that direction. *Splash*.

The others searched beyond the wall for targets to shoot. More settling water. More rustling chainmail. More creaking leather.

Aiming at the top of the tower directly above Bennett, Spectavi on the wall fired silver musket balls. Bennett heard swords slice flesh and bone, but no metal clanging against metal. *Splash, splash.* No sounds of bullets hitting their marks. *Splash, splash.* By his count, eight guards had fallen, and twelve remained.

To Bennett's left, streaks of black shot down through the roof of the long narrow barracks.

Inside—*tyn-tyn!*—swords clashed. *Fshwt-fshwt!*

"Agh! Ugh." Distinct male voices were followed by thumps of bodies hitting the ground.

Tyn-tyn! Fshwt. Spectavi on the wall watched and listened with Bennett.

"Agh!" A third body hit the ground.

Tyn-tyn! Tyn-tyn! Fshwt! And a fourth. Four balls of silver flew out of smoke-filled barracks windows.

"Ungh." Two hit a guard on the high front wall—one chest, one forehead.

"Agh." The other two hit the guard beside him.

The Spectavi crumpled to the ground. Six remained.

The barracks door swung open, and Caterine stepped out, twirling her katana menacingly at her side. Ariane followed, dropped a musket, and drew her sword. The six guards rushed the twins, while Bennett held his position in front of the tower.

Tyn-tyn! Fshwt. Fshwt. The ancient demons made short work of the youngest two Spectavi, then fought far faster than their last foes. *Fshwt. Fshwt.* Caterine and Ariane both stood ready. The final two guards glanced at each other, then fled over the castle wall. Bennett gripped his sword tightly with both hands.

"Bennett, is it?" Caterine asked as they approached him.

"You are braver than those two," Ariane said. "Though I have made short work of many brave vampires." The pair attacked.

Tyn-tyn. Bennett repelled their first strikes.

Tyn-tyn! Tyn-fshwt.

"Agh!" Bennett's hacked-off hands fell to the dirt. Blood spouted from his wrists, and his blade clattered to the ground. Ariane slammed him against the tower wall and sank her fangs into his neck. The bleeding from his wrists slowed. She sucked, and his eyes grew heavy.

From the tower above, two Spectavi dressed like Tristan broke through narrow windows, and Ariane stopped drinking. A second pair of Spectavi followed, and all four leapt out of the castle in different directions. Letting maimed Bennett crumple to their feet, the twins watched, poised to chase, when another two Spectavi darted from the tower. Then two more pairs came and jumped over the walls. North, south, east, west, and in between, the ten Spectavi, all dressed the same, fled the castle in ten different directions.

"Clever, Edmond. Clever." Caterine turned to Bennett and pressed her blade into his neck.

Ariane sheathed her katana on her back, crouched, and pushed Bennett until he sat upright against the wall. "Where is Edmond taking those papers?"

"God *damn* you!" Bennett cried.

"Shhh… shhh…" Caterine put away her weapon and crouched. "No need to yell. We are all alone." She bit into Bennett's arm near where it had been severed.

He closed his eyes and labored to breathe. She stopped and licked her lips, while a trickle of blood spilled out of the cut end of his arm.

"In the name of the Lord," Bennett commanded, "go back to Hell!"

Shock filled Caterine's face. "Do you hear that?" She shifted her gaze skyward. "No." She looked left. "I hear nothing." She looked right. "No God here, my friend." She faced him. "Nor His son."

Bennett sprang to his feet. Ariane slammed him down to the ground. She bit into his neck, and he strained as his blood was sucked out of him.

"Lucifer fell to Hell, it is true." Caterine grabbed Bennett's wrist, bit in, and slurped. "Into those fiery depths, he plummeted, with all his loyal followers." Caterine sipped again. "God did damn those radiant angels to call that foul place their home, but they were not defeated."

Ariane stopped drinking and got up from weary Bennett.

"From that pit, we rose." Caterine stood tall. "God has His Heaven. Lucifer reigns in Hell. But this world is *ours*."

Ariane sneered at Bennett. "You will tell us where Edmond intends to hide that Greek fire. As many nights as it takes, however much pain we have to inflict, you *will* tell us."

In the kitchen, the back door opened.

"Grant?" I called.

"Yes," he answered. Soft gunshots sounded before the door closed.

I finished that part of the story for my audience. "The twins left the castle with Bennett as their prisoner."

Grant and Alice came into the living room.

"The gunshots?" I asked.

"A few blocks away. Not for us," Grant explained. "Are you hungry?"

I almost cried, "Yes!"

Grant clarified, "Luke? Caleb?"

"Yeah," Luke answered.

"I could eat," Caleb agreed.

"I'll go with them," I said, intensely jealous that their hunger would soon be sated.

"There's a 7-Eleven down the street, three blocks," Grant said.

Renshu stood. "I'll go, as well."

On the way to the kitchen, we all stopped when Luke did. "What's it like, Alice? Being a vampire."

Her face lit up. "Indescribable."

Luke squinted. "Could you try?"

Alice beamed. "The people, the blood—I wasn't scared that I'd have to drink to live, but I had no idea how amazing, how vivid the drinks would be. And the confidence that comes with being—"

"Let's go." I pushed Luke toward the kitchen.

Caleb and Renshu followed us. An urge to be angry with Alice for her lack of discretion surfaced, but then subsided. She had merely stated her opinion. In fact, in spite of the thirst driving me mad, I believed that all she had done was state the truth.

I sat in my coffin, holding my katana in its scabbard. The vampire-forged Japanese sword dated to the fifteenth century. As Vera, when Victoria had given it to me, I named it Tomori, after a Latin phrase reminding that all are mortal. From the sharp point, down its polished, slightly curved blade, to the electric-blue collar and leather-wrapped handle, I loved that sword completely.

While no longer being parted from my katana brought some calm comfort, an agitated aching for blood spread through me. Changing clothes sounded appealing, but that my vampire body didn't perspire gave me one less reason to worry about it.

Renshu and Zhilan walked past a disorganized pile of

Grant's free weights and up the stairs. Renshu hadn't changed from his tux, but his bowtie was gone, and his top shirt buttons had long since been undone. At her house the night before, Zhilan had switched to black pants and a sleeveless, red turtleneck. That the pair had already risen came as no surprise. According to Zhilan, for most of us, the older we got, the earlier we rose.

Grant sat up in his coffin. Alice followed, and their long kiss produced a trickle of blood on his chin. Alice licked it clean, and they shared another kiss. Discretion was clearly not her style. I ran my dry tongue over my parched lips to no effect and headed up to the living room.

Caleb sat on the couch—alone.

"Where's Luke?" I asked.

Caleb shrugged.

Out the window, the sun had set, of course. Luke wasn't safe. My eyes shifted to Caleb, who was perfectly safe and only a few short feet from me.

"Try his cell?" Zhilan suggested.

"Right." I pulled out my phone and tapped Luke's name in my contact list.

Brring… brring… brring… brring… brring… Hey, it's Luke, leave a message. I hit End. "Come here." I extended my hand to Caleb.

Caleb came and took it with his soft, human fingers. I led him to the stairs and up. Zhilan and the rest of them knew what I was—a young Sanguan dying for blood in a world where the life-giving nectar had become dreadfully scarce. One step after another, I struggled to take my time.

Out in the darkness somewhere, Luke *might* have needed me, but I needed blood. That was certain. And closer. *So close.* Step after step, we climbed. Caleb wasn't in a band or tending a bar, which meant I didn't have to bite somewhere he could conceal. *So close.* I could bite him anywhere. *Almost there.* Or everywhere! I reached the top.

I grabbed Caleb from the last stair, and he smiled while we darted down the hall and into a bedroom with one piece of furniture beyond what I had expected—a dresser with a mirror above it. Maybe Grant had it for the women he brought home with him, who might sleep in that room. But what did it matter?

The wall screamed for me to slam Caleb into it, to position him perfectly for my drink, but that would have been loud. The next instant, the bed creaked, absorbing his back when I laid him beneath me. He brought his hands to my bare legs under my skirt. I sliced my fangs into his neck.

"Mmm…" His whole body relaxed.

I sucked—*fire!*—then stopped and sat straight with my head tilted to the ceiling. Caleb ran his hands over my thighs. I enjoyed the boiling blood flowing down my throat and where traces flickered in my once-more moist mouth.

Caleb's hands stopped on my knees. "Last night was torture."

"For you?"

He smirked.

"You have no idea." I leaned down for another sip, and then we kissed.

"I missed that taste," he said, meaning his blood.

"You could miss it, I suppose. But not like me."

He sat up to embrace me. "I *could* miss it the same way. We could leave all this fear behind. If I were a vampire, you wouldn't have to worry about me like you do now."

I shook my head.

He held me from leaning away. "This world is evil, and it's getting worse, but together, forever, we wouldn't have to be afraid."

I chomped into his neck and sucked hard.

Caleb had lived a privileged life—he recognized it, and I felt it in his blood—yet he often dwelled on the bad in the world. Why all the pain? Why all the death? And since the red rain had fallen, why did I refuse him the drink by which he would overcome the world's latest unexplained hardship?

I stopped, and amid a deep breath, savored the simmering fire within. "No, Caleb." I got off the bed. "Come on."

He followed me downstairs, where the others were watching the news on TV. As I hit the last step, Luke opened the front door. He spotted me and Caleb, and likely Caleb's fresh bite mark. Luke turned away.

I reached him before he got off the porch. "Hey." I grabbed his arm.

Luke shook my hand off. "Hey what?"

The familiar sirens whined in the distance.

"Where are you going?" I asked.

"Uh… I don't want to be here."

"Why?"

"Really, Erin? Come on. You obviously don't need me here."

"I do! I'm sorry." I sighed. "Actually, I'm *not* sorry. I *need* blood. There's no way around it."

"Last night was unbearable with him around. Tonight's going to be worse."

Not for me or Caleb. Not as much anyway. Luke was right. I started to pull him close.

He pushed me away. "Not now."

"Okay." His refusal was a first. "But you can't go."

"Why?"

"I *need* you here. With me. I need to know you're safe. I couldn't stand it with you out there on your own."

"Make me a vampire," he shot back. "I wouldn't be so helpless against those twins—I could run, at least—and you wouldn't have to worry about me all the time."

I shook my head. "It's not that simple."

"Because of Caleb?" he asked.

"Because blood's running out."

He inched toward me. "We'd find blood, Erin. Zhilan, Grant, and Alice have blood. You don't think you and I would find our own? You think my fans wouldn't eagerly share theirs with us?"

"What if there are no more fans?"

"The worse things have gotten, the more popular we've become. People need music, and people like my band. Our fans aren't going away."

"*What about* your band?" I knew he had already thought it through, but maybe something had changed. "They'd play with a vampire?"

"Yes! You know the other groups with vampires in them.

A bunch of them are decent, but so many are shams. Their music's garbage, and they're only famous 'cause of the Sanguans. But we could be great. We know we could. *I* know we could."

I didn't doubt him. "You can be great—beyond great—as a mortal."

"I know, I know… if we catch the right break. And if I'm alive when we do."

"So stay with me. Let me keep you safe."

He glanced toward the street. "How long?"

"All night," I said.

"No, I mean, how many nights?"

"I don't know." It was a good question. "Until we're sure what the twins are up to."

"Will we ever really know?"

Another good point. "Yeah, well, at least for a few days. Let's see what happens."

He shook his head.

"Please?" I urged.

He threw up his hands. "Fine." He angrily stepped past me.

I followed him inside.

"General Sharpe called," Zhilan said. "He will meet me tonight."

"Where?" I asked.

"My house."

"What about us?" Luke asked.

"Here is safe," Zhilan said.

"There's the rest of the twins' story," Caleb suggested.

Luke's shoulders slouched.

"I wouldn't mind meeting the general," I said. "And, Zhilan, your place is safe."

Zhilan squinted, then nodded. "We'll all go."

Luke and Caleb perched on bar stools at the marble-topped island in the kitchen of Zhilan's two-story brick home. With Tao gone, the food in the half-empty fridge was old, but mostly unspoiled. Regardless, after looking around, the guys stuck to glasses of tap water. I sat on the counter near the sink, after finally having a chance to change into black pants and a matching short-sleeved shirt on the way there. My sheathed sword lay beside me. The others were in the living room. General Sharpe, whose office was nearby in the Pentagon, had yet to arrive.

"Who took over the company after your brother?" Luke asked Caleb. I appreciated Luke's attempt to be civil.

Caleb answered, "Mr. Tillman. He's a good guy. He's been there for years, and he'll do a good job. I just wasn't ready for the responsibility. Or particularly interested, to be honest."

"Then you get the money without all the stress? That's not so bad," Luke said.

Caleb sipped his water. "No, it is not so bad."

Someone knocked on the front door.

Zhilan answered it. "General Sharpe. Please, come in."

I slid off the counter, grabbed my sword, and, with Caleb and Luke, headed to see.

The general, who wore civilian clothes, stopped when he noticed us at the edge of the kitchen and the others standing in the living room. He retreated a step.

"It's fine." Zhilan gently placed her hand on his shoulder. "These are my friends."

"Why are they here?" he asked.

"Because with what is going on out there, we all wanted to be with our friends in here." Zhilan motioned to an ornate, red-cushioned chair. "Please."

The general gave Caleb a long look, possibly recognizing him from the tabloid coverage of his extravagant club-going nights—a life Caleb had grown bored of and after meeting me, had left behind. The general took a seat. "I shouldn't be here."

While I remained in the entranceway with Luke and Caleb, Zhilan sat in the chair next to the general, and the others settled back into their seats.

"But you are here," Zhilan said. "And you are safe."

"Like I told Renshu," General Sharpe said, "I don't know what you think *I* can do for you."

Zhilan asked, "What do you think of us?"

"Well, I'm grateful Renshu saved my son. But…" He looked around the group. "I've seen a lot of bad Sanguans do a lot of bad things, and more often, I only see the results."

Zhilan nodded. "What do you think of the Spectavi?"

"We'd be lost without them."

"Why?" she asked.

"Sanguans," he said. "The attacks and the murders. We can't fight them. Without the Spectavi, things would be worse. Much worse."

Zhilan shrugged—for her, very demonstratively. "*We* don't kill humans. Yet my friends and I, and those like us, are chased down city streets by Spectavi, run from our homes, and when we are unlucky, killed. The Spectavi justifications for their persecution are lies."

The general shook his head. "They're not all lies. I've seen the bodies."

"No, they are not all lies," Zhilan conceded. "And it is easy to take what the Spectavi say at face value. But it is not right. What can we do to show this government that we aren't all killers? That we truly are not all evil?"

The general took another look around the room. "You know, I've seen the stories lambasting the Spectavi kangaroo courts. I read about the synthetic blood in San Francisco when it was all over the news, months ago. I even heard something about a few Sanguans having a hand in the gang leader Alexander's downfall. And sitting here, I trust that I'm not in danger from any of you, which I pray is not a massive misjudgment. But it makes no difference. You'll never convince the president, or the Secretary of Defense, or enough people that matter."

Alice's smile slipped away.

"It's wrong," Grant said. "I was *in* one of those courts. In chains. The crime they charged me with—and convicted me of—was heinous, and it was nothing but a lie. Since then, I've been constantly on guard, knowing that at any moment, I or someone I care for could be snatched off the street or executed on the spot under the pretense of another lie. It's no way to live."

"I hadn't ever considered that," the general said. "I can't imagine."

Rustling came from out back, near a window. Grant sniffed deeply, then Alice followed his lead.

"Spectavi," Zhilan said, surely catching the same whiff of sterile-smelling synthetic blood that I did.

We all looked at the general.

He stood and whispered, "I have no idea, but if they're after you, they can't know I came here voluntarily."

"I understand," Zhilan said quietly.

"Meaning what? He's our prisoner?" I asked. "I don't like the sound of that."

"We need to get him out of here," Grant said.

"Yes," Zhilan confirmed as soft shifting and shuffling continued outside. "Unseen." She asked the general, "How did you travel here?"

"I walked," he said.

"We don't know how many they have, so we cannot stay and fight," Zhilan said. "My car is in the garage for Luke and Caleb. We'll put the general in the trunk."

Grant, Renshu, and I nodded. Caleb's car, which parked down the street, would have to be left behind.

"Run!" I grabbed Luke and Caleb around their waists and headed across the kitchen toward the door to the garage.

Zhilan already had the general. Renshu followed her. Grant and Alice flashed puzzled looks my way, but I had no doubt. A sudden, inhuman sense had told me that if I didn't run, it would mean my end. Grant and Alice figured it out, and last into to the garage, Grant pulled the door shut.

BOOM! The explosion rocked the center of the house. I crashed into the side of Zhilan's red Ferrari with Luke and Caleb. Flames shot out around the kitchen door. A chunk of the garage wall fell, revealing the blaze inside the house.

"The Mercedes," Zhilan said.

Caleb pulled open the passenger-side door and got in the back, while Zhilan opened the trunk.

Luke said, "I'll drive." He took the key from her and got in the front.

The general started, "You're sure—"

"It is your best shot," Zhilan interrupted, "if you do not wish to be seen leaving this house."

He shook his head, climbed in the trunk, and lay on his side.

Zhilan slammed the trunk closed. "Alice, go with Erin and the guys."

Alice began, "But—"

"Go," Grant said, his face sober. "I need to fight, but Zhilan's right. You aren't ready."

Alice got in the back of the car.

Zhilan unsheathed her sword. "Renshu and I will go first to the left, then Grant to draw their fire. The rest of you, go right, then make your way south. When you're sure you don't have a tail, drop the general somewhere. A taxi stand would be good."

Grant added, "Try not to let anyone see you getting him out of the trunk."

Zhilan finished, "Then head for Fort Washington, in Maryland, off the Beltway. The park is closed to the public this late. Wait for us there, and Grant or I will see you inside when we arrive."

"You think they'd be safer without us?" I asked. "Just the humans in the car?"

Grant answered, "Who knows what the Spectavi will do to *anyone* coming out of this house? And the twins could be out there, anywhere."

I got in next to Luke, who prepared to turn the key. I grabbed his hand and stopped him. "Wait."

Caleb buckled his seat belt. In the house, through the hole in the garage wall, glowing red and orange flames raged. Chunks of brick wall had fallen. Renshu exchanged glances with Zhilan, then, shoulders first, they broke out opposite ends of the closed garage door.

Guns fired, and metal clanged with metal. Grant drew his pistols.

"Luke, open the door." Alice pushed his seat forward and got out of the car. "Be careful," she told Grant.

Grant wrapped his arms around her, and they kissed. "You, too."

When Zhilan yelled to Renshu, Grant sped out of a fresh hole in the garage door, further weakening the lower half for us. Alice got back in the car.

I still had one hand over Luke's on the ignition. "Not yet." With my other, I pulled my knife off the holster around my leg.

Swords clashed. A fresh rattle of shots sounded.

Grant called, "Renshu!"

I took my hand off Luke's hand. "Now!"

The car roared to life. Luke hit the gas, and I flipped open my knife. We broke through the garage door into the melee. A swarm of Spectavi to our left and down the street fired at my friends.

While Luke sped right around the circular driveway, Zhilan, with red splattered on her face and arms, met swords with Reinald, who was also bloodied.

Renshu dealt with gunfire in addition to his own one-on-one battle. He ducked under a white katana blade. Konrad—Reinald's extremely pale-skinned, bald, blue-eyed second in command—swung again, and Renshu blocked. Away from them all, Grant's opponent with a longsword faced away from me.

When Reinald missed with a swing, Zhilan raced away to slice apart two Spectavi shooting at her. She took a bullet to her thigh on the way back to reengaging the Spectavi leader.

"Jesus," I said, watching out the back window.

Caleb stared at the same mixed fire and sword fight. "Does Victoria know about this?"

"I can't imagine."

Renshu held a wound in his side with one hand and fought with his other. A bullet hit his chest while he repelled a blow from Konrad. Fangs out, Grant lunged at Gavin, Victoria's youngest fledgling. I hadn't seen him since his transformation and training at Eure. He was big, and his black hair as messy as always.

Grant punched twice, and Gavin dodged, spun, and swung, but Grant avoided it. Gavin spotted us.

Alice grabbed her knife. "He needs me."

"No, I'll go." I folded my knife closed and strapped it to my leg before lowering my window all the way. "Don't stop, Luke. Whatever happens, I'll catch up." I threw my sword scabbard over my shoulder, connected it to my belt, and pulled the diagonal strap to tighten it to my back. "Just get to the fort." I got my hands around the window frame and turned my whole body to it.

Luke placed his hand on my hip. "Be careful."

Gavin ducked under a punch from Grant.

"Good luck, Erin," Alice said.

I glanced at Caleb, then Luke, but couldn't sort out what to say, or to which of them. "Protect them, Alice." Visions of starving Sanguans flashed to mind. "If the twins are out there, run with Luke and Caleb."

"And the general?" she asked.

"Leave him." Pulling off the window frame, I launched myself at Gavin. My shoulder drove into his chest, and he fell to the ground. He jumped to his feet and readied his blade.

Grant fled from Spectavi pursuers, while Zhilan and Renshu battled on.

I drew my sword. "Where's Victoria?"

Gavin relaxed and stood straight. "After so long, no hello, Erin?"

"Hi. Where's Victoria?"

"New York. *Surely* she told you."

I nodded at the burning house. "Does she know about this?"

"You think she cares to be told the details of *every* Sanguan we round up? And if you must know, we're after Zhilan. She's the threat to society, not you."

"Threat to society?"

He smirked. "She's quite old."

"I'm stronger than you, Gavin. And I'm faster." With a quick flick of my wrist, I twirled my sword at my side. "You don't want to fight me."

"We'll see." He charged and—*tyn*—our blades met high and—*tyn*—low.

Tyn-tyn. He swung, and I ducked, spun to the side, and slashed at his back. *Tyn.* He barely blocked it. How angry would Victoria be if I killed her Gavin? He lunged into a swing.

With one hand off my katana, I caught his arm and flipped him to the ground. "I told you. This won't end well for you."

"Renshu!" Zhilan yelled.

Renshu lay bloody at Konrad's feet. Red dripped off the pale victor's blade onto his foe's unmoving body. Zhilan charged, and despite the rage mixed with silver from gunshots that had to be coursing through her, she fought Reinald and Konrad with powerful precision.

I took a step that way, but when Gavin got to his feet, I froze between rushing to Zhilan and staying between Gavin and Luke and Caleb

Reinald called, "Gavin! Let's go!"

Konrad sheathed his sword. He and the Spectavi with rifles darted out of sight, while Reinald battled Zhilan alone.

"See ya soon, Erin." Gavin raced after Konrad, and then Reinald finally left the scene.

Zhilan, bleeding from slowly healing wounds, rushed to Renshu and crouched beside him. I ran to join her. He wasn't breathing. He had been shot and slashed all over his legs, midsection, and face. The accumulation of wounds had left little blood to run out of the large gash in his neck.

"Renshu," Zhilan whispered, then glanced up at me. "His whole life, mortal and immortal, his bravery eclipsed his skill in battle. I adored it—the foolish irrationality." She kissed his cheek. "All the decades apart, I never stopped loving him. Our love had changed, but I never stopped. And when he returned…" She shook her head. "He returned during such dark times."

Dark because I let Caterine and Ariane free and darker because they kept me from reaching the True Cross before David Sartori. "I'm sorry."

"The Spectavi are headed to D.C." She stood and watched the bricks above a front window crumble into the blaze gutting her house. "The twins are causing trouble."

"How do you know?"

"Konrad yelled it to Reinald." She lifted Renshu's body and, limping, carried it toward her house. We stopped at a newly low section of wall in front of an especially active area of fire.

"You won't bury him?" I asked, relieved that the twins weren't after Caleb and Luke.

"His body has already been long enough of this earth. Were it another night during another time, I might spend a moment or two more with him." Fast enough to avoid her own burns, she placed Renshu in the fire. Flames rolled over his lifeless skin, which grayed and blackened before being consumed. His insides and bones burned quickly, and then Zhilan's fledgling and a hundred years of her love disintegrated to ash. "But it is no other night. Let us get to Fort Washington."

4

We took Zhilan's Ferrari to Fort Washington, eight miles south of the Beltway around D.C. The first fort on the site had been destroyed during the war of 1812. The current dark concrete-and-brick structure had been built in 1824, then remodeled later that century. Two three-sided bastions on its face overlooked the Potomac River from the east side.

Grant, Alice, Luke, and Caleb were standing around Zhilan's other car when we arrived.

"Where's Renshu?" Grant asked.

"He didn't make it," Zhilan said.

Grant shook his head.

"Why us?" Alice asked.

"Zhilan," I explained. "They targeted her because she's old and powerful. They're afraid of her, basically. Gavin told me. He's the one you were fighting, Grant. I knew him back at Eure."

"They waste their time." Zhilan, who had healed significantly since the battle, crossed her arms. "However, I do fear for the younger ones." She looked at Grant's fledgling. "Who aren't so powerful."

"I'll be fine," Alice said.

"Damn right," Grant agreed.

"Let's go." Zhilan led us to a path on the fort's nearest short side.

I brought up the rear with Luke and Caleb. "You guys okay?" I asked them.

"Yeah," Luke answered.

"Yup," Caleb said.

"The general?"

"We dropped him off halfway here," Caleb said. "And why here, anyway?"

I called to the front of the column, "Zhilan, why here?"

"The fort is maintained by the National Park Service these days," she said. "It was turned over by the military in 1946. Before that, while it protected Washington's approach by river, the Spectavi built a secret stronghold of their own a little deeper underground, farther inland. The Spectavi abandoned their post when the humans did."

"Is it safe?" Caleb asked.

"Yes," Zhilan said.

Grant added, "It's as safe as anywhere. The old entrances are gone. Sanguans engineered the new one up ahead in the fort and the other one out back in the woods. Very few know of them."

"Secret entrances?" Caleb asked.

"Yup," Grant confirmed.

Caleb nodded. "Cool."

"What about the cars?" I asked.

"We'll move them around to a smaller secondary lot

later," Grant said. "There are usually a few cars there all the time."

"Ferraris?" Luke asked.

"No one will trace either car to me," Zhilan called back, then stopped. "You are correct about the Ferrari. Will you drive it from here after sunrise?"

"Sure," Luke said.

We came to an open drawbridge before the gatehouse, which fronted an arched entranceway in the fort's side. Inside, the path cut across a grass lawn that ran down the hill to the long front wall facing the water. Beyond the wall, a low lighthouse stood at the river. On the other side of the Potomac, lush trees lined the Virginia shore, blocking most of the view of a highway.

Almost halfway into the fort, we deviated from the path and moved onto the lawn. Black gates enclosed two identical entrances to concrete staircases into the earth, facing each other. We descended the nearest staircase, which ended on a brick landing before a large green door.

I pointed at the door. "There?"

"No," Grant said. "That leads outside, down to the river."

Facing the wall, Zhilan crouched low, spread her fingers, and placed six of them on carefully selected bricks. She pushed, and with a loud *thunk*, the unoccupied half of the landing dropped slightly. Dirt surrounding the descending slab crumbled onto it as she continued pushing. Then the slab shifted toward me, revealing stairs that continued down.

When the entire slab had slid out of sight, Luke peered into the hole. "Pretty dark."

Grant started down with Alice behind him. Caleb stepped in front of Luke to go next. At that, Luke didn't hesitate to follow. As I went, minimal light from above shone into an otherwise pitch-black hallway with brick walls, a matching ceiling, and a smooth floor. I doubted Luke and Caleb could see anything at all.

Halfway down the stairs, Zhilan tapped another set of bricks. The landing at the top of the staircase slid shut faster than it had opened, plunging us into darkness. The air was heavy, and my vampire eyes made out faint silhouettes of everyone.

"Are there torches?" Caleb asked.

"In a manner of speaking," Grant said. Yellow lights running along the edge of the ceiling came on, dimly illuminating the area. Grant's hand rested on a pulled-down lever on the wall.

"We're beneath the middle of the fort," Zhilan explained as we walked. "This hallway runs away from the river and ends under the woods."

"When were you last here?" I asked.

"Two years ago, Tao and I swapped out the canned food for a fresh supply," Zhilan said. "Human visitors are rare because of the risk of their memories revealing the secret entrances, but when circumstances dictate, we like to be prepared."

Grant added, "Most of that food should still be good, but our mortal guests will probably also want some fresher options. We can stock up tomorrow."

Luke gave me a concerned look.

"It'll be safe here," I assured him, hoping it wouldn't turn out to be an empty promise after what had happened at Zhilan's.

The hallway kept going, but we turned off through an open entrance on the right leading to a large square room with overhead lamps, two doors at the end, and one door on the side.

Grant pointed out the various amenities. "TV"—very big, and significantly thicker than a flat panel—"couches"—three cushions, leather, and another with two cushions—"you see the tables"—one long, rectangular table, and the other round, both surrounded by wooden chairs—"a small kitchen"—a fridge, a sink, a microwave, and a narrow stovetop in the corner—"and a bathroom"—beyond a side door.

"The other doors?" I asked.

Grant pointed to the left. "Coffins behind door number one." He pointed right. "Eh... basically an all-purpose room. More tables, but they had been pushed off to the side last I saw, and a couple of laptops, which are pretty old, but should work. Oh, and we've stashed some weapons in there."

Zhilan headed right. "Alice, come with me. You need to practice. Grant, if you're finally ready to fight with something other than a gun, you should join us."

He considered it, then followed Alice into the room. I thought it wasn't a bad way for Zhilan to cope with Renshu's death, and Grant and Alice could surely use the practice.

Luke fell into the far corner of the big couch. "We're just gonna hide here?"

"For now," I said, sitting on the smaller one.

Luke checked his phone. "At least there's service down here."

Caleb sat on the other end of the same couch as Luke. "Wanna tell us the rest of the story?"

"Sure," I said, noting the eerie quiet during the moments no noise came from the other room.

The place felt cozy. Like Luke, all the waiting, fleeing from one place to another, and, in a sense, being hunted, really didn't sit well with me. But with him and Caleb—human him and Caleb—running had certainly been the only choice.

I started back into my story. "It was a few nights after Bodiam Castle, so still 1698. Victoria told me this part with considerable pride."

———————————

With the wind at his back and a mile to go on horseback, Tristan raced through the woods for the town of Niaux in the South of France. Leaves kicked off the wild ground as Caterine sped past, slashing his poor steed's side. Tristan fell, tumbling forward, then rose and attempted to sprint away. Ariane got in front of him, knocked him back to the forest floor, and with her mouth open wide, leaned down to him. He sprayed a handful of dirt and leaves into her face.

"Agh!" She spit and let him go.

Tristan ran. When Caterine blocked his path, he leapt over a thick tree limb. Her katana cut the branch and nicked the sole of his right boot. Tristan emerged from the woods and reached the open entrance in the low wall at the town's edge. He kept going, and when the sisters charged through the same entrance, electric-blue flames shot out from cauldrons at the base of the wall, barely missing their backs.

While people in Niaux hurried into their simple houses to hide, and those already inside slammed wooden windows and doors shut, the twins abandoned their pursuit and admired the fire.

"He has already made some," Ariane said. "Such a weapon…"

"So Edmond *will* permit its use," her sister noted. "But solely to our peril, I expect."

"We *must* have it," Ariane said.

Alexander and Erec le Roux leapt over the wall, avoiding the blue blaze.

"You're both terribly slow," Caterine said.

Erec shook his head. "You are faster than we are. It has always been so, and it will always be so."

Ariane smiled.

Alexander asked, "Where is Tristan?"

Caterine pointed her sword at the center of town. "That way."

A man in that direction forced open a stuck door and slammed it closed behind him.

"What are we waiting for?" Alexander licked his lips and, with his longsword in one hand, walked that way.

The others followed—Ariane and Caterine with their katanas lazily at their sides and Erec the most ready, holding his longsword in both hands.

"Where would he hide?" Erec asked.

"Let's start with the church," Alexander suggested.

Down two blocks of desolate street, then around the corner, Alexander and Erec crept to the rear of the small, triangular-roofed church.

Caterine pushed open the front door and called cordially, "Tristan?" She stepped inside. "Father?"

Her sister entered. "Faatheeer…"

A scuffle broke out to the left of the simple alter, where a middle-aged, robed priest appeared, shoved forward by Alexander.

"Demons!" the priest yelled.

"Where is Tristan?" Caterine demanded, the pleasantness gone from her voice.

The priest began, "I command you, unclean spirits—"

Caterine chomped into his neck, and his entire body slumped. She withdrew her fangs. "He spotted Edmond in town earlier." Caterine threw the priest to her twin. "Good to know, but nothing more useful."

Ariane drank from the other side of his neck, then let him fall to the floor, face-first, but still alive. "You have sinned, Father. *My*, how you've sinned."

Blue flame raced from the edges of the church roof to its central apex.

Ariane watched it burn. "Such a weapon…" She darted out the rear door, and her blade met Victoria's.

The other Sanguans fled the church. Sofie's longsword found Caterine's katana.

"Not her, Sofie!" Victoria called to her hundred-sixty-year-old fledgling, while swinging her sword wide to keep the other three at bay.

Sofie's blade again clashed with Caterine's.

The shorter warrior flashed her fangs. "I want *her*!"

"And I want you, my dear," Caterine called. "*I* want *you*."

With quick cuts, Caterine drove her foe to the defensive, then cracked the back of her hand across Sofie's face, launching her down the street.

Edmond arrived and took over for Sofie against his sister. Sofie turned her attention to Alexander, and when a Spectavi named Jardan showed up to take on Erec, the eight immortals fought one-on-one outside the burning church. Victoria lunged to slash Ariane's side, at the expense of a deeper cut in her own arm. While Victoria bled, Ariane's side healed completely.

The older vampire heckled, "Careful, *wench*."

Victoria swung her long blade. "One arm's enough for you."

Sofie darted from place to place faster than Alexander, inflicting a series of small cuts in her larger foe. She grazed his neck. "You're too slow."

Her blade gave a dull sound when she repelled a thunderous blow. She barely blocked another before Alexander stabbed into her chest, inches from her heart.

"*You* are far too weak," he parried.

Sofie retreated and kept her distance, grimacing as her wound partially closed.

Edmond's blade met Caterine's in the most even contest. He asked, "What did you do with Bennett?"

"We talked to him."

Edmond shook his head. "Does he live?"

She shrugged.

Edmond yelled, "Does he live?"

"He lives," she said. "Because he is weak. After enduring *a tremendous* amount of pain, he broke and failed you. *He* is the reason we found you here. If he finds his way home to you, handless and horribly burned, remember he lives only because he failed you."

Enraged, Edmond came at her. "This secret will not be yours!"

She swung, he blocked, and she stepped back, pointing her katana at him. "Do you know what day this is, brother?"

"I do, sister."

"It is ordained. It is destiny. On the same night as our glorious rebirth… on the night that miraculous blood wet our dry, cracked lips and made fair our hideously grayed skin… on the night Satan's fire returned to us strength that your *good Lord* saw fit to steal from us. On *this night*, we are to have a *new* fire. It is fate, brother. Make no mistake."

"Agh!" Jardan cried, blood gushing from his stomach. Erec beheaded him.

Victoria turned to look, then couldn't avoid Ariane's cut across her already-wounded arm. With the limb dangling uselessly, she raced down the street, over a hill, and farther into town. Ariane chased, and Caterine rushed to catch up to them. Edmond pursued his sisters, with Sofie, Erec, and Alexander not far behind.

Victoria barged her good shoulder through the door of a house on the left.

From the top of the hill, Edmond yelled, "Not—"

The twins raced in after her.

Tristan leapt out a window of the same house and darted down the hill. Inside the house, blades clanged and clattered before Caterine rocketed out the window. Ariane shot from the doorway, and they both chased Tristan.

Edmond spun and stabbed his longsword into Alexander's chest. Alexander jumped back and fled in the direction of the church.

Sofie was holding her own against Erec, and when Edmond joined that battle, Erec parried a few blows before deciding better of continuing, outnumbered.

"We shall meet again," Erec said and ran after Alexander.

Far down the dark street, the twins closed in on Tristan.

"It is *hopeless*!" Ariane screamed.

"Give it to us!" Caterine yelled.

"Never!" Tristan called behind him. He cut off the road and sped to the right, into the woods, up a steep hill, and toward a line of houses at the forest edge. The twins raced after him. Climbing the hill, Tristan weaved around trees and darted out of the forest and between two houses. The twins closed the gap.

Tristan raced for a cave in the face of the hillside. The twins followed him in.

"It is *ours*!" Ariane's scream echoed against the rock surrounding them.

They ran on.

"Ours!" Caterine's cry echoed louder.

Boom! The twins skidded to a halt.

Boom, boom, boom! The faint glimmer of moonlight reaching into the cave disappeared.

"No!" Ariane screamed.

Boom, boom, boom!

"No!" Caterine yelled.

Rubble from the mountainside covered the cave entrance. In front of the cannon-filled row of houses that had been constructed specifically for that night, Victoria stood with her arms folded and her hair blowing in the wind. "Keep firing."

Boom, boom, boom!

Blasted rock tumbled onto the pile.

"Higher."

Boom, boom, boom!

Edmond and Sofie came to Victoria's side. Spectavi in the houses lit fires.

Boom, boom, boom!

"Enough," Edmond said. "The other entrances are sealed?"

Boom, boom, boom!

Edmond turned and yelled, "Enough!"

"They are," Victoria answered.

Edmond shook his head. "A few months, you think?"

"Longer," Victoria said. "Far longer."

Edmond grimaced. "They will have air to breathe?"

"Yes," Victoria confirmed.

Edmond nodded. "Tonight, we will say a prayer for them all—Caterine, Ariane, brave Bennett, and poor, brave Tristan."

Victoria tested her arm. "Sofie, bring me someone." While Sofie sped off, Victoria grabbed her sword and walked to the pile of rubble.

Boom! She spun to the houses before realizing that the

sound had come from inside the cave.

The twins battered the rock blocking their way out. *Boom!*

Victoria held her mighty blade in front of her, its tip cutting into the earth. Before long, Sofie returned with a man from town for her to drink from.

The thunderous pounding of Caterine and Ariane's efforts to break free continued until sunrise, then filled the night and the next many nights. Victoria had her coffin brought to the nearest house in the row the cannons remained in and spent the days there. Summer gave way to fall, and Sofie kept her company most nights. Two dozen Spectavi stayed in the houses, and Edmond, William, and others occasionally joined Victoria's watch. Edmond and William often discussed strategies for how to calm the twins upon their release from the cave. William spoke very optimistically of recent developments in microbiology and pulmonary circulation, and his enthusiasm buoyed Edmond's spirits.

That winter, Erec, Alexander, and a host of Sanguans attacked Niaux in an attempt to rescue the twins. The Spectavi were prepared for the assault and, with Victoria and Edmond leading the defense, won an easy victory.

Aided by Tristan's blood, the twins kept up the relentless racket in the cave for over a year before their wails, screams, and moans came more often than their pounding of rock. Another year later, even those cries were rare. Edmond grew nervous and frequently urged Victoria to let his sisters free. Victoria steadfastly refused, threatening to kill the twins if he or anyone let them out before she deemed it time. Edmond always relented.

Ahmose returned from a twenty-year seclusion and spent two nights in Niaux. Victoria remembered one conversation in particular, between him, herself, and Edmond.

Ahmose asked, "Once you have them prisoner outside this mountain, Edmond, what then? Tell me you do not still believe you can make them human once more."

"In my heart, that remains my sincerest wish. Failing that, we will discover how to heal them of their terrible rage," Edmond answered.

"What if they do not want to be healed?" Ahmose countered. "What if they love their rage? What if... they have become their rage?"

"No," Edmond said. "They were good—so very good—before they were *changed* into what they became. That is absolute proof that they can change back."

Ahmose stroked his smooth chin. "How long will you keep them prisoner?"

"As long as it takes," Edmond said. "If we cannot heal them quickly, time will give us a cure."

"Time?" Ahmose asked.

"Technology advances, my friend. The steady march of time—"

"The *steady march of time*," Ahmose scoffed. "You would keep them prisoner for so long that the steady march of time will be your solution?"

"*However* long it takes," Edmond reiterated.

"And you, Victoria?" Ahmose asked. "I suppose you fully support this imprisonment?"

"You do not?" she replied.

"I do not judge," Ahmose said. "I have questions. I seek to understand your goals and motivations, but ultimately, all I will do is watch."

Edmond said, "I do miss these conversations, my dear Ahmose."

"I will *not* be staying long, I assure you," he said. "Victoria?"

"While I would prefer we take this chance to end Caterine and Ariane's lives, short of that, I support anything that will see them removed from society—if possible, for all time."

As promised, Ahmose departed Niaux soon after and returned to seclusion. A year later, a second large Sanguan attack brought a bloodier battle than the first. But again, the Spectavi prevailed.

Years passed, and Edmond left often for long stretches to tend to business in France and other countries. Victoria's watch never faltered, and except when sent on errands and missions by her maker, Sofie remained ever at her side.

After Caterine and Ariane had been under the mountain for nine years, for the last two hardly making a sound, Victoria finally ordered that the cave be opened.

Spectavi pulled away the boulders, needing to work in groups for the largest. Others rushed a pair of steel coffins from the houses. Dozens more stood ready, with swords drawn.

As the entrance neared being uncovered, Edmond, who had left his longsword in one of the houses, asked, "You're sure we should not bind them in chains when they emerge?"

"No," Victoria said, her blade on her back. "I do not care

to listen to that metal clattering against their coffins night after night."

With a few boulders to go, Sofie and the others grew tense.

Victoria called to the workers, "Do not hesitate to strike. We have but one shot at this."

The last massive boulder, pushed by two Spectavi, slid inch by inch. Slowly, more of the cave's mouth uncovered until the opening grew large enough for a thin body to fit through. They kept pushing.

A pair of gaunt wraiths with katanas shot out of the hole. Victoria grabbed Caterine's darkened arm and slammed her to the ground. Ariane got a few steps farther before Edmond caught her, ripped her sword from her hand, and threw it away.

With Caterine struggling beneath her, Victoria snatched the twin's katana and chucked it out of reach.

Ariane flailed at Edmond. He tripped her and drove his knee into her back on the ground. "I am sorry, my sister."

Victoria smashed the side of Caterine's head into the dirt, and the Sanguan went limp.

"They are so weak," Edmond remarked.

"Keep heart, my king!" Victoria urged.

"They look as gray as they did"—he leaned on his knee to keep Ariane down—"so many years ago."

Caterine rasped, "E... Edmond... Greek... f... fire..."

The coffins were dropped between the twins and their hinged lids opened by two Spectavi.

Victoria whispered to her captive, "There *is* no fire.

There *was* no fire. There will *not be* any fire for you or your sister while you rot in these boxes." She lifted struggling Caterine into the coffin and slammed the lid shut.

The lid flew open. Victoria pushed it down, then closed the six latches around its edge.

"Ariane!" Caterine screamed, summoning new strength to batter her prison walls. "Gragh!"

"Caterine!" Ariane called, still fighting to break free.

"Ariane!" Caterine yelled, while Victoria strode to her sister.

Ariane screamed, "Cat—"

Victoria punched Ariane's face into the dirt, then lifted the feeble creature and threw her in the second coffin. Victoria slammed it shut and latched it closed.

"Rraargh!" the twins growled.

While the pair beat on the coffin walls, Edmond said, "Rest, my sweet sisters. Find yourselves."

"Grahh!"

"GrrAh!"

Edmond finished, "Let the Lord guide you to your *good* selves."

The Spectavi took the coffins into hiding, and a decade passed before Victoria judged the twins had grown sufficiently weak for the coffins to be opened. In her presence and Edmond's, William conducted his first experiments on Caterine and Ariane.

————————

"So it was all a trick," Luke said.

"Yup," I replied. "The Spectavi don't have the secret of

Greek fire, at least as far as Victoria told me. The blue fire in Niaux was regular fire, chemically colored."

"What happened to Tristan?" Luke asked.

"To no one's surprise, he was found drained and torn apart in the cave."

"And the twins were locked up for *three hundred years*," Caleb said.

"They were," I said. "Occasional attempts to locate them and free them were all thwarted." I half-smiled. "Until I succeeded."

Grant returned, carrying the handle of a weapon more than a foot long. Alice and Zhilan followed him.

"How'd it go?" I asked.

"Alice is coming along," Zhilan reported. "Grant needs quite a bit of work."

"What's that?" I asked him.

From the handle, a shorter length of black folded out, and at the end, two ax heads—nearly rectangular, but widest at the edges—extended and locked into place.

Luke leaned forward. "Awesome."

"You carry it on your back?" I asked.

"Indeed." Grant moved his thumb up the handle, then pressed in, and the ax folded inward. The two heads kept the long pieces of handle from being perfectly flush, but the weapon would no doubt fit on his broad back.

"The sun will rise soon," Zhilan said. "Caleb, Luke, come with me. I'll show you to the other entrance in the woods behind the fort. You can return that way before nightfall."

5

Seven nights before the Spectavi would run out of synthetic blood, I emerged from the room that held our coffins and found Caleb alone, watching the news on the big television.

I checked my phone. "Crap."

"What is it?" Caleb asked.

"Luke isn't coming."

Grant and Alice rose and went to the long table.

Zhilan came out last. "What did he say?"

"That his boss at the bar is mad at him, and so is his band." I got no answer when trying to call Luke. I returned to my coffin, grabbed my sword, and strapped the scabbard to my back.

"Where are you headed?" Zhilan asked.

"I have to go after him."

"Have a seat," she said.

"What?"

"Relax. You cannot force him to stay here."

"Uh, yes I can."

Zhilan shook her head. "For how long?"

"As long as I have to. Until the twins aren't a threat to him."

"They're old, Erin," Grant said.

"So what?"

"I mean, they're fifteen hundred years old. They could be around, and a threat, for quite a while."

Caleb pointed at the TV. "The twins might have already moved on."

While we all headed over, Alice asked, "What do you mean?"

"Late yesterday, they apparently caused a lot damage downtown," Caleb explained.

"Turn it up," I said.

The anchorman asked the reporter, "And there were more than the two of them?"

Broadcasting from D.C., the pretty reporter stood in front of a smashed in, burned-out office building surrounded by yellow police tape. "Witnesses reported between four and ten Sanguans involved—a wide range, but it seems likely it was not the French twins by themselves."

The anchorman asked, "And no video of the attack exists?"

"That's correct. The surveillance system command center has been completely destroyed. Data from the system is typically backed up off-site. However, the most recent video, which would include the attack, was stored in this building. There was no time to make a backup."

The anchorman nodded. "Disappointing news, but thanks for the report." He spoke to the studio camera. "We need to take a break. More on the attacks after a check on the weather."

Caleb lowered the volume. Todd, my ex-boyfriend from when we were humans, ran the surveillance system, but thankfully, didn't work at that control center. My phone rang—Victoria.

I walked away from the group and answered, "Hi, Victoria."

"Erin, where are you?"

It was encouraging to hear her voice, the voice of one who had stood up to the twins time and again. "Maryland."

"Did you see what happened last night in D.C.?" she asked.

"Just now."

"I could use your help."

"Sure," I said. "With what?"

"It concerns the surveillance system."

I wondered if that meant it concerned Todd, as well. "What about it?"

"I'll explain when I see you."

"You're coming back from New York?"

"Yes, I'm on my way to Eure."

My heart skipped a beat. "Where do you want to meet?"

"There."

I looked around the group. "I'm not sure that's a good idea."

"Why not?"

"Reinald came after us last night."

"Not you. Zhilan," Victoria said matter-of-factly.

"You knew?" At my raised voice, attention in the room briefly shifted to me.

"I learned of it after the fact. Erin, I'm glad you are all right, but let's save all that for later. I promise you'll be safe at Eure. Will you come?"

I never wanted to go back to that place. And I had to find Luke. But rescuing Todd meant eventually getting involved with Eure. And *doing* something sounded significantly better than hiding out. "I need to bring someone."

"Who?"

"Caleb."

Victoria remained quiet for a moment. "Fine. I will see you in two hours."

I hung up. Everyone had refocused on the TV. "What is it?" I asked, heading over to join them.

"The president's going to speak," Grant replied.

In the White House Press Room, while President Hughes approached the podium, the microphone picked up reporters shifting in their seats and preparing pads and pens. The elderly second-term president appeared a little pale.

He opened a folder and began, "Tonight, I want to assure residents of Washington, D.C.—my fellow residents—that they are safe. In the wake of yesterday's incidents, you will find an increased police, military, and Spectavi presence patrolling the city."

He glanced at his papers. "I am deeply saddened by the loss of lives in the attack on our defense network and grieve with the families of those who fought so valiantly. In close cooperation with the Spectavi, we are aggressively pursuing the Sanguan criminals who perpetrated the attacks. D.C. residents, and all Americans, if you see any violence or anything suspicious, go indoors and call the police. I am confident that nationwide, our increased standing defense presence will allow us to respond to Sanguan violence more quickly than ever before. Last night was tragic, but this night sees our country better prepared because of it." He closed his folder and ignored a barrage of reporters' questions on his way out of the room.

Zhilan asked, "What did Victoria want?"

"She wants to meet me at Eure."

"Why?"

I shrugged. "Something about the surveillance system in D.C. She wouldn't tell me what."

"You think it's related to yesterday?" Alice asked.

"The twins, yes," I said. "The Spectavi coming after Zhilan? No. But I don't really know for sure."

"Will you go?" Zhilan asked.

"Yes, with Caleb. And I'm going to try to find Luke on the way. And there's Todd. I'm hoping he's there."

"Did Victoria indicate Todd might be?" Zhilan asked.

"No," I said. "And I didn't ask because I'm not sure how to handle it."

Grant huffed. "Like you need *more* to worry about."

"Who's Todd?" Alice asked.

"My ex-boyfriend," I explained. "When we were both human, he and the company he founded—Snap Safe— created the software that runs the surveillance system. Except Todd didn't want it to operate the way the Spectavi did. He figured, rightly, that the system, if it was always on, watching everything, would be used far beyond its stated purpose of tracking criminals. The Spectavi forced him to become one of them and used their synthetic blood to make him forget that they had done so. Then, with the synthetic, they altered his mind to make him go along with their plans for the cameras."

"That's awful," Alice said.

"Yeah," I agreed. "Oh, and in the process, his memory of me got wiped away. *That* was really awful."

Grant asked, "Are you going to tell him what happened if he's there?"

"I don't know. Probably eventually, but I think it'll take some planning to find a good moment, you know?"

Zhilan said, "He's surely been programmed to be content with his current life as a Spectavi."

"Exactly," I said. "Plus, aside from writing the software, he's important to them because he knows the locations of all the cameras. Between that and everything going on, telling him isn't going to be simple. Anyway, what are you guys gonna do?"

Alice looked at Grant. Grant looked at Zhilan.

She answered, "We'll all go for a drink and then have more practice."

While Caleb drove—he had picked up his car from Zhilan's street during the day—I texted Luke. He didn't answer.

We stopped at my house so I could change. Caleb asked if I wanted a drink, and I did, but with Luke on my mind, I held out.

The drive into D.C. was unlike any before. Soldiers, police officers, and Spectavi lined the Fourteenth Street Bridge, where the speed limit had been reduced to a strictly enforced fifteen miles per hour. A group of Spectavi had a Sanguan out of his car and were searching his trunk.

"Try to look human," Caleb suggested.

"Yeah," I said, wishing I had put on a little skin-darkening makeup, despite the fact that I passed for a pale mortal as long as I kept my fangs hidden and didn't move too quickly.

Over the bridge, more of the same mishmash of authorities were spread out everywhere. I had never seen so much military equipment anywhere, let alone in downtown D.C. Their parked vehicles blocking lanes made the trip slow, but significantly fewer civilians than normal were driving, which helped.

"I guess this is their version of a manual surveillance system," Caleb remarked. "With the other one out of commission."

We stopped two blocks from Luke's apartment. Waiting while Caleb went inside felt odd, but it was easier than dealing with the Spectavi guard out front.

Caleb returned alone and opened the car door. "Jonathan was there, but not Luke."

I called on my cell, but again, Luke didn't answer.

"I'm sure he's fine," Caleb said. "You try the bar?"

I appreciated him being helpful. I called and, after five rings and no answer, said, "Let's see if he's there."

Caleb started the car and hit the gas hard.

"Don't." I put my hand on his leg, and he slowed. "We don't want the attention. Just get us there."

"Okay."

Patrolling police and military watched us, block after block, during each of Caleb's very gradual turns and non-threatening accelerations. Finally, I spotted the bouncer standing outside the bar. Though he waved us away, Caleb stopped in front of him beside a No Parking sign.

I got out of the car.

Desislav quit waving. "Oh, Erin." He opened the bar door for me.

I asked, "Have you seen Luke?"

"Nope," he said.

Inside, three customers sat at the bar. Behind it, the bartender wasn't Luke.

"Have you seen Luke?" I asked him.

"Yeah," the bartender said. "He was here this afternoon."

"Where's he now?"

"No idea."

"If you see him again, tell him to call me."

He nodded. "Yes, ma'am."

I left and got back in the car.

"Anything?" Caleb asked.

"No."

"Should we head to Eu—"

Shvmp! My fangs sliced into the far side of Caleb's neck. I drank and leaned so my chest drove his firm body into the leather seat.

Joy! The emotion had surged through him at word that Luke would not return to the fort, then again, more gently, when he found Luke not at home, and it lingered. Caleb didn't like me being worried, but he couldn't help how he felt.

The blaze built, fueled by his rich, juicy blood. I leaned in harder, bit deeper, and sucked faster.

Caleb *couldn't* help wanting me.

The fire roared! I *couldn't* help wanting him.

I withdrew my fangs and licked my lips clean. "Yes. Let's head to Eure."

He gulped and put the car in Drive.

6

West of Washington, near Tyson's Corner, on the long road that led through a thick forest to Eure's entrance, I pulled up my picture with Todd on my phone. The photo had been taken on our boat trip on the Potomac on a warm, sunny day. He had been handsome—no doubt about that—a bit taller than I was with neat brown hair.

An email arrived from Blaine... finally. I switched apps to read it.

Erin, sorry! I'm fine. I'm in Miami on my friend's computer. I lost my phone. And my job, ha! I'm looking for work, but no luck yet. We might go to Key West soon. Figure everywhere's dangerous, so if we aren't working, we might as well be someplace fun.

And that was it—no new phone number to call him, no hope to see me soon. But I didn't blame him. What would the point have been, really? At least he was safe so far.

With the campus in sight, Caleb asked, "What if Reinald's there?"

"Victoria confirmed that they were after Zhilan, not us."

"I know, but still..."

"We'll be fine," I assured him. Caleb didn't appear convinced, so I added, "I'm going to ask Victoria about it."

At the same guarded entrance gate I had leapt over to escape the cursed place, and then raced back to, to drink the life out of my first victim, Caleb stopped and lowered his window. An armed Spectavi stepped out of the booth and leaned down to the car.

"Erin Rose," Caleb said. "And Caleb Sartori."

The guard reached into the booth, and the gate slowly slid aside. "Go ahead. Victoria is at home. Do you know the way?"

I stared straight down the lamppost-lined street. "Yes." Did the guard know I had worked there? That I had caused Edmond's death? "Go," I said to Caleb.

Caleb raised his window and drove on.

"It's up a ways, then to the right," I directed, while thinking of the twins' capture hundreds of years before. My responsibility for their release weighed heavier on me as we drew nearer to Edmond's home. We drove past white office building after white office building, deeper into the campus, closer to that damn courtroom where I had spent one long night after another.

We passed the building with my old room in it. That place was where I had read news coverage of Todd and his software team on my laptop and had grown to despise him, wrongly, based on his Spectavi-engineered actions. That was also where I had last lived as a human.

"Is this weird?" Caleb asked.

"You have no idea."

Spectavi guards at occasional street corners and outside building entrances represented a subtle, but noticeable heightening of security since I had been there. We turned toward Victoria's imposing mansion built of black stone with round porch columns. I counted the same twenty windows across the front, ten on each of two levels, all with metal bars covering them.

Caleb gawked at the house. "She lives *there*?"

"Yeah... well, I'd imagine her coffin is in there somewhere, but the place was pretty dusty last time I was inside. So I don't know how much *living* she's been doing there recently."

"Gotcha." He parked the car and unbuckled his seat belt. "How's she been since Switzerland?"

"Normal, I guess. We've only discussed the True Cross a little. She's been focused on the twins and then was in New York."

I got out of the car, and Caleb did the same. I had my knife strapped over my pant leg, but decided to leave my sword. After climbing a short set of stone steps, I knocked twice on the large door.

When no answer or sound came in response, Caleb looked to me.

I pushed open the door, and he followed me inside. The wood floor creaked, and dust still covered the antique furniture.

"Victoria?" I called.

No answer.

Caleb made his way to the corner, where a statue stood on a pedestal. The carved angel had his wings spread wide and held a sword above his head.

"Who is it?" I asked.

"Michael," Caleb said. "The archangel. He's often considered the leader of God's armies against evil."

"Fitting for a veteran of the Third Crusade. Edmond described Victoria as a 'powerful weapon for Christ.'"

Caleb turned to me. "Where do you think she is?"

"Come on." I led him out the back of the house, down another set of steps, and across a dirt path to a high wooden fence.

Sounds of metal striking metal inside confirmed my suspicion. We made our way through an open entrance in the fence to an inner ring around the arena.

"Who's fighting?" Caleb asked.

"Probably Victoria and some Sanguan prisoners." My heart fell as I recalled vivid scenes from that disgusting, sweltering courtroom: arguing defendants put to death on the spot, others dragged away, struggling violently, and those resigned to their fate, who sulked off without a single word. The uncomfortable courtroom chair, signing my name as witness to the proceedings again and again… "Most of them are murderers, but some of them aren't."

Caleb stopped. "Then what did they do?"

"Nothing. I don't like it, but at this point, the Spectavi would just be killing the Sanguans out on the street if they weren't bringing them here. I don't like that, either, but *that* is why we fight them. If we succeed against the Spectavi out there, innocent Sanguans won't be slaughtered in here."

We walked up a steep staircase and down a short tunnel, then stepped out into the middle of rows of benches overlooking the central arena, where Gavin fought a lone Sanguan. In addition to the six Spectavi guards evenly spread around the circular wall, Victoria leaned against the side, observing, with the sleeves of her black blouse rolled up her arms. Caleb and I took seats, and after spotting them, I made a conscious effort to avoid looking at the set of six high-backed leather chairs where Edmond and I had always sat to watch. Where he had fed on me, over and over...

Gavin spun and cleaved the Sanguan in two.

"Good," Victoria called, while Gavin's foe bled onto the dirt. "Very good." She glanced up at us and told Gavin, "That's enough for now."

He nodded and marched out of sight beneath us. A guard from the wall collected the two Sanguan body halves.

Victoria leapt up to the aisle at the first row of benches. We stood as she approached, and I noticed her ever-present chain necklace and pictured the red cross that hung under her top.

"Thank you for coming," she said.

I folded my arms. "I fought Gavin, you know. At Zhilan's."

"How'd it go?" she asked.

"How do you think?"

"I'm not surprised, but he knows what he's doing. He's strong and vastly improved from when you watched him here last. He has tremendous potential."

"If he comes after me or my friends again, I won't hesitate to end him."

She wagged her finger. "It would be a mistake to

underestimate one of my blood."

"It would be a mistake for *him* to underestimate *me*." I uncrossed my arms. "Why'd you guys attack Zhilan?"

"I did not. *If* I had been involved, *if* I knew you were with her, I would have put off the attack. Before it came to that, to what extent I could have, I would have lobbied against the mission. But I was not involved, and Reinald deemed her a threat because of her age. You might say she's been on our list for a while, and with me out of town, he took the opportunity to go after her."

I shrugged and tried to sound nonchalant. "I thought you commanded more respect than that."

She bristled. "I am respected plenty. But that is the nature of war."

"Konrad killed Zhilan's fledgling."

"War." Victoria glanced at Caleb. "I am sad for you, Erin, that these are your first nights as a vampire. But the fact is, as truly as ever among immortals, this is a time of war."

"Meaning Reinald will go after her again."

"Perhaps." She shrugged. "But in my estimation, it will not be soon. Not after last night."

"What happened?"

"Come with me." She led us back through the tunnel.

I couldn't help but ask, "You know those you fight in this arena aren't all guilty, right?"

"I know that a small number did not commit the crimes they were tried for, yes."

"And that doesn't bother you?"

While we went down the stairs, Victoria said, "If they did not meet their end in my arena, they would be executed in the sun or done away with at the hands of another Spectavi on this campus."

"That's no excuse," I countered.

"I seek no excuse," she said. "I fight in the name of Christ, for the good of His people, in a war that I find just. I count myself a Spectavi, and because we have set ourselves upon a course that aligns with my ultimate goals, the details of the life of each individual Sanguan are of no consequence to me."

I shook my head as we exited the arena and headed for her house.

Victoria asked, "You saw that the surveillance operations center was destroyed?"

"Yes."

"It is not that simple. It is worse. Caterine, Ariane, and the Sanguans with them stole most of the equipment from the building before they set off their explosives."

Caleb opened the back door to her house and held it for us. "So they can use the cameras?"

"Yes." Victoria led the way in.

"Can't you shut them down?" I asked.

"At the moment, no," she said.

"Destroy the whole system," Caleb suggested. "Camera by camera."

"No. It took a lot to get those cameras installed. A lot of time convincing the government to let us. A lot of lobbying. We are not in a hurry to destroy them. More importantly, we're going to need the system to defeat the twins—to kill them, or short of that, to drive them from Washington."

Todd *had* to be involved. We walked out her front door and headed for the main street of office buildings.

"They're in D.C.?" Caleb asked.

"At this particular moment, I do not know where they are. But they will return to Washington, I have no doubt, and they must have plans for the city, or else why steal the surveillance operating hardware? I fear for the residents and your government leaders, Caleb."

"What does this have to do with me?" I asked.

"I believe you know who wrote the software for the system?"

"Todd?"

"Yes," Victoria said. "He'll help me explain."

What would I say when I met him? Before Victoria called earlier that night, I had usually imagined my next meeting with Todd as part of a hurried escape attempt. But could I get him to leave Eure with me after our meeting? I wondered if he'd come willingly. To try to convince him of what had happened, I could show him the picture of us on the boat. But what if he was completely content in his current situation? In that case, especially considering the state of the world, perhaps he was best off working at Eure.

At the nearest white office building, we climbed a short staircase to opaque glass doors, one set among the many I had failed to enter while trying to investigate the campus. The locks clicked open when Victoria neared.

Regularly spaced white doors with silver control panels

and no handles broke up a long plain hallway of white walls and bright fluorescent lighting. The familiar filtered air hit me, as did the lonely sounds of our footsteps.

"Which one?" I asked to interrupt my memory's assault on my senses.

"At the end," Victoria answered.

More sterile hallway. More quiet. At least Caleb and Victoria walked alongside me.

When we arrived, the door slid open. Inside, at the middle of a long white conference table, Todd, who wore slacks and a blue button-down, stopped his conversation with William. On the table, a silver metal briefcase was eerily similar to the case I had seen bald, narrow-faced William flee the complex with, which carried the initial batch of the additive that permanently erased Todd's memory of me.

I felt very Sanguan, walking into a room full of enemies on their home turf. But I stopped short of seething. I didn't attack the scientist who had spent years brainwashing his own kind. Maybe because it had been a while since Todd had been taken from me, I didn't ache at the sight of him or fume at William. Or maybe it was because I had Luke and Caleb.

Both Spectavi at the table stood, Todd with his hands on his hips.

"Is this Erin?" he asked.

"It is," William said. "And Caleb Sartori, if I'm not mistaken."

"You aren't," Victoria confirmed.

"Victoria thinks you can help us," Todd said.

I crossed my arms. "You really don't know me?"

William frowned. Caleb shoved his hands in his pockets.

"Uh, no," Todd said. "Have we met somewhere?"

"Yes. We worked together before we were both vampires."

"Erin!" William glared at me.

"We lived together for a little while," I added. "In your apartment."

William shifted his attention. "Victoria?"

She smiled. "That's enough, Erin."

I took a seat at the table, and the others followed suit. Todd appeared befuddled.

I wasn't done. "I let Caterine and Ariane loose, you know."

"You did *what*?" Todd asked.

William shook his head.

Victoria's smile widened. "Another time, Erin."

I *was* angry, as it turned out. And yet, Todd seemed to be all right. His mind was clearly tricked, but the trick seemed... successful. He didn't look like a prisoner held against his will.

"Fine." I relaxed. "But what am I doing here?"

Victoria said, "I mentioned the cameras and the operating hardware. In short, Caterine and Ariane, and those with them, have access to the entire surveillance system in D.C. They can see everything in the city—every vehicle movement, any person, essentially everything outside. Todd?"

He shook his head, still looking confused. "There's no

S.M. PERLOW

way to hack into the computer network the cameras are on. We could destroy all the cameras because I know where they all are. In fact, I think we *should* destroy them all."

"And so do the president and his advisors," Victoria said. "But I do not. We need those cameras."

"If you can't use them, what good are they?" I asked.

Todd answered, "There's another control center. We could use the cameras from there."

"Then what's the problem?"

Todd shrugged. "I don't know where it is."

"Who does?"

"The president, the vice president," Victoria said. "Others, I'd imagine, but we are certain that those two know."

Todd leaned forward. "Vice President Turner hated the idea of the surveillance system from the outset. But despite considerable effort, he failed to stop it from being built. The second control center was a concession to him, so the government would have their own access. We set up the computers and the software for them here at Eure, and then they disassembled it and moved it. Somewhere."

"I see." I tore my gaze from Todd and looked at Victoria. "That's all moderately interesting, but again, what does it have to do with me?"

"They won't tell us where it is," Victoria said. "I have a hunch that despite how hard Turner lobbied against the system, since they have access to it, they're using it. And that's fine. The problem is, now that we *don't* have access, they want to keep it that way." She tapped her finger on the table. "I expect things to grow far worse in Washington. Our relationship with the United States is already strained, and it will become quite tenuous if we cannot protect their capital. We need to regain use of those cameras."

"You think one of them will tell *me* where the second control center is located?"

"We don't think you'll make it near the president," Victoria clarified. "But the vice president, maybe. If you do, you could use tactics to persuade him, tactics that we Spectavi are not able to use."

"You mean drinking his blood?"

"His blood will not tell you anything these days," Victoria said. "But there are other methods of making a person talk."

"What makes you think I'll be able to get close to the vice president?"

"Because he's intentionally keeping a high profile," Victoria explained. "Almost to the extreme President Hughes has avoided public appearances of late, Vice President Turner has sought them out. My sources tell me the strategy is for Turner to stay visible and portray the administration as confident and unshakable, despite Hughes being quite scared."

"Got it. So where's Turner?"

"I can point you in the right direction, but then it'll be up to you to track him and acquire the information we need."

"I'd imagine the rest of the Spectavi will be trying to stop us?" I asked.

"They will," Victoria said. "If the vice president suspects

we've relaxed in our defense of him to accomplish this mission, our relationship with the government could fall apart."

"What about reporting his whereabouts?"

"No. Turner trusts the Spectavi, but based on decades of fear that one bite would reveal countless national secrets, the Secret Service monitors the vice president's vampire guards and their communications closely. The situation is simpler now that Turner's blood has changed, but I won't risk trying to get messages past his human protectors."

I nodded.

"Will you do it?" she asked.

I asked William, "What's in the case?"

He slid it toward me. "Victoria will explain on your way out."

I pulled it over by the handle. "What about Caleb?"

"Surely he has somewhere to stay," Victoria said.

He did, lots of guarded locations—many secret—his late father had set up at or near their corporate offices around the world. Any of them would have been safer than his apartment in D.C.

Caleb said, "I'll go with you."

Victoria shrugged. "Take him along if you wish."

The mission sounded exciting, and I loved that Victoria trusted me with it, but my thoughts drifted to Luke. "I need to think about it."

"Tell me tomorrow, early," Victoria said.

"Okay."

She got up, and we all followed her to the door.

"Erin," William said, after it slid open. "A word, please."

Caleb gave me a worried look, but I nodded, and he left.

"Sure," I said, turning to the scientist, then scanning the rest of the room more carefully. The door closed behind me.

"Vera." His small smile grew. "Vera…" He shook his head. "I promise to cease calling you by that name, but… I could not resist."

I folded my arms and raised an eyebrow.

He sighed. "I've missed you. I wish you would show some discretion with Todd. He has no idea what you're talking about. But I find myself not really caring. I have missed working with you."

I prepared—irrationally, I knew—for a wave of memories of our time in the lab together to come rushing back. When none did, I asked, "Who did it to me? To wipe my mind, I'm assuming someone injected me with something."

His smile departed. "I did. And I am very sorry." He clasped his hands. "I will share more if you would like. Or if not, I will apologize again and refrain from troubling you with further details."

"How old are you?"

"I became a vampire in 872."

"Tell me more," I said. "About me."

He pulled out a chair. "Have a seat."

Once we were both settled back at the table, he said, "Victoria tells me you are a great warrior. You always possessed tremendous skill in that arena, but you were young and mortal. You were tall"—another brief smile—"yet scrawny. But in the lab?" He shook his head. "Your mind was not restrained by any limitations of the human body. You were truly a gifted scientist."

The past tense, describing a *me* I couldn't remember, remained peculiar, despite being nothing new.

He rested his elbows on the table. "For a while, we were able to broadly influence the minds of those drinking the synthetic blood. We have experienced, brilliant scientists here—many, pioneers in their respective fields. But we struggled to pinpoint specific changes, and we could never make the changes stick once a subject stopped with the synthetic.

"Even while Edmond's sisters attacked your mind in retaliation for the work you did on them, *you* cracked the code. From there, we had a lot of refinement to do, but your discovery was the breakthrough that allowed us to permanently alter the minds of Spectavi. And as you surely have already concluded, your breakthrough led to the process we used on you."

"You're a monster." Gripping the table tightly between my thumbs and both palms, my nails poised to dig in, I forced myself back in my chair. "How could you do that to me?"

"I am many things, Erin, but I am no monster." William's eyes unfocused, and he seemed to be searching inward. "Or perhaps your wisdom prevails yet again, and I was, at minimum, monstrous. But what I did, I did at Edmond's bidding and out of compassion for you. Caterine and Ariane tormented you. Near the end, you didn't sleep. You cried out in terror when you tried to rest. And we *knew* the torment you felt because we drank from you. Edmond made me, to ensure I fully understood your pain. Once I had, I didn't understand how you could bear it and not simply end the twins' lives. Enough silver in their bloodstream would doubtless have been the end of them. The pair could not tolerate that sacred metal any more than the rest of us, and you could have done it in a matter of minutes."

I relaxed my arms and let go of the table. "I didn't think those wretched creatures deserved to die?"

"The thought crossed your mind. But in your heart, above all, you loathed the idea of admitting defeat in your efforts to help them, and you cared too much for Edmond to bring yourself to take from him ones so dear to him."

Bastard! Edmond had no trouble taking *my* life from me.

William went on, "Then, when Edmond asked me to prepare the chemicals for use on you, I said no. You knew how you could end their attacks on your mind. You knew full well that becoming a vampire would end that suffering. And while when you were younger, you did dream of such a life, you had changed your mind. For a time, I respected that you preferred being mortal, despite the pain. But in the end, compassion and Edmond's persistent framing of the act as one of mercy persuaded me. Looking now on those nights, I made the wrong decision. And yet…" He shook his head.

"And yet?"

"I find myself full of joy to be sitting across from you, with you as an immortal."

"But I'm not that me. I'm not who I was."

"You're different." He shrugged. "But what's wrong with different? Who's to say Erin isn't better? Who's to say she's worse? You are different. And that you are a vampire and will be with us for all time makes me truly happy."

My notion to despise him faded. The most terrible new detail—that I had made the discovery that led to my doom—was a cruel twist, yet far less cruel than Edmond using it on me. And despite any uncertainty over what fate the twins had deserved back then, I had grown quite certain since setting them free.

"Thank you for telling me what happened." I took the silver case, and we stood to leave. The door slid open, and we headed into and down the empty hallway. "I have another question."

"Of course," William said.

"The synthetic blood for all the Spectavi... have you been able to make more?"

"Unfortunately, we have not," he said. "Across the globe, nearly all of our scientists are working on the problem."

"What's going to happen when you run out?"

"Well..." He might have been organizing the words of some lie.

"Victoria trusts me," I said. "So should you."

He nodded. "In case we cannot produce any fresh supply, we are incorporating a set of instructions into the remaining blood we have."

The prospect of Todd being further "instructed" sickened me. "Don't do that to Todd."

"What?" William asked.

"If you do run out of synthetic, let him have a clear mind—no instructions, no nothing."

"I don't—"

"If you really regret what you did to me, that's how you can show me." I opened the door to outside. Todd had gone.

"Did you explain that?" Victoria asked, gesturing at the case I carried.

"No," William said.

I took a closer look. It had two latches and, apparently, no lock.

Victoria said, "It's a canister of clean synthetic blood."

I dropped the case to the ground.

"It won't affect your brain," William hastened to explain. "But for a night or so, it will give your blood that synthetic scent expected from Spectavi."

Victoria picked up the case. "Your mind will be untouched, Erin." She held it out to me. "I promise."

"I won't drink it," I said. "No way."

"Take it," she urged. "It may allow you to gain access somewhere you otherwise could not."

I shook my head.

She handed it to Caleb. "You never know."

He took the case, but I couldn't imagine myself trusting such a thing from Eure.

7

We spent the day at my house, a few blocks south of the Pentagon in Virginia. Deciding against the two upstairs bedrooms, Caleb slept on the living room couch. I awoke in my finished basement, and while in my closed coffin on my dark-gray, satin-lined mattress, I checked my phone—nothing from Luke. June had called and left a voicemail:

Erin, it's June. Zack and I are going to stay with my aunt in Fairfax. All classes are suspended, so we decided to leave D.C. Be safe, and we'll see you soon.

Good. I rolled onto my side and ran through the events of the prior night.

I had asked Victoria and William what had happened to my old friend Jennifer. They said she had become a vampire, as I had expected, and that she worked in a lab in Los Angeles with her boss and maker, Mr. Roberts. Becoming a Spectavi had been her dream for so long that I figured it safe to assume she was happy.

I also inquired about my boss from Snap Safe, Mr. Oliver, who had been made a Spectavi at the same time as Todd. He had switched to a new project based out of

Toronto. William claimed that with his managerial oversight of Snap Safe no longer needed, Mr. Oliver and his wife had embraced the transfer of their own free will.

To satisfy Caleb's curiosity, I endured a short walk around the campus with him. Scaffolding covered portions of Edmond's white stone house. Apparently, Reinald had moved in and was renovating. I wondered what had become of the steel-lined basement that had held the twins, and especially Edmond's old wooden coffin with the cracked edge that had saved my life and given me an immortal one.

When Caleb and I reached the underground cathedral's above-ground entrance, which replicated the lower portion of the west entrance of the original cathedral in Edmond's home town of Chartres, I let Caleb go down the long staircase alone while I waited at the top. He returned extremely impressed.

The synthetic blood William had given me never made it farther than my doorway. The silver case lay on the wood floor in my living room because I didn't want it near me while I rested. Trusting Victoria was one thing. But William? He had probably been truthful about my past, knowing I could verify his story with Victoria. Likewise, regarding the substance in the case. Since Edmond's death, Victoria had offered sincerity and truth, and I sensed the same from William. But drinking that fake blood? If it had come from Victoria directly, I would have hated the prospect.

William had played his part in what had happened to me, and there was no excuse. Yet, as always, I deemed Edmond by far the most villainous, the most dastardly character in the tragedy of my life as Vera.

Certainly, William should have refused to help Edmond wipe away my memory, and Victoria should have stopped them both from doing so. At least Victoria and William admitted their failings, and as usual, new insight into my past made me feel more complete in the present.

I could never decide if I had forgiven Victoria. Since *I*, Erin, wasn't the one she had wronged, how could I be the one to forgive? Just the same, how could I harbor an eternal grudge against her? She had beaten me to a pulp; I did remember that. But the attack and what came after transformed me into the vampire I loved being, and at the end of the day, I was the result of all that had happened to me, both as Vera and as Erin.

So I didn't think I had *forgiven* Victoria as much as I had left her failure to stop Edmond in the past. Not carrying that burden allowed my relationship with her to grow and strengthen. I decided to treat William the same. He would have to earn my trust, first by not subjecting Todd to any instructions in the last of their synthetic blood, but I would not hate him based on the events of another lifetime.

Interrogating the vice president, regaining access to the surveillance system for Victoria, and even defeating the twins didn't seem like certain objectives toward my goal of helping the world recover from the red rain. But the twins were evil, and whether they targeted me or Washington, they had to be dealt with.

Plus, the mission gave me access to Todd. While he might

have been doing fine, with the synthetic blood near to running out, whether William would do as I had asked or not, I had a new reason to worry about Todd. Snatching him away from the Spectavi seemed more realistic if I took the mission.

Maybe most simply, I doubted I could actually say no to Victoria. I just had to figure out what to do about Luke.

I pushed open my hinged coffin lid, climbed out, and went upstairs, where Caleb was watching the news.

He looked up. "FBI Headquarters is pretty well destroyed."

I sat beside him on the couch. "That's not good."

"Witnesses think six to twelve Sanguans this time. A lot of people who had stuck around so far gave up and left the city during the day."

"Any mention of the camera system?"

"They noted how, if it were functional, it might have helped prevent the attacks and definitely would have identified the perpetrators, but nothing about the twins having control of it."

An anchorwoman read from a paper handed to her. "And as night has fallen, this statement from the president: 'We continue to do all we can to ensure the safety of the citizens of Washington, D.C.'" The anchor flipped over the page. "That's it. That's the whole statement."

My phone rang—Luke. I hurried through my kitchen, pulled open the sliding glass door, and from my fenced-in backyard, answered the call. "Hey."

"Hi, Erin." A scattering of drums sounded briefly on Luke's end.

"Are you all right?" I asked.

"Yeah, I'm fine. I got all your messages and wanted to let you know that I'm fine."

"Where are you?"

More drums and two guitars. They softened as Luke must have been getting farther away from them. "I'm with my band. We're practicing. We might do a show tomorrow or the night after."

"Downtown?"

"No, out in Virginia," he said.

"It's still not safe."

"Erin—"

"Luke, I'm sorry, but it's not—"

"Erin!"

"What?"

"We're gonna play. I miss you, but right now, I need to play." He sighed. "You've been to the shows. Remember the last one? The energy in the crowd? You *had* to have felt it. That room, the people… it was incredible."

"I know. It was."

"Everything's crazy," Luke admitted. "The city's a mess, but we've gotta play."

"Let's talk about it in person."

"I have to go," he said, and the music in the background grew louder. Someone was doing a reasonable job at Luke's piano—and then hit a horribly off note.

I knew where they normally practiced, but it really sounded like he didn't want me there. "Luke, I'm going to be on the road for a little while. There's something I need to help Victoria with."

"Okay," he said.

"Be careful." I implored him, "*Please* be careful."

"Is Caleb going with you?"

"Yes. But—"

"It's fine," he said. "I was just wondering."

"Good luck, Luke."

"Bye, Erin."

"Bye."

I stared at my phone for a few moments before texting Victoria that I'd take the mission.

———————

At Fort Washington, I asked Zhilan, "Will you stay here?"

"It is a good base, and my house is in ruins," she said. "So, yes, I will call this home for the time being."

"What will you do?" I asked.

"Ensure Grant and Alice are safe, for starters. Alice is strong—not as strong as you, but respectable. And she is strong willed, which I was unsure of but am pleased to see. And yet, she is dangerously young. Grant is a good teacher for her, and he'd die to protect her. I aim to ensure that he does not have to."

"They're lucky to have you around. Like I was."

Her warm smile quickly faded. "Houjin, Hayden, and Max are on their way here. It is a delicate game. How do we take advantage of this Spectavi weakness, when at the moment, the humans need them so much?"

"Well, how do we?"

"We shall see."

8

In desolate Annapolis, Maryland, Caleb and I parked two blocks from St. Anne's Church and walked east toward the Naval Academy. Compared to D.C., far fewer police and Spectavi patrolled on foot or in cars and SUVs. The passing vehicles had flashing lights but no blaring sirens and horns. Aside from the academy, there was far less military, as well. We crossed paths and exchanged nods with one other Sanguan, who strolled by, going in the opposite direction.

Vice President Turner had spent the day at the academy, where he had been a student from 1982 to 1986. The Naval Academy was a three-hundred-thirty-eight-acre yard where the Severn River met the Chesapeake Bay. A gray brick wall with numerous guarded gates surrounded the yard.

Turner was meeting with the school's superintendent and planned to speak to the midshipmen at some point that night. A small press corps had traveled with him to cover the event, which had been scheduled for nighttime as part of the effort to highlight the vice president's—and thus the administration's—unwavering confidence.

Caleb and I were two blocks away from one of the academy's larger, guarded entrances.

"I met the vice president when I was at Eure, you know," I said. "I went to a dinner with Edmond to honor a woman who fought off the Sanguan who killed her husband. She identified the attacker so he could be arrested and tried in their court. Thinking back, it sounds pretty absurd. The whole thing was probably a lie."

"What was the vice president like?" Caleb asked.

"All I did was shake his hand. He seemed pretty confident, I guess, which isn't surprising. But I honestly wasn't paying close attention—to anything really."

"What time is his speech?"

"I don't know," I said. "Victoria didn't say."

We rounded the corner and spied two Spectavi guards and a man in a suit—probably Secret Service—standing at the entrance. The vampires caught my scent immediately.

One guard aimed, while the nearest raised his hand. "Halt!"

We stopped.

"Let's go," I said quietly.

Caleb gave me a surprised look, but turned as I did and walked away with me. I didn't hear or smell the Spectavi following.

Back around the corner, I told Caleb, "I wasn't going to barge in, anyway. We don't have a clue where Turner is in there, and I have no idea how many Spectavi are with him."

Caleb nodded.

We headed for Main Street—a strip of shops normally

crowded with tourists. Before we got there, from the far side of the street, we passed a smaller entrance to the academy with two Spectavi guards. I made out four Spectavi beyond the gate, which, considering how little of the place I could see, hinted at many more being around.

On Main Street, we made our way down the hill toward the water, past nearly empty bars and restaurants. One place had a Sanguan bouncer out front who appeared quite bored until taking an interest in Caleb. I kept ever vigilant and ready to grab my knife and defend my friend.

"Where are we headed?" Caleb asked.

"Water taxi," I said. "For another vantage point on the academy."

At the end of the street, south past a closed restaurant, I led us down an alley and out onto a wooden dock. Inside a silver motorboat, an old man wearing a wrinkled, off-white dress shirt and a weathered captain's hat sat reading a paperback book.

He looked up. "Hello there."

"Are you working?" I asked.

He stood. "I'm in the boat, aren't I?"

"Right." We stepped aboard. "How much to get to the other side and back?"

"Six dollars each."

It was less than a mile. "We'll make it an even twenty, if you go slow."

He peered to the dock and the alley. "Sure. I'm not very busy at the moment."

Caleb and I took our seats, and we started away from the

dock. A soft breeze blew. It wasn't much of a boat, but it had plenty of room for the three of us. I enjoyed bobbing in the calm water.

Out the rear, to the right over at the Naval Academy, I noticed no flashing lights, helicopters coming and going, or any other sign of exceptional police or military force—except for all the Spectavi. I stood for a better view and saw the place was crawling with them.

"There's a lot more vampires there than normal tonight," the captain announced.

"The vice president's there," Caleb explained.

"Oh. How do you know?"

"Uh…" Caleb began.

"It was on the news," I finished for him.

"Good man, Vice President Turner," the captain said. "He attended the academy in… 1982, I think it was."

"Really?" I wondered if the captain had any information about him that I hadn't already found online.

"Yup, then he flew fighters off a carrier in Desert Storm. Good man."

I knew that, and biting the captain probably wouldn't tell me anything. I spotted nothing else important the rest of the way. We reached the dock on the other side.

The captain asked, "How long until you want to go back? I'll probably wait here."

"Now's fine."

"Are you sure? There are a bunch of bars and restaurants over… but most are closed, now that I think about it, because of everything that's going on."

"We're good to go. We just wanted to take the ride."

"Suit yourself." He increased the throttle, and we headed back.

Despite the certain thrill, with all the Spectavi in addition to all the military students, barging into the academy seemed like the wrong move. Since we didn't know where, precisely, the vice president was, he might manage to escape. After he did, his plan to remain high profile could come to an abrupt end. I needed to wait for a better opportunity.

Caleb paid the captain, and we made our way through the alley back to the main street.

"What next?" Caleb asked.

"I dunno. I'd like to watch the academy and see if Turner leaves. There are a few exits he could take, though. We could watch all night and still might miss him."

Caleb scanned the rooftops. "I have an idea."

"Good idea," I said, lying on my stomach beside Caleb on the flat roof of a waterfront hotel.

"You can see that far?" he asked.

"Yeah." I couldn't spot all the different gates the vice president might use to leave, but we figured I'd notice the commotion of Spectavi reacting if he exited any of them. "I just realized that when the synthetic runs out, all those Spectavi may not be protecting Turner, and he might not keep up the bold nighttime appearances. That gives us five nights."

"Uh huh." Caleb moved his upturned, unblemished

wrist in front of me. Without shifting my gaze from the yard, I took hold of his arm, cracked fresh skin, and sipped.

Bliss. It saturated him. Being on the rooftop with me, that I had taken him along for the mission, that I had revealed how the twins became imprisoned—he was in heaven.

A whiff of the bay water lent its salty flavor to a small sip, and from my toes, gradually up my legs, out to my fingers, and up to the tip of my head, I burned.

I drank, and my eyes watered. I loved not being alone up on that roof.

Vice President Turner never left, or if he did, we didn't notice. According to Victoria, his watch and class ring had GPS locators built in for the Secret Service to track him, but she didn't have access to that real-time information.

Victoria had provided us with a black Chevy Suburban with deeply tinted windows and a gray leather interior. As the last minutes of nighttime ticked away, Caleb drove us out to a quiet street that ended overlooking the Chesapeake Bay. The flat, seatless back of our SUV contained the small bags we had each packed, the silver case from William, a case with supplies, and a coffin bolted to the driver side. I sat in the front, watching the sky to the east lighten to purple and then progress to shades of blue.

Caleb recapped our plan for the day, which was designed to minimize our traveling during the short summer nights. "I'll check for news online and see where the vice president is going."

"Right," I confirmed. "And drive us there. And then find a safe place to wait until sundown."

"Okay."

"If Turner goes somewhere far, and we need to fly, call John Womack. Zhilan let him know that you might." John, Zhilan's friend who had flown us to Memphis a few months before to steal a case of Spectavi synthetic blood, remained happy to help.

"Got it," Caleb said.

"Don't go after the vice president yourself," I added.

"It hadn't crossed my mind to try."

"Well, don't."

"I won't."

"And try to get some sleep," I said. "Either now or later in the day."

"Will do. I just hope… I just hope nothing happens with you back there."

I took a sharp breath. The sky was quite light, and my eyes and body grew weary. Heavy. I summoned the energy to climb to the coffin and open its lid. "I'm counting on you. I'll be fine—as long as you keep me safe."

I darted to Caleb for a few seconds of a kiss. "Keep me safe," I whispered, then rushed into the coffin, and my world went dark.

9

I raised the coffin lid. Caleb lay next to me, with his head on his arm, in place of a pillow.

He opened his eyes. "Hey."

"Where are we?" I asked.

He blinked a few times. "Norfolk. Downtown."

"All right."

He climbed behind the wheel, and I crawled into the passenger seat. We were in a parking garage.

I turned to him. "How long were you back there with me?"

"Since we got here."

I felt my face glow, and my throat became parched. "Thank you." I gave him a quick peck on his stubble-covered cheek.

"You're welcome."

My dry lips found his neck. He gulped. I bit.

Vwoosh. Sweet Caleb's blood sizzled on my lips, in my mouth, and down through my body. The blazing liquid burst into firecrackers that popped into strands of tiny sparks.

He had kept me safe. He took pride in having made it that first day—learning of the vice president's visit to Norfolk on Twitter, completing without incident the four-and-a-half-hour drive south on the east side of the Bay, never straying beyond arm's reach from the car when he stopped. His confidence had grown.

I drank, and Caleb urged himself to enjoy that moment with my fangs at his neck, even as he found himself failing, and not caring that he was failing, looking ahead to future nights on the mission. I pulled my fangs out of him, awash with Caleb's dreams of an endless string of nights as an immortal, with me all to himself.

I pictured Luke, and fear oozed through me. I saw him on his own in Washington in four nights, when the Spectavi synthetic ran out—and then on his own for many nights after. I forced a smile and pulled out my phone.

Caleb wiped sweat from his forehead. "Anything from Zhilan?"

"No." I held my phone to the side so he couldn't see and loaded the Shattered Nights website. Scrolling down and checking a few subpages, I found no indication they had played a show the previous night. "Nothing from them."

In addition to eleven aircraft hangars, Naval Station Norfolk boasted fourteen piers extending west into the water. We parked in a nearby neighborhood of small homes and headed for the base's main entrance.

With the piers and docked ships on our left, we passed

small gatehouses guarded by both humans and Spectavi. In between, the numerous parking lots were mostly full, in stark contrast to the desolation of Annapolis.

"Can you see it?" Caleb asked.

"No, but it's there." I slid my hands into my jacket pockets. "Probably at one of the piers on the end." The aircraft carrier USS *Dwight D. Eisenhower* had just returned from the Middle East, and the vice president had gone to welcome its sailors home. "Turner's picking some pretty well-defended places; that's for sure."

"Yeah, he's no fool," Caleb agreed. "You against so many of them sounds—"

"I could fight 'em. That wouldn't be a problem. Or I could snatch Turner and run. But it would be a lot to run from. With so many chasing, it'd be hard to get what we need out of him."

From the direction of our car, a gunshot rang out, then another began a series of shots. I grabbed Caleb and rushed us that way. Human screams and a vampire growl came from inside a house, and we stopped.

"Ugh!" I lurched forward when a bullet ripped into my back and came out my front.

Eight Spectavi surged toward me from the naval base, seemingly unconcerned with Caleb, who ran for our Suburban.

Blood streamed out of me. "It's not me!" I yelled.

A bullet grazed my side. I grabbed my knife, flicked open the long blade, and charged. I sliced apart two Spectavi on my way through their line. Those with pistols holstered them. Others threw rifles to the street. The six drew swords and surrounded me.

I stood ready. "There's another Sanguan in that house. *He's* the one you want."

The Spectavi attacked.

Tyn! I blocked the first, spun—*tyn-tyn*—*tyn-tyn-tyn!*—and engaged the others. I ducked and dodged and—*fshwt!*—chopped off a leg and—*fshwt!*—then a sword arm. I ducked—*swoosh*—and a Spectavi nearly beheaded his companion. I hacked across the careless Spectavi, then darted away. "I didn't attack that family!"

The three remaining Spectavi came at me, and while one fought more quickly and powerfully than the other two, I didn't know why any of them expected to fare better than their fallen comrades. When I found time to trade successive blows with one, I sliced his chest diagonally from his shoulder. He slumped to the ground in a puddle of blood. I cut off the hand of the next Spectavi, who fled. Only one remained.

"I'll kill you if you stay and fight," I said. "But if you go, I won't follow." It wasn't mercy. I had to catch up with Caleb.

The Spectavi attacked, and a flurry of sword strikes proved I had underestimated him—he was *far* better than the rest. But it didn't matter. I struck back hard, and at the first opening, after driving him off balance, I slashed across his neck, sending his head rolling down the street.

A silver SUV came out of the naval base. Caleb rounded the corner in our Suburban and stopped next to me.

I pulled open the door. "Go. I'll be fine on my own."

"No," he said.

"They might not chase you, alone."

He took his hands off the wheel. "I'm not going without you."

I climbed in and shut the door.

Caleb turned the car around. "Where to?"

From the SUV behind us, a Spectavi leaned out a side rear window and rattled off shots with a submachine gun.

"Just go." I pulled my jacket off and threw it in the back.

Bullets peppered the side of our reinforced vehicle. Cracks radiated when one hit the rear glass.

"Victoria didn't skimp on the car," Caleb said. We lurched to the right before Caleb regained control. "Tire?"

"Yeah." I grabbed my scabbard. "But it's fine. She said we could run without air for a while."

The Spectavi withdrew into his vehicle and re-emerged with a rocket launcher. I unsheathed my sword and flung open my door. Flame shot from the rear of the launcher's tube. I leapt that way and sliced apart the projectile coming at us, then swung again and got the retreating Spectavi on the way past. I ran and got back in next to Caleb.

"You okay?" he asked.

"Yup."

Our huge engine roaring, we sped south onto the highway, with our pursuers shooting at us sporadically. I watched for any sign of the rocket launcher. Caleb avoided the minimal traffic. Another bullet cracked the rear window.

"I've given Grant a hard time about sticking to guns," I

said. "And he's finally trying to learn with an ax. But at the moment, I wouldn't hate having something to fire back."

Caleb checked the rearview mirror. "You could throw your knife."

"Psh! On the highway? Don't be silly."

The Spectavi SUV sped up. A passenger climbed out, leapt toward us, and—*thud!*—landed on our roof, stabbing down into the car, a foot in front of Caleb.

I lowered my window. "Keep driving, no matter what."

As the Spectavi pulled up his sword, I flipped onto the roof and kicked the intruder off to the highway. He jumped back up, and I dodged and sliced him apart, leaving his halves to fall to the road.

I counted two Spectavi in the SUV behind us and launched myself at the driver. He took his hands off the wheel too late, and I chopped through the car and his body. Our last pursuer climbed out of the veering vehicle with the rocket launcher, aimed, and fired at Caleb.

I cut through the Spectavi. "Caleb!"

Our SUV braked hard, and the rocket flew in front of it, into the roadside concrete barrier.

Boom! The explosion lifted the Suburban off the ground, sending it flying toward me. I dropped my sword and, with all the speed of my immortal body, ran to Caleb.

"Uah!" My face slammed into the bullet-riddled tailgate when I caught the vehicle. Holding it there, I took a slow breath, crouched, and set it on the ground. I went around the side and pulled open the passenger door. "You good?"

Clutching the steering wheel, wide-eyed Caleb turned to me. "Ya."

I retrieved my sword, and we drove off.

———————————

No one followed us into North Carolina. From the highway, we turned onto South Mills Road. Shortly after it became Old Swamp Road, I said, "This looks good."

Caleb pulled into an old out-of-business gas station and stopped in front of the rusty garage. I got out and lifted the door—a mess of tools and used car and truck parts, but empty enough. Caleb drove in, and I lowered the door. Stepping carefully around and over all the clutter, I returned to the passenger seat.

He clicked on the interior light. I clicked it off, pulled his shirt over his head, and carried him into the back, beside my coffin. Straddling him, staring at his hard body and sitting up straight, my head inches from the low ceiling, I took off my shirt. Our eyes locked.

He unfastened my black bra and slid the straps off my shoulders and down my arms. With a wide-open mouth, I licked from one sharp fang to the other.

He held my waist, then ran his hands up my back, pulling me to his chest until my tongue tasted his skin. His hand on the back of my head brought my lips onto him, and my fangs pierced his flesh.

Fire! Fire everywhere—in my mind, in my blood, in my body. I sucked and—*vwoosh*—the blaze built.

That fire couldn't hurt me, and it couldn't hurt Caleb.

Vwwoosh!—that fire, I could sip and—*crack*—*boom!*—make burst when I sucked hard. Those flames, I could love.

Thank God Caleb had made it. *Boom!* Thank God for the glorious flames of his blazing blood.

10

In the garage, while Caleb stayed in the car, talking with work the next evening, I checked my phone for updates.

While we had been fleeing Norfolk, Shattered Nights played for an hour, "headlining" an impromptu show in Virginia that featured two other local bands. According to blogger recaps, the industrial warehouse was packed by the time Luke came onstage. I hated that I had missed it, and when all the posts described a Sanguan attack in the crowd, I hated it more. Apparently, the fifth she drank from quenched her thirst, and she left without killing anyone.

I called Luke. He didn't answer, so I texted, *How are you?*

To my surprise, he responded immediately. *Fine.*

I tried calling again. No answer. I texted, *I heard the show went well.*

I waited for his response, wishing he would answer his phone, so I could congratulate him and tell him how excited I was for him. I wrote, *I miss you.*

He responded, *I miss you, too. Good luck with your mission.*

Caleb got out of the Suburban and stretched his arms above his head. "Everything all right?"

"Yeah." I noticed the fresh red of the fang marks on his neck. "You must be hungry."

———————————

We had parked behind the nearby diner to hide our bullet-riddled SUV from the road. Along with the waitress, two men at the counter gave us suspicious looks when I didn't order, but paid us little further mind, perhaps on account of Caleb being perfectly at ease with me.

Caleb bit into his thick cheeseburger and chewed quickly.

"Take your time," I said.

He ate in a far bigger rush than usual when we were out at a restaurant. His neck expanded when he gulped down the mouthful. "Okay." He drank some Coke.

His flesh hid a river of blood... that skin asked—no, pleaded—to be bitten... "So nothing at all about the vice president?" I would have gone crazy doing nothing but staring at him.

"Nope. Like I said, our chase made the news, and so did the attack on that family near the base, but that was it." He shook more salt on his fries. "It's a little surprising that I couldn't find anything on Turner."

"They didn't mention either of us by name on the news, did they?"

"No." Caleb stopped short of taking a bite of a fry. "You think the Spectavi are out looking for us?"

"I hope not. I hope they realize that it'd take a lot more than they already lost to catch us, and they decide they don't have the resources to spare to bother trying." I had said *us*, but I meant *me*. While *I* would be hard to get, protecting Caleb seemed a lot less of a sure thing. One of his father's hideaways was increasingly sounding like the best place for Caleb. The trick would be convincing him to go.

My phone chimed with a text from Victoria. *Where are you?*

I responded, *North of Elizabeth City, North Carolina.*

Change vehicles. I'll have another one dropped off in an hour and will text you the address. The same set of keys will work. Leave the shot-up one there.

Caleb asked, "What is it?"

"Victoria," I said. "She's dropping off a new car for us. Somewhere nearby."

"Nice."

I responded to her, *OK. Thanks.*

"But how do we find the vice president?" Caleb asked. "We're down to three days."

"I don't know."

Caleb bit and spoke with his mouth full. "What about General Sharpe?"

"What about him?"

"You think he'd know?"

I pulled out my phone. "Good idea." I called Zhilan.

"Erin, hello," she answered. "How are you?"

"We're fine. We think..." I glanced at the men at the counter, then spoke more quietly. "We think our friend in the military might be able to help us. Do you know how to get in touch with him?"

"I do. What shall I say it is about?"

"We're not sure where we should head next. I'll explain it to him."

"All right," Zhilan said. "I will call him now and ask him to contact you."

"Great, thanks." We both hung up, and I told Caleb, "Zhilan's going to call him."

"Cool." He sipped his drink. "What's the plan for the twins once we have access to the camera system?"

I leaned back. "I don't know."

"You wouldn't try to capture them again, would you?"

"I don't see the point. With Edmond gone, I think Victoria and Reinald would be just as happy with the two of them dead. Victoria would be happier, for sure."

"Would you fight with Reinald against those two?" Caleb asked.

"Maybe." I considered it. "To kill the twins, I think I'd do pretty much anything."

He nodded. "Any more thought about why my blood is still normal?"

Phew. I had feared him launching into the 'me turning him into a vampire' question. "Well... Zhilan and I had one idea."

Caleb set his burger on his plate. "Which was?"

It would be awkward to spell out, but continuing to hold back during such uncertain times felt wrong. "I love you." His face brightened. "And Luke, both of you, very much, which could explain it." His reaction tempered at the mention of Luke, but only subtly. "But I also love June and

Zack." And even Blaine, I thought. But June and Zack, certainly. "So I'm not totally sure how 'love' explains it, or if it does at all."

My phone rang. Instead of an incoming number, it read, *Blocked*. I answered, "Hello?"

"Erin, this is General Sharpe."

I surveyed the scene at the diner, then slid out of the booth and whispered to Caleb, "The general. I'll be right outside."

Caleb nodded. A line of windows would allow me to keep an eye on him from out front.

"Erin?" General Sharpe asked.

"Yes, hi. Sorry." I made my way to the parking lot.

"I just spoke with Zhilan," he said. "I'm sorry to hear about your friend Renshu."

"Thanks." I never knew what to say to things like that, but didn't want to say nothing.

"So what can I do for you?"

"Well, a few other friends—Spectavi, actually—sent me looking for someone, and I've hit a bit of a dead end."

"Oh, who are you looking for?"

"Vice President Turner."

"Turner? The Spectavi are in touch with him all the time."

"He… he hasn't been forthcoming with some information they need."

It sounded like the general shifted in a chair. "What's this about?"

"You know the surveillance system in D.C.?"

"Yes."

"The Spectavi think the twins didn't destroy the control center. They think the twins stole it and are using it to access the cameras, to watch the city."

"Uh huh. I heard something like that."

"There's another control center somewhere, but the Spectavi don't know where. It was built for the government, and the president and vice president know its location, but won't reveal it."

"So they've decided to send a Sanguan," General Sharpe concluded, "to try to be more persuasive, and the vice president is the easier target of the two."

"Exactly."

I heard a noise like someone knocking on a door. "Hold on," the general said.

I watched Caleb eat inside the diner and considered those who had been snatched off the street for their blood and what it meant if my theory was correct. Somewhere, when the red rain had fallen, a vampire loved those men and women. Did those mortals go out alone after sundown because the feeling wasn't mutual? Feelings changed, of course. People moved on. And those vampires couldn't be around them *all* the time. I missed Luke.

"Sorry about that," General Sharpe said. "Hmm... I certainly understand why the cameras are so important to the Spectavi. A lot of people are nervous—hell, beyond nervous at this point—about their ability to keep the city safe. All our cities are in trouble, but Washington is not just *any* city."

"Of course."

"But I have to disappoint you. I don't have anything to do with the office of the vice president. I don't know where he is."

"I see." *Damn.*

"I have to go, but can I ask you a favor?"

"Sure."

"My son Eli—the one Renshu helped. Since then, his questions about vampires haven't stopped. I've tried my best to answer them, but he has so many, and I really don't know what to say to most. Strange as it is, I trust *you* more than a lot of the Spectavi I work with. Would you mind if Eli texted you with a few of his questions?"

"Um, okay."

"Great, thanks. I'll give him your number. I've gotta run." He hung up.

I put away my phone and went back into the diner. A few fries remained scattered on Caleb's plate.

"How'd it go?" he asked.

"He understands what's at stake. He says he trusts me, but he can't help."

"Can't or won't?"

"Can't, I think. He said he didn't know where Turner was."

"Damn."

"It was a good idea, though," I said.

Caleb shrugged.

My phone chimed. A text from an unknown number read, *Is this Erin Rose?*

Eli hadn't waited long at all. I responded, *Yes, is this Eli?*

"Who is it?" Caleb asked.

"The general's son, I think. He has some questions about vampires or something."

No. My name's Colin. I'm a friend of Zack's. He's in the hospital. A Sanguan attacked. He told me to text you. June's dead.

I dropped my phone to the table and stared at it.

"What?" Caleb asked.

June's dead. The words on the screen hadn't been misread. They didn't go away. They didn't change.

My eyes watered. "June's dead."

"How?" Caleb put down his last fry.

"A Sanguan." Of course a Sanguan had done it, probably one starved for blood. June and Zack's couldn't have even helped.

"Where? Who was that?"

"I don't know where. Zack's alive. The text was from one of his friends." My phone seemed immensely foreign and mechanical when I picked it up. I typed my response on the heartless device. *Where?*

Her aunt's house. He's at Northern Virginia Hospital in Fairfax.

"In the hospital in Fairfax," I told Caleb. *How's Zack?*

Beat up pretty bad, but the doctors said he made it through the worst.

We're on our way.

Colin wrote, *I don't know if that's a good idea.*

I typed, *I don't care*, and hit Send.

We switched to a dark green Suburban outside Richmond, which was roughly halfway into the four-hour drive to Fairfax. Time was running short to find the vice president, but I couldn't ignore Zack in the hospital, not after turning my back on him and June since the red rain.

While Caleb drove, I spent a lot of time staring out the window, teary eyed, with Zack and June's memories flooding my mind. They'd arrived at school as freshmen and didn't know each other, or anyone. They made some friends, had some hook-ups, and went on a few dates, but nothing serious. Then they met, and it had been different than when they had met anyone else. They both noticed it. They both felt it. They went on their first date and then another. They spent more and more time thinking about each other—in class and out, when they should have been studying. June fell harder for Zack, but he fell, too. His first instinct had been correct—June *was* different. And so was Zack, at least to June. Their love took root.

Less than a mile from the hospital, I asked Caleb, "What if I was wrong, and there is no hope? Maybe you and those like you really were left unchanged so that God could punish His world more slowly."

Caleb turned to me. "I refuse to believe it."

My phone buzzed with a text from a new unknown number. *Is this Erin? This is Eli.*

Bad timing, but I responded, *Yes.*

Cool! My dad said you looked like a new vampire, but I want to know for sure. Are you new or old?

New. I figured Eli to be on the young end of "teenager"—as Renshu had described him—based on how he had phrased his question.

We pulled into the circular drive of the trauma center entrance, and I was out on the pavement before Caleb had completely stopped. Two Spectavi guards with rifles came through the automatic sliding doors.

One aimed at me. "Stop!"

I reached back to my seat for my sword scabbard. "I need to get in there."

The other aimed. "No way."

Caleb slowly walked around the vehicle.

"I'll leave my sword," I offered. "My friend's a patient."

"It doesn't matter," the first guard said.

"Then I *won't* leave my sword, and I'll cut you both down on my way inside."

The guards' trigger fingers tensed. The second said, "There are more of us inside."

I wrapped my hand around my sword's handle. "It doesn't matter. I'll kill you all." I began pulling out the blade. "I'll tear this place apart if I have to, but one way or another, I *am* going to talk to my friend."

"Wait!" Caleb shouted. "What if Zack came out?"

I finished drawing my sword and held it down at my side. "All I want is to talk with him. I don't care where. Outside would be fine." I calmly and deliberately grabbed my phone and tossed it to Caleb. "Text his friend."

Caleb typed.

The guards glanced at each other, and the first shook his

head. "I can't let you do that."

Caleb looked up from the phone. "Sent."

I pointed my katana at the guards. "You can't *stop* him from doing that."

My phone chimed. "Colin's inside," Caleb said, typing some more.

"Who are you?" the second guard asked.

Erin? Vera? A Sanguan on a mission for Victoria and William? An immortal who loved her sword and any remotely justifiable chance to use it? "Just a friend of a patient I will be seeing tonight."

Caleb announced, "He'll come out. In the back."

"Well?" I asked the guards.

The first lowered his rifle. "I'll go with you." The second lowered his gun.

I sheathed Tomori. "Fine."

The guard pointed at me. "If you try anything—"

"Whatever. I won't." I stuck out my hand, and Caleb returned my phone.

After walking down the long building side, we rounded the corner to the hospital's rear. A startled doctor in a lab coat threw away her cigarette and went inside through a beige metal door.

General Sharpe's son texted, *I saw a comic book with a vampire detective on the cover, but I can't remember the name. Dean something. Do you know his last name?*

Why didn't he google it? I asked Caleb, "Do you know the name of some vampire comic book detective? First name's Dean."

"Castle," Caleb said. "I used to read all those. Dean Castle. He's awesome."

I typed, *Castle*, and hit Send.

A door opened. Zack, pale, bruised, and wearing a hospital gown, was pushed outside in a wheelchair, presumably by Colin.

"Zack!" I rushed to the bottom of the ramp.

I heard the Spectavi readying his rifle behind me. Zack's left eye was swollen shut and his other halfway. Plaster covered his right forearm and hand. His right leg had been similarly cast.

"Erin," he said, not as weakly as expected.

I crouched in front of him. "I'm so sorry." I wanted to *hold* him and to *protect* him.

"It's not your fault. It's good to see you. Thanks for coming." His face contorted. "June's... June's gone."

I hadn't protected him. Or her. I had failed them, and their lives were lost to me forever. "I'm sorry."

"It happened so fast. He went for her first, then me. Her uncle had a shotgun and got the vampire with a spread of silver. I stabbed him, he threw me against the wall, and then he fled. By the time we got to June, she was already dead. They said her neck"—his voice cracked—"they said her neck was broken."

That sweet neck. Her sweet blood. Her sweet feelings for Zack and all their indescribable nuances. I had glimpsed the first sparks of that caring and was supposed to experience its growth. The couple seemed destined to be married, and I would have felt every emotion on their journey. Their love was going to be *glorious*. "I'm so sorry," I said. "She loved you. She truly did."

His face contorted again, and he began to cry. "I should have protected her."

I gently placed my hand on his thigh. "You did all you could. This world… that Sanguan… I don't know. *I* should have protected her. But you did all you could."

The door they had exited swung open. Two men and a woman came out—June's parents and Zack's father—followed by the other Spectavi guard.

June's mother screamed, "Who are you? Go away!" She pointed. "Shoot her! She's a Sanguan!"

June's father held her mother from running down the ramp.

Zack's father called, "Zack, what's going on? Colin, get him away from her."

I stepped away from Zack.

Colin looked at me.

"Go," I said.

"Bye, Erin," Zack said as Colin wheeled him away. "Be safe out there."

"You, too, Zack."

Returning the way we had come, the same Spectavi accompanied us, but didn't aim his rifle along the way.

In our Suburban, Caleb asked, "Where to?"

"I don't know. Away from here."

Caleb started driving. "I'm sorry about June."

"So am I," I said. "But I don't feel like I thought I would."

"What do you mean?"

"You know what I liked about her most of all?"

"What?"

"Her sweet blood, her soft skin, her blue eyes… it had all been really great. But I loved her love of Zack and *his* love for her. I've hardly seen them recently, and *their love* is what I miss more than anything else."

My phone chimed.

Another text from Eli. I read it aloud. "Where's your coffin? At least tell me the state!"

I certainly would not tell the peculiar boy anything more specific than that. *Virginia*, I wrote.

Caleb changed lanes to pass a stopped car with blinking hazard lights. "Strange question."

"Yeah." I scrolled up on my phone and paraphrased them all. "Are you a new or an old vampire? The comic book detective, do you know his last name? What state is your coffin in?"

"Wait. Read me just the answers."

"New. Castle. Virginia."

Caleb glanced at my phone. "New Castle, Virginia. It's a location—south."

I reread everything. "That would explain the absurdity of the questions."

"I think the general is trying to tell you something."

"How far is it?"

"Four hours, maybe? It's a tiny town, but they built a fancy resort there a few years ago. Château Forêt."

"I'll get directions." Before I did, I texted the general's son. *Yup, Virginia. Got it. Thanks for the great questions! Let me know if you have any more!*

11

New Castle, in southwestern Virginia, was so small that the vast majority of the staff of Château Forêt commuted from out of town to get to work. The sprawling, luxury resort, named for its secluded location in the middle of Jefferson National Forest, lay straight ahead.

The main, red-brick hotel building extended to wings off an imposing three-story mansion. Large, almost contiguous guestroom windows made up the face on every floor. Formal meals were served in the Grand Dining Room, and the expansive grounds included two golf courses and an equestrian center.

"Keep going," I said as we drove past a side entrance.

Caleb did. "I could go in without you."

"What?"

"To check it out. If we're right, and the vice president's here, the Spectavi and the Secret Service won't let you anywhere near him."

"No." I couldn't lose Caleb next. "It's too dangerous." After the hospital, I had begun seriously plotting where he might go when the time came for me to confront Turner.

"What about that synthetic William gave you?" Caleb asked.

I waved away the notion. "No way."

"But if they thought you were Spectavi, we probably wouldn't have trouble getting close at all. We only have two nights before who knows what's going to happen with them."

"I don't care. I'm not using it," I said. "It's a good idea, but who knows what's in that case? William could have lied to Victoria. He could have some other, awful agenda. I doubt it, but after what I've been through, I won't risk it."

"Okay. I understand." He shook his head. "I'm sorry I brought it up."

"No, like I said, it was a good idea."

Caleb smiled. "I just really wanna get this guy. I want to get what we came for."

I smiled. "Me, too. Turn around. Let's take another drive by."

He drove back past the main entrance, where beyond a small parking lot and lush lawn, a lone Spectavi stood guard. We opted not to drive closer, in case they or the Secret Service were on the lookout for us after Norfolk. The road curved, and after less than a half-mile of small shops and offices, woods lined both sides.

I pointed ahead. "There."

Caleb squinted. Two women wearing matching staff uniforms chatted while walking to their car in the parking lot of a general store. Caleb parked a few spots away.

"See if they know anything?" I suggested.

"Yeah."

"I'll head into the store, but I'll be watching."

He opened the door before I could instruct him to be careful. I got out and, on the way past, guessed the two women were in their thirties.

"Hi," Caleb said to them.

I looked back, and they had stopped to talk with him. One of the women's glances sent me facing forward, continuing to the store while Caleb told them I was going to buy us snacks. The women explained that they worked as waitresses at the Château. There hadn't been many guests lately, and they had been forbidden from talking about it, but with a little of Caleb's prodding, they revealed that there was a special event going on the following night.

I held open the door to the poorly stocked store and watched. The same woman peeked my way again, and I went inside. The lone cashier—a man reading a magazine—had a shotgun beside the register. He interrupted his reading to nod at me. I nodded in response, then resumed watching Caleb through the window.

The women appeared to be enjoying the conversation. I checked my phone to confirm Luke hadn't written, then I texted, asking how he was doing.

Two car doors closed. The women drove off, but the one in the passenger seat turned around. Even if she guessed what I was, would she do anything about it?

I met Caleb at our SUV.

"Turner's got to be there," he said. "They wouldn't spill all the beans, but they said there's a big dinner tomorrow. They rely on tips for the most part, and they're excited to get a decent crowd for a change."

"But you aren't sure?"

"No, but after the general led us here and the way Turner's been off the grid, out of the news, this just feels right."

"Probably." I texted Eli, *Any big plans tomorrow night?*

"How do we get in there?" Caleb asked. "He's finally not at a military base, but I'm sure the place will be crawling with Spectavi."

The synthetic in the case would certainly have made things easier, and time was short. I imagined bringing the unknown substance my lips—the sterile taste I had smelled so often. I shuddered and considered it no more.

Eli responded, *Anniversaries are extra special shared with good friends!*

"It's the vice president's anniversary," I said. "His friends will be there." I began a text message. "Maybe some of ours should be, too."

———————————

Soft thunder cracked into a long quieting roll. Down the street from Château Forêt's main entrance, partially protected from the steady rain by the trees, I watched for Grant's rented red-and-black Dodge Viper. In addition to my sword on my back and my knife on my thigh, I carried a flare gun in a holster on my hip. I had arrived early and might have sat if the ground wasn't wet.

Caleb was in Myrtle Beach at a heavily guarded compound. Like other similar destinations, the vacationing population there had dwindled of late, and fewer people meant fewer Sanguans on the hunt. I had drunk my last sip from Caleb moments before dawn, after barely convincing him to go. The car rental company picked him up from the general store.

We figured we had a decent plan, and on the last night before the Spectavi ran out of synthetic, we had no choice but to give it a shot. I couldn't protect Caleb during the upcoming events, and he eventually agreed that it was pointless to risk him being associated with the most criminal portion of the mission.

I hated being apart from him, out in the woods by myself, uncertain if blood that would sustain me existed nearer than hundreds of miles away. But Caleb was safer in South Carolina.

A buzz on my belt—an unknown number. I answered my phone below my tilted head, trying to keep it as dry as possible. "Hello?"

"Is this Erin?" a male voice asked.

"Yes." I pushed my phone against my ear to hear better over the rain.

"Erin Rose?" He sounded familiar.

"Yes, who is this?"

"It's Todd."

"Oh, wow. Hi, Todd. How'd you get my number?"

"Victoria."

"Are you calling from Eure?"

"No," he said. "I bought a prepaid phone."

"Ah ha."

"So how's everything going with the mission?" he asked.

"Good. I'm optimistic about tonight."

"Are you outside?"

"Yeah, and it's raining. Hold on a second." I put my cell on my belt and connected my earbuds, which had a microphone on the cord. "Okay. How's everything going with you?"

"Well, things have been a little different since your visit."

"Oh?" Had his memory been jogged after seeing me? Had William altered his synthetic?

"Yeah. I mean, at first, it didn't make a whole lot of sense—all the things you said in the conference room. But later, I realized that Victoria, and even William, didn't deny them. She seemed to enjoy it, and he just got mad. So I did a little digging."

"What did you find?"

"Not surprisingly, no *record* of us being together, and no record of you setting the twins free, either. By all accounts, they escaped during a training exercise gone wrong."

"I cut the tubes of synthetic blood running into their coffins," I said. "I pulled out the cords and the cables. I wish I hadn't, but I did."

"Well, then I investigated the events on the Golden Gate Bridge a few months ago—those Spectavi that set a couple cars ablaze and marched into the fires, to their deaths. The Sanguan explanation never made any sense to me. I had seen the reports a few times, but I always brushed them aside. After what you said, I decided to take a closer look at the science myself. While I was, it dawned on me that I had never gotten that far because I *always* stopped myself for some reason. It was totally unlike me not to satisfy my curiosity. Those were Spectavi—my co-workers, and a lot more than that, really. Why hadn't I seriously investigated before? It was like... something always stole my attention away."

"Uh huh."

"Well, with what you told me in mind, I pressed on," Todd continued. "I'm no chemist, so the most technical details were a little hard to grasp, but the Sanguans laid things out pretty clearly. It certainly looks like those Spectavi followed orders to end their lives."

"They did," I said.

"You're totally sure?"

A white car raced by—not Grant.

I explained, "I helped steal the batch of synthetic blood we used for that operation. I met the scientist who did it. He did the same kind of thing that was done to you, and before that, to me."

Silence filled the line, so I kept going. "Before I met you, I was a different person, with a different life and a different mind. Edmond wiped it all away, along with any memory of me from the Spectavi. After that, I woke up as Erin Rose, and I got a job at your software company, Snap Safe."

"Who did I use to be?" he asked.

"Todd," I said. "My case was extreme, but you were always Todd."

"Then what happened to me?"

"You had recently sold your company to the Spectavi. You were still human, and as they pushed you to use the surveillance system more extensively in D.C., you grew uneasy. You thought the invasion of privacy was too great."

"I don't," Todd said. "I just think that if the twins have control of the cameras, destroying them would be best."

"Well, back then, you *did* judge it wrong to use the cameras like the Spectavi planned," I said. "We had been dating for almost two months, and since you couldn't stop them, you got more and more frustrated. Finally, you gave up and told me you wanted to quit. We were going to move out west, probably to San Francisco. The Spectavi turned you into one of them and made you willing to build the system as they asked."

"Unbelievable," he said.

"I know. But it's worse."

"Worse?"

Thunder boomed.

"Things could have been better. The changes to your mind weren't permanent. We captured a software developer on your team—Sagar Kapoor—and once the synthetic blood had faded from his system, he remembered what had been done to him. After that, I wanted to rescue you, but... by the time I could have, William had altered the synthetic so the changes to your mind *did* become permanent."

"Jesus. Why on earth are you helping us?" Todd asked. "How can you stand to be in the same room with William, with all you know?"

"Yeah, it's complicated. But this is about getting the twins. That's more important to me than anything else."

"They need to be stopped."

"Exactly."

"And going after the vice president of the United States doesn't scare you?" Todd asked.

"Nope."

"*Victoria* couldn't make him talk."

"I will."

"What'll you do?"

"Whatever it takes."

A car appeared in the distance.

Todd asked, "Were we in love?"

"What?"

"When we were going to move to San Francisco, were we in love?"

The red car had a black stripe and a spoiler.

"I… I have to go," I said.

"Sure, sorry."

"No," I said. "It's fine. I don't know. I don't know how you felt, and me… I just don't know."

"Sure, sure."

The car was the Viper. Grant had on a tux, and Alice wore a red gown. She had been as eager to participate as he had, but their imminent arrival might have been getting to her because she sat very straight and looked nervous.

I asked Todd, "What are you gonna do?"

"Check our records for Sagar. I don't remember him, but if this is all real, that doesn't mean a whole lot."

"Correct. If you can't find him, let me know, and I'll see if I can track him down."

Grant turned into the Château.

"Thanks," Todd said.

"No problem. And let me know how it goes."

"Will do."

"Okay, gotta run." I hit End.

I felt good, really good, to have finally had that talk. Todd seemed to have taken it well, but I had no time to dwell on it. I put away my headphones, ran into the rain, and leapt over the outer wall. I landed in a small patch of trees across the parking lot from the hotel entrance and found a spot against a wide trunk.

Grant parked the Viper under the long front awning, and a valet opened Alice's door. They both stepped out, then Grant threw his keys to the staff member. Slender Alice stood nearly as tall as Grant, whose tux fit his muscular frame perfectly. Her gown had a long slit in the side, and I guessed she had hidden a knife higher on that leg. Her long hair was straight, and she really did bear a close resemblance to me.

A Spectavi rushed out to meet them. Grant waved his hands, apparently arguing. Lightning flashed in the clouds. Alice turned sideways, the slit in her dress away from the guard, and whispered in Grant's ear.

From up on her thigh, she pulled the expected knife, spun, and sliced across the Spectavi's neck. Blood sprayed as he crumpled to the ground. When another Spectavi appeared, Grant reached into his jacket and brought out his unfolding ax. He chopped it into the guard's shoulder and out the opposite hip. What a waste of my friends' fine attire.

Spectavi reinforcements neared the entrance. Alice flashed a smile to Grant, then darted away from the hotel with Grant and gunshots following. One after another,

Spectavi streamed out, pursuing the pair across the side parking lot, then over the wall. I counted seventeen in total, and as they got farther away, the downpour drowned out their gunfire and all the noise of the chase. I waited, hoping everyone in the opulent dining room would calm down. Thunder rolled again, and I replayed my plan in my head.

I stepped out of the woods, grabbed my knife, then raced to the hotel and through a revolving door into the lobby. The nearest Spectavi fumbled with his rifle. I flipped open my knife and had his head off before he got organized.

"Never a dull moment in the company of the vice president!" a man in the Grand Dining Room called.

Laughter and hearty cheers drowned out the piano's resumption.

Two Spectavi guards at the dining room's entrance fired their rifles. Two more raced out from inside.

"What the—" the same man yelled.

Ignoring the pair drawing long knives, I darted to the shooters. A silver bullet hit my arm, and another grazed my leg. I sliced a Spectavi neck. The other fired into my chest before I slashed his midsection. Silver-fueled pain radiated from my wounds.

I spun and blocked a guard's knife, then kicked the one behind me, driving him back. I cut down the Spectavi near me and whirled to the one returning to the battle. *Tyn-tyn-fswht!* He didn't last long.

My wounds were closing, but less quickly and fully because of the cursed silver. I limped into the dining room. It hurt to swing my arm, but I could bear it.

The guests at the black-tie affair crowded the narrow back exit. Others ducked and hid under tables. Handguns drawn, police and Secret Service surrounded the vice president and his wife. Conflicting instructions yelled to and by the screaming crowd added to the confusion. The interested woman from the general store parking lot stood gaping, while the two remaining Spectavi attacked with swords.

Fswht! I stabbed my knife straight into one and sliced up through his neck. He fell to the floor.

I leaned low to avoid a sword strike from the other, parried his next blows, then dodged to the side and— *fswht*—chopped off his sword hand. I cut across his stomach, and he collapsed into a pool of his own blood.

The vice president, his wife, and their guards were trying to push through the crowd at the rear of the room. A bullet grazed my cheek, and I glared at the policeman who had fired at me as I put away my knife.

I ran and drove my shoulder into the nearest Secret Service man, then bowled over the vice president and most of his protectors. I punched one and kicked another into the wall. I picked up the nearest chair and hurled it through a tall window that faced the front of the hotel.

The vice president's fist smashed my face, sending blood shooting from my nose. I grabbed his arm and ripped off his watch and ring, dropping both to the floor. Holding him, I took his wife around the waist and raced with them for the broken window. I leapt out, dragging them into the rain. Sharp glass sliced my face and arms, but when we landed, a quick glance told me the humans were mostly fine.

From behind me, someone shouted, "Hold your fire!" doubtless afraid of hitting those with me.

Still carrying my captives, I ran across the street and into the woods. I expected screams from the woman, if not from both, but none came. I jumped a wide river, landed us in stride, and kept going. I splashed through puddles and passed a huge uprooted tree, then the decomposing remains of a deer. I ran and ran until it seemed far enough, then I dropped the couple at the base of a tall tree with a wide, thick canopy that blocked some of the rain.

The vice president got up, and I brought my katana to his neck.

The Navy man stood firm. "Who are you? What do you want?"

"The surveillance camera system in Washington. There's another control center. Where is it?"

He didn't respond. His wife inched away on the ground.

"Stop!" I called to her, and she froze. "And you'd better not scream." To her husband, I repeated louder, "*Where* is the control center?"

Thunder rumbled.

The vice president rubbed his wrist where his watch should have been. "They'll find us."

"Not for a while." I glanced at the treetops. "Not out here."

"I won't tell you," he said, his eyes scanning my wounded body. "And my blood won't, either."

"Why is it so important it stay secret?"

"The cameras should never have been installed in the first place. Those twins have access to the system, and *our* access is one of the only things we have to fight them. They're evil. You Sanguans are *all* evil."

I pressed my sword into his skin. "You're right. We are all evil." I eased up, then took my blade off him. "But we want to fight the twins. That's why we want to know where it is."

"Who's *we*?" he asked. "You look familiar. Are you Spectavi?"

"*We* includes some Spectavi. *We* intend to kill the twins."

He shook his head. "The Spectavi had their chance. My answer is no."

I squinted at him. "Do you know where the evil you speak of comes from?"

"Yes. Edmond, who maintained order a far cry better than this Reinald, explained the horrific experiment gone wrong fifteen hundred years ago. On a night like tonight, in the middle of a lightning storm, vampires came into existence as the result of some... some kind of mutation."

I almost laughed. "Caterine and Ariane's power comes from Hell, the same as the rest of us, Sanguan and Spectavi. Edmond lied. The twins were the first vampires. They are his sisters."

The woman gasped.

"I don't believe you," the vice president said.

"You hold Edmond in such high regard, but he was a liar. I look familiar because I met you briefly when I was a human, pathetically hanging on his arm, following him from event to event. He lied to me, just like he lied to you and everyone else."

He shook his head. "I *will not* believe you. God would never—"

"God did." I stepped close. "God did, and here I am."

"I won't tell you."

I returned my katana to his neck, then formed a wry smile and moved it to his wife's.

She gulped, pressing herself against the wet bark behind her. "Don't tell her. She's a demon. I *knew* they were all demons."

I pushed in the blade until blood trickled down her neck with the rainwater. When her husband tried to pull the sword away, I switched it to my left hand and pinned him against the tree with my right.

"Burn in *Hell*!" she demanded.

He grabbed my arm with both hands, but failed completely in his attempts to move my sword. "Stop!"

"No!" she urged. "Don't tell her!" Her blood ran more quickly.

"Stop! Please stop!" he pleaded.

I moved my sword an inch off his wife's neck. "Where?"

He hung his head. "Annapolis."

With the flat side of my blade, I lifted his chin. "Where?"

"Michelson Hall. In the basement."

"If you're lying to me…"

"I'm not. I swear," he said.

I lowered my sword, and he covered the wound on his wife's neck. He hugged her and kissed her cheek.

I sheathed Tomori, stepped away, and called Victoria.

She picked up. "Yes?"

"I want Todd," I said.

"What?"

"I've got the vice president. He revealed the location. I'll tell you if you let Todd go."

"Hah!"

I imagined her with a smile—a satisfied one. At least I *hoped* she was smiling.

"That's not the way this works." She sounded serious.

"You never should have kidnapped him in the first place," I argued. "You—"

"Erin—"

"You erased his memory of me!"

The vice president and his wife appeared surprised at what they were hearing.

I continued, "I just… I just want him to have a normal future. A future where his mind is his own."

"We need him," Victoria said.

"Why?"

"To run the software. He wrote it. He knows it better than anyone."

"How hard could it be?" I asked. "Have him write a manual."

"No, we need him. I'm sorry."

"Then *I'm* sorry. I won't tell you where the control center is."

"You will," Victoria insisted.

"Why?"

"Sanguans are running wild in Washington, D.C. We're doing our best, but as you can see, it isn't enough. And frankly, most of those Sanguans have become secondary concerns. I don't have time to worry about them with Caterine and Ariane focused on Washington. Every hour—every minute—you keep the location from us, those two have an insurmountable advantage in that city. I don't know if they rest there during the day, but we might discover that with the cameras."

I turned to face away from my captives and spoke as quietly as possible. "You'd have them attacked during the day?"

"Anyone else, probably no. But them? Yes, I would explore that strategy."

"What if they leave the city every night, so they aren't vulnerable that way?" I turned back to the vice president and his wife.

"They probably do," Victoria admitted. "But each night they return, the remaining civilians, the president, and the nation's government are in grave danger. I can fight the twins, and *you* can help me fight them. Three hundred years ago, I could have put an end to them, and without Edmond to stop me, we *finally can*. But not while we are blind to their movements in the city, and they use the cameras to know all of ours."

"It'll be a stalemate," I said. "We'll each have access to the cameras."

"Not necessarily. They will not know we have access to the system, and we can use that to our advantage. Todd believes he can ensure that remains our secret."

"It's wrong, how you've used him."

"Perhaps, but we need him for a little longer."

"When this is over, when the twins are dead or driven out of Washington—"

"Then Todd can write his software manual, and you may have him back."

It was better than no deal at all. "The basement of Michelson Hall, at the Naval Academy."

"Thank you. And, Erin, good job. I'm very proud of you."

She couldn't see it, but I smiled. "Thanks."

"Keep Turner there. We've got others at the academy already. They'll check it out, and I'll let you know." She hung up.

The vice president asked, "Who was that?"

"It's not important." I walked over to them. "In a minute, if everything checks out at the academy, I'll let you go."

"It's there," he said.

I nodded. "Good."

"Is it true?" he asked. "What you said about Edmond and the twins?"

"It's true, all of it. Including that we mean to fight them and kill them."

"Can you really do it?"

"I think so."

His wife moved her hand off her neck. The bleeding had slowed.

He asked, "Do you know why everything changed after that red rain?"

I glanced skyward. "Only He knows for sure."

Victoria texted, *We got it. You can let him go.*

The vice president and his wife flinched when I pulled my gun from its holster and fired a flare at the treetops. I put away the gun and ran off.

12

After the bright sun next slipped beneath the horizon, I awoke in my basement. The Spectavi had run out of synthetic blood. The night had come.

I climbed out of my coffin, turned on the shower, got undressed, and found that the silver-laden bullet wounds in my chest and leg had healed to the point where each resembled an ugly bruise. A little blood would get me back to normal, and one way or another, I'd have that drink before long. While the water warmed, I scrolled through my received calls and messages.

A text from Caleb asked how everything had gone. Grant had also texted, letting me know that he and Alice had evaded their Spectavi pursuers and were going to spend the day in Winchester on their way to Fort Washington. There was a missed call from Caleb, then another text, noting that he assumed things hadn't gone disastrously, since he hadn't seen anything about me or the vice president on the news. He hoped I would fill him in with the details soon.

I got into the steaming shower.

Regarding Todd, it had become clear to me that I

couldn't get him "back," as Victoria had put it. While he had absolutely been stolen from me, like Vera, that person was gone. There was no getting *that* Todd back. There was no resuming the same relationship we had, and there would be no making him suddenly remember me. No switch existed to flip that would restore his feelings for me.

I wondered, not for the first time, if everything in my life would have been different if I had said yes when Todd asked me out initially, weeks before I eventually agreed. Would a divergent chain of events, leading me to another fate, have been set in motion? Or would I have ended up running to that bus stop shelter in the rain, petrified when imposing Grant came near because I didn't know him or his intentions, eventually following him so his friend James could drink from me and show me a photograph of Vera and Edmond and then finding myself working at Eure, regardless?

I reminded myself that my decisions *had* worked out well with Todd, for a while. My waiting had led us to a good relationship, before it all went wrong.

And that Todd had been lost for good. There were no two ways about it. Freeing him from the Spectavi meant saving him from their sinister ways for *him*, not for me. Considering the strength and skills I possessed, along with my access to the Spectavi, I certainly owed it to Todd to try.

I grabbed a towel, got out of the shower, and went straight for my cell to text Luke. *You around? I'm back in D.C.*

I threw on baby-blue pajama pants and a tank top, then went upstairs and turned on my TV.

"Details are still coming in," the anchorwoman said. "But all indications are that the senator and his family were murdered in their Cleveland Park home early this evening. The Sanguan attack comes just hours after surprise legislation was rushed through the House and the Senate and signed by President Hughes, doing away with the legal window from four to six a.m. for vampires to hunt. It is unclear if the attack is related."

She added, "And here again is the picture from a witness, who was driving by and heard screams inside the home."

Full screen, a blurry image showed three large male vampires headed away from a house. The one most in focus had a tall, pink mohawk and a grin for the camera.

The image disappeared. "That picture is from earlier. Police and Spectavi are currently on the scene, and the street has been closed off. Speculation is that the Sanguans took advantage of the early hour to attack the senator and his family before Spectavi had fully spread out to their usual patrols."

Maybe the Spectavi hadn't fully spread out to their patrols. Though I strongly suspected that, driven by a thirst that suddenly had no factory-made cure, fewer of them had gone out on patrol at all. That the Spectavi blood supply had been depleted would surely be in the news soon. I texted Victoria, *What will happen now that you're out of synthetic?*

Things were clearly getting worse. The senator's entire family had been murdered *in* their home. June had been killed where she assumed she was safe, far from Washington. The Spectavi couldn't be everywhere, even before they ran out of synthetic. And the attackers had apparently not even been the twins. If they had been, the Spectavi's presence probably wouldn't have mattered at all.

No raging fire torched the streets, and no stench of rotten brimstone polluted the air. The pits of Hell remained a place apart from the earthly world. Yet the world's descent into a different kind of hell continued relentlessly. In fact, to humans especially, that descent might already have been completed, and I didn't expect the repeal of the legal window for hunting to help.

Victoria responded, *We'll see.*

The reporter outside the senator's said, "And this just confirmed—two additional bodies have been found in the backyard. At this time, it is not known if they were guests of the senator or what exactly they were doing at his home. We do not have their names."

On the long list of messages I had ignored on my phone, I responded to Caleb's most recent. *Sorry, things got hectic. I'm fine. So are Grant and Alice. Turner had the information we needed. Did you see the news about the senator?*

My phone rang—Caleb. I muted the TV, then considered sticking to texting because it would have been easier. But on the fourth ring, I picked up. "Hey."

"Hey. So you're all right?" Caleb asked.

"Yeah."

"How'd it go? And is the vice president okay?"

"He's fine. The control center was at the Naval Academy, where we started. Victoria had it moved somewhere."

"Good, good."

Luke texted, but I couldn't read it while talking on the phone. I said, "Crazy about the senator."

"Very."

"D.C.'s a mess. How are things down there? Any trouble?"

"Nope, no problems here," he said. "I'm getting ready to head up your way."

"I'm not sure you should."

"What?"

"Not yet, I mean." I didn't have any great plan to convince him. "The Spectavi are out of synthetic. It's really dangerous here."

"If they're out of synthetic there, they're probably also out here. And there are Sanguans everywhere."

"I know, but... there, you've got guards. And the twins! They're up here. You've *got* to be safer there."

"You said you weren't afraid of the twins," he argued.

"I'm not *afraid*, but that doesn't mean it's not dangerous with the two of them around." I hated admitting the next part. "And even one-on-one, confident as I am, I know fighting Caterine or Ariane could end really badly for me."

"I'm coming back," Caleb said.

"No, please. At least not for a few nights. Now that Victoria can access the cameras, she can go after the twins. Maybe the worst of this will be over soon."

"I miss you."

"And I miss you. But please stay there. It's safer."

Silence.

I urged, "Please, for me?"

"Fine."

"Good. I have to run. I'll call you later, or tomorrow."

"Okay." He sounded defeated. "Bye."

I ended the call. He *had* to be better off down there than tagging along with me.

I read Luke's text. *Yup, in D.C. Leaving the bar.*

I wrote, *Can you meet?*

I need to practice, Luke responded.

I'm alone. Please?

That did the trick. He wrote, *OK. Where?*

I glanced at the news on the quiet television. *Can you take a cab to my house?*

Sure.

———————

I stood in my pajamas at my living room window, awaiting Luke's arrival, somewhat seriously curious if scores of bloodthirsty Spectavi would amble into view.

A taxi pulled up, and Luke got out.

I pulled open my door. "Hi."

He stepped inside.

I closed the door. "I missed you."

He kissed my cheek and tilted his head.

I gently took hold of him, pushed aside his hair, and bit into his neck. While his blood flowed over my fangs and his body relaxed, I refrained from sucking. His skin heated my lips, and my tongue tasted the salt in his sweat, but I didn't draw out more of his luscious blood than what trickled into my mouth on its own. Satisfied enough to hold off on my first deep drink for a few moments more, I pulled my fangs from him, held his hand, and led him up to a bedroom.

In my living room, with the news muted on the television, Luke plopped down on my couch and moved his hair out of his face. "I'm exhausted."

I sat at his side, curling my legs beneath me. He grabbed the remote and raised the volume.

At a podium, a high-ranking police officer said, "We have no further information at this time."

A flurry of questions came from reporters. One stood and spoke above the rest, "What about accounts saying that fewer Spectavi are out on patrol than normal tonight?"

"I have no comment," the officer said.

The reporter added, "It certainly seemed like less to me."

"No comment."

Luke yawned. "I'm gonna need a cup of coffee."

"You still want to practice," I recalled from the blood I had drunk.

"Yup. It's going to be a late night."

I muted the TV again. "What's this concert you're planning?"

"You know what I know. We wanna do something big." He nodded at the TV. "The whole country's watching D.C. even more than normal, and we want to play a show that's sure to be noticed."

I wrapped my arms around his arm. "I worry about you."

Luke kissed my forehead. "I know."

I kissed his cheek. Then he held my back while I climbed on top of him.

I kissed his forehead. "I worry so much."

I kissed his neck, then the other side and bit—*vwoosh*—and saw his vision of himself inside a packed Robert F. Kennedy football stadium downtown. I sipped while the crowd rocked along with him and his band, perfectly in tune with their beat—and then to a different song, jumped and danced in a raucous furor. *Boom!* The fire in my mind burst. *Boom!* I sipped as a drum hit, and then—*boom—boom—boom*—on and on to the thunderous beats of Luke's music. It was loud. It was hot—Luke, his band, the crowd, the flames roasting my mind and enveloping the entire stadium. Luke burned, the crowd burned… everything *burned*.

I pulled my fangs out of him and swallowed. A tear slid down my cheek. I wished the world was different. "It's not fair." I got off him and curled up on the couch again.

He wiped his forehead and worked to catch his breath. "What's not fair?"

"It's an amazing vision—that concert at the stadium. But these are dark times."

He lit up. "No, no. Don't you see? This is our chance. Our band's doing okay. Better than we all thought we ever would, when we're really honest with ourselves. But not better than we hoped. We *all* hoped we'd catch some big break. I wouldn't be playing with those guys unless they dreamed big, and they do. And here we are. *This* is our moment. We're staring right at it."

"It's dangerous."

"It is, but will you make me a vampire?"

"I can't," I said. "I just… can't."

"Then I say the risk is worth it."

"You do. I know. You truly think it's worth it. To your core."

"Uh huh."

I took both his hands. "Promise me you'll tell me whenever you play. Every time. I need to be there. I need to know you're safe."

He nodded. "I promise."

13

The next night, I searched Twitter for "Spectavi synthetic."

The results contained links to articles I had already read:

Spectavi running out of synthetic?

From a reliable source: the Spectavi can no longer make synthetic blood and will be out soon.

The articles were correct, except for the timing, based on what I had been told.

I searched for "Spectavi blood" and scrolled down tweets of rumors and links to articles like the others. Then, one with a lot of retweets caught my eye:

Saw a Spectavi IN UNIFORM drinking blood from this chick outside a bar. Ran away so no picture, but it's TRUE!

That, unfortunately, was what I had expected.

I went upstairs, outside, hopped into the Suburban, and drove south to Fort Washington. I used the entrance in the woods, and from there, the dimly lit, brick-and-concrete hallway to the main room was shorter.

At my arrival, Hayden, the lean, spiky-haired Texan-turned-vampire in the eighteen hundreds, stood from his chair at the long table. "Erin."

"Hayden," I said. "Houjin."

At the head of the table, at a laptop, the older immortal nodded. It comforted me to see them both. Houjin appeared quite youthful, but was more than seven hundred years old and very pale because of it. Purportedly, he was an excellent sword fighter. In Alexander's throne room, I had seen Hayden valiantly battle the twins. He had been cut and bloodied, but not beaten. Months later, in Europe, he had helped me on the trail of the True Cross.

Max—an old friend of Grant's and Zhilan's whom I had gone on a few missions with—walked in from the back room we used for sparring. Max hailed from New Jersey and had grown up in New York City at the same time as Grant. The two didn't get along as humans or young vampires, but when I asked Zhilan what had changed, she revealed nothing beyond that something had and that they had been close friends since. I would ask Max for the details when the time was right.

Alice and Grant followed him out. Zhilan trailed them, slipping her arms through the sleeves of a loose pink floral kimono that went over her black shirt. While Renshu's absence was impossible to ignore, the group gave me confidence. I reckoned we could handle anything.

"Alice, Grant, thanks for the help in New Castle," I said. "Everything went all right?"

"Yup," Grant said. "You?"

"Yup," I echoed.

"Good. And yeah, no problems at all. We lost 'em eventually."

"We *could* have lost them sooner," Alice said, "if I wasn't waiting for you all the time."

Grant put on a sober face. "I think she's faster than you, Erin."

I took a seat at the table. "Really?"

He sat. "Well, maybe *as* fast."

Alice sank onto a chair, and she and I exchanged smiles. It didn't bother me. She could be faster. I'd be surprised if she were, but frankly, speed like that sounded very valuable, and in fact, already had been. The others joined us at the table.

I asked Hayden, "Bored of Europe?"

He smiled. "Worried about America."

Houjin spoke up. "Erin, Grant explained the mission you undertook for Victoria. Did you acquire the information she sent you for? And have you shared it with her?"

I leaned forward. "Yes and yes. I told her what the vice president told me—that the second control center was at the Naval Academy in Annapolis."

"I see." Houjin brought his hands together. "Did you ever consider *not* sharing the information with Victoria and instead, bringing it to us?"

I almost laughed. "I tried to keep it from her to bargain for my friend Todd's release from the Spectavi, but I couldn't."

"No?"

"She wants to use the cameras to go after the twins, and I agree with her. For the sake of D.C. and everyone there, they need to be stopped. She convinced me."

Houjin nodded.

"Would *you* have kept the information from her?" I asked. "Knowing how she planned to use it?"

"Perhaps, perhaps not. I merely sought to understand your rationale," he explained. "And that means Todd remains with them?"

"When this is over, they'll let him go."

"Reasonable," he said.

I also found consolation in the fact that Todd had learned the truth and could contact me again if need be. "Have you ever fought her?"

"Victoria?" Houjin asked.

"Yeah."

"Long ago."

"How'd you do?"

"Not well. She's too tall for me. Her reach plus her longsword—I could not overcome the disadvantages."

I considered the group with me—Hayden had fought beside Victoria, as had Zhilan, months after she fought against her. And that, after hundreds of years of holding Victoria responsible, in part, for her father's death. And then there was me. We were decidedly Sanguan at that table, but it never seemed quite that simple.

"So what's the plan?" Grant asked.

All eyes went to Houjin, who shrugged.

Max asked, "What does that mean?"

Zhilan answered for her maker, "It means there is no plan."

"Why not?" Grant asked.

"Why should there be?" Houjin argued. "The Spectavi are in trouble. They have already run out of synthetic in most of the world. Everywhere else, it will happen any time. I am at ease here, watching it all unfold."

Watching didn't sit well with me, and hearing Houjin suggest it surprised me. "I thought you had some respect for humanity and that you didn't want a 'catastrophic loss of human life.' That seems to be where things are headed—or already are."

Apparently remembering the same conversation, Hayden corrected me. "He said he didn't want to *cause* something like that."

"Precisely," Houjin confirmed. "Since the thirteenth century, I have seen towns and cities burn, and I have witnessed governments fall and nations be wiped from the map. The world keeps turning. I have seen the Spectavi celebrate victories over groups of Sanguans, large and small. And I have also seen Sanguans win victories against the Spectavi. History is full of winners and losers. Change is the only constant.

"But most recently, I've seen the Spectavi attempting to eradicate our kind for no reason other than that we are not 'with them.' We cherish our freedom, those in this room and those like us. And in fact, the Spectavi have gone beyond merely 'attempting' in their pursuit at eradication. They are well on their way.

"I have lost many friends these last few decades, friends who sought nothing more than to live their lives as they saw fit. If thousands or even millions of humans have to die for the Spectavi to suffer a massive, crippling defeat that drastically diminishes their influence, I am willing to stand by while it happens."

"But *I* let those twins free," I said. "And they've caused a lot of this mess."

Houjin waved his hand. "I think not, Erin. Blame Edmond for how he ruled the Spectavi—his ideology and how he used his synthetic blood to bend others to it. Blame Edmond for what he did to you that compelled you to free Caterine and Ariane. And surely, if you judge that the twins should die, blame Edmond for not taking his chance at *any* time during the three hundred years they were his prisoners to wipe them from the face of the earth."

"And God," Zhilan added. "David Sartori committed serious crimes, but God's red rain has pushed the world into this horrible situation. Caterine and Ariane terrorize Washington, but people suffer everywhere and will suffer more, because the Spectavi cannot produce synthetic blood. Some say that the Lord has a plan, but if He does in this case, I do not see it."

"What if it was the Devil's rain, not God's?" I asked.

"That would be worse," Zhilan concluded. "It would mean the Devil has the upper hand in a meaningful way."

I had another idea. "What about love? Maybe it *was* God's doing, and the point was to teach our kind to love those we drink from. The two I truly love have blood that still nourishes me. Alice's was the same with Grant. It's a lesson."

"Perhaps," Houjin said. "And perhaps a fine one. But if

so, it is quite a price for all of humanity to pay to teach our kind a lesson. Let me ask you, Erin, what will *you* do?"

"Fight," I said. "Someone. The twins, the Spectavi, ruthless Sanguans. I don't know, but I won't sit around here watching."

Zhilan began, "Very reckl—"

"Not all on the same night, not wildly," I interrupted, wondering if their willingness to wait and watch reflected a detachment from humanity developed over the long years since they had been mortal. "I don't know how to fix everything or how to change things back to the way they were before the rain—and maybe things won't ever change back. I have Luke and Caleb to worry about, but I'll figure out who to fight next, and then I'll get to fighting. I won't have my *plan* be to do nothing." I looked at Hayden. "What about you? Surely *you* don't want to sit around here waiting."

"I don't like seeing my nation's capital under siege." He grew stern. "And I'm looking forward to paying Caterine and Ariane back for Alexander's and Switzerland, so you can bet your ass I'm not here to sit around waiting. However, I also am not here to rush straight into battle."

"Well," Houjin said, "the beauty of this group is that you each may do as you wish. But I offer these words of caution: We have already lost dear friends to this intensifying conflict. Know that our war ebbs and flows. It always has, century upon century. Many of our kind who have survived the longest have managed to do so by choosing very carefully when to be involved in the fighting and when to stay out of it. Act if you will, but do not discount *that* course of action, either."

Houjin's phone buzzed. Zhilan's and Max's chimed at the same time, then Grant's did. I realized most of *my* contacts were at the table with me.

"What is it?" Alice asked.

"Eure's headquarters is under attack," Max announced, while responding to a text.

I got up, grabbed the remote, and turned on the television, which was already tuned to the news. A video shot from the middle of the woods surrounding Eure's campus panned from bright, blurry patches on the road outside the main entrance to a hazy light above the white office buildings. The lens focused—the place was ablaze. My friends left the table and came over to watch.

The scene cut to the anchorman in the studio. "Tom, can you hear us?" Coverage shifted back to the shaky camera in the woods. "Tom?"

A tan reporter wearing a crumpled shirt smudged with dirt—presumably Tom—came into view. "Are you hearing anything?" he asked the camera operator. "No?" Tom glanced at the fire over Eure.

"Tom?" came the anchor's voice.

Tom said, "If you're speaking to us in the studio, we're not getting it, but we're going to keep broadcasting. We're going to try to get closer."

With Tom still on screen, the anchor said, "We seem to have lost the ability to communicate with them, but we'll stay with their feed as long as we can."

Tom started toward the blaze. *Boom!* Fire burst atop an office building in the shaky camera view. Tom glanced back, but didn't stop.

I texted Victoria. *Are you at Eure? Do you need me there?*

Boom! The camera shook again. Burning buildings filled the screen. Lampposts crashed to the street. A silver jeep raced out of the complex.

Tom turned to the camera. "I can feel the heat from the fires growing." Tom flinched at a growling scream piercing the night. "I don't see anyone." He pressed on, nearing the tree line facing the main entrance. "There!" He pointed, and the camera followed, but picked up nothing except burning buildings.

Another shrieking growl.

Tom took a few quick steps ahead. "Do you see that?" He pointed again.

"Where?" the cameraman asked.

"That far building. Come around."

The camera bobbed and got some of the forest floor while its carrier caught up with Tom.

"My God," the cameraman said as the view settled on a burning building at the front of Eure and focused near the top, on a body. Stuck to the side, with arms outstretched and feet pinned together, it looked like William, cut open, bleeding, chained between windows, and unmoving. Surely, it had been done by the twins in retaliation for hundreds of years of experiments while imprisoned. Unless a group of Spectavi had done it because they were out of synthetic blood and somehow knew what William had done to them. The fire closed in on the body.

My phone buzzed—Caleb. *You see what's going on at Eure? You're not there, are you?*

Victoria hadn't responded. I decided asking her about Todd could wait and answered Caleb, *Watching on TV. I'm not there.* I almost included "yet" at the end.

Todd couldn't handle anything like what I saw on the television—all that fire. But Todd could have already run. *Todd, I hope you had the sense to run from that fire.*

"There!" Tom pointed at a dark object approaching. Tom fell, then so did the cameraman, and the screen went black.

"Tom?" the anchorman shouted. "Tom? Phil?"

The black picture persisted.

"Tom! Phil!"

Tom and Eure flickered into view. "It was just a vampire," Tom said. "She's gone. We're all right." Tom brushed himself off. "We're going to keep going."

They crept forward and reached the forest's edge. A group of vampires moving faster than the camera could clearly capture battled on the field between the office buildings and Reinald's and Victoria's houses.

I moved close to the television. Tall, long dark hair—one of the fighters must have been Victoria. The two blond-haired females had to be the twins. Another combatant might have been Reinald. I wasn't certain. Among the others, one was extremely pale and bald, which probably meant Konrad. The Sanguan with the pink mohawk whipped a long chain at Victoria, who dodged it. The expected warriors appeared to be present, and the scene largely removed any doubt about how William had wound up on that building side, but the lack of more Spectavi surprised me.

Boom! Ba-boom!

The camera panned to fire engulfing the entire building where William's body was pinned.

Behind that building, a ball of flame roared skyward, and the TV went blank.

"Tom? Phil?" The broadcast switched to the anchorman, who stared into a side monitor. "Tom? Phil? Can you hear me?" The anchor's attention returned to the main studio camera. "We're trying to get them back."

I remarked, "If they couldn't even defend their own headquarters…"

"It was an office park," Houjin said. "Not a military base. They have many of both. This is a long way from over."

The anchor held his hand to his ear. "I'm… yes, we've heard from Tom and Phil. They're fine. They're on the way to their truck." The anchor's body relaxed. "Tom and Phil are okay."

Expecting that to be the end of the updates from the scene for a while, I made eye contact with Zhilan and tilted my head to the other side of the room. She followed me to the far wall.

"Should I go?" I asked quietly.

"No," Zhilan said.

"But Victoria and the twins—"

"Victoria can take care of herself. And that is not the setting for you to engage those twins. You will have better opportunities, or perhaps Victoria will prevail tonight, and you will never have to."

"I hate doing nothing."

"I understand. Trust me, I do. But *that*"—she pointed at the television—"is not your fight."

"What about Todd?"

"If he were smart, he fled that place when the attack began."

Alice approached. "I hope I'm not interrupting."

My gut told me to obey Zhilan's council. If Victoria reached out to me, I would go in a heartbeat. Otherwise, I'd stay out of it and pray to hear from her soon. I answered Alice, "No, not at all."

"I don't like just sitting here, doing nothing," she said.

"That is *definitely* not *your* fight," Zhilan said.

"I know." Alice folded her arms. "But…"

Zhilan rolled her eyes. "Practice. Shall the three of us go spar?"

"Sure," I agreed. It was a reasonable way to shift my focus from Eure until Victoria responded.

"Okay," Alice said.

Zhilan motioned to the back room. "I'll be right there."

Alice followed me that way.

Inside, I asked her, "How is everything?"

"Good."

"No trouble, no…" I realized her background was nothing like mine. I didn't *really* know what went on inside her head—what she experienced when she drank or what she felt in between drinks, especially when the cravings grew desperate. "… no problems with anything?"

"No. It's different… so different." She bit her lip. "But I love it. I love every single night. I've met so many incredible people and vampires. I've been so many new places, and all the places I had been before are like a whole new world."

"It's a grim world," I said. "Everyone apologizes to me for the state of things, and you're even younger."

"Yeah, but it's always been grim, and I don't have to be scared of it anymore." Her eyes lit up. "I imagine what it would be like if the red rain hadn't fallen and *all* blood still burned hot—if I had my pick of anyone." *There* was her craving—her lust. "But it doesn't matter. And Grant's been with me every step of the way. He's taught me so much."

I smiled. "Good." I pointed at another door in the far corner of the room. "What's in there?"

"A gas-powered crematory." Zhilan came in from the main room. "The heat and exhaust are dissipated and expelled through underground ducts. Many let out near the water south of the fort."

"Why do we need a crematory down here?" I asked.

"No reason that should surprise. Vampires die. Mortals die. We need to dispose of the remains discretely." Zhilan grabbed two wooden knives from a side shelf and lobbed one to me. "Alice, watch Erin and I to start. Notice how we leave ourselves ready for our next moves, as we finish the ones before. After, I will work with you on that."

Alice nodded.

Instead of charging with all my speed, I moved slower to help Alice understand. She was so young, so inexperienced, and the nights were so dark.

14

"We will not abandon this city. *I* will not abandon this city," President Hughes said in a statement early the following evening. The networks were replaying it repeatedly. "Washington is safe, and I will remain here in the White House."

I hit Power, threw the remote on the couch, then went out and sat on my front porch steps. My knife was on my thigh. My sword, beside me. My block, totally quiet. All the houses lay dark, without illuminated windows or porches. Only a few solar-powered outdoor lanterns glowed.

Despite the president's proclamation, most viewed the destruction of Eure's headquarters as the last, ominous straw and had fled the terror of Washington, D.C. While attacks and murders like June's made it clear that nowhere was safe, Interstate 95—north and south—had been full of bumper-to-bumper traffic almost the entire day, according to news reports. Luke's bar, one of the last in the city to remain open, had finally closed.

My neighbors on both sides were gone, but not quite every last person had left the area. From the Reeds' house across the street, which was as unlit as them all and had its curtains drawn, when I really tried, I could hear the family's faint mortal pulses. I wondered if I should let them know.

For the first time in a long time, a glass of wine sounded nice. Not for the taste and not for the alcohol. I just wanted something to do while I sat there, awaiting answers from Victoria. Todd was fine, she had said, but she had yet to respond to my follow-up about him, what had happened, and if it had really been William horrifically burned on the building side.

Caleb had texted during the day, practically pleading to return to Washington. After the events at Eure's headquarters, I simply refused. If he had been safer in South Carolina before, he certainly was after what had happened at Eure. While estimates varied, by all accounts, far fewer Spectavi had gone out on patrol in the city than in recent nights.

When I had called Luke shortly after sundown, he said he couldn't meet me because he had skipped out on his band for so long last time to be with me. I felt weak. I had a headache. My image of red wine had changed to a vision of thick viscous blood filling a crystal-clear glass. I began to doubt that my earlier craving had actually been for wine at all. If I didn't see Luke the whole night, I resolved to do so first thing the next evening.

A siren to the east broke the neighborhood's calm. I stood, slung my sword over my shoulder, and began walking. Around the corner was another deserted street and different lifeless houses. I made my way up the hill toward Zhilan's place.

Very few cars lined the road. The small park overlooking the highway, the Pentagon, and downtown was empty. Every window in two apartment buildings was dark.

To the left, the burned-out ruins of Zhilan's house still stood. Her neighbors' houses had charred side walls, but no major damage. Nevertheless, they seemed abandoned, and I sensed no living scents or pulses inside. I walked close and peered into Zhilan's basement—all the weapons had been removed from the walls.

Another siren—not far and west. I continued south on the sidewalk. What a nightmare. What an utterly placid nightmare. I envisioned the terrible calm advancing out from the city, enveloping all in its path like water from a broken wave that never finished running ashore. I had grown used to the sirens, I realized. Yet they sounded, and the nightmare must not have been as peaceful where they came from.

I walked down a hill and through the middle of an empty intersection. Without hesitation, a car far to my right ran a red light. I kept going, passing an empty Laundromat and a strip mall with unlit stores and every door chained shut.

I sniffed—Sanguan. Not crossing paths with the vampire would have had its advantages, but I continued on, unenthusiastic about changing course to make that happen.

An old maroon car with two young men in the front seat sped into the intersection ahead and lurched to a stop when a Sanguan darted out and slammed his hands on the hood. Both men screamed.

A Spectavi in gray fatigues raced to the near side of the

car. Another went to the far side—no synthetic odor. The Spectavi really had run out. The men frantically tried to crawl into the back of the car while the two Spectavi pulled open the front doors. The Sanguan growled and dove at the Spectavi on the passenger side, shutting the door in the process. While the vampires grappled, each trying to sink their fangs into the other's neck, the second Spectavi pulled out the driver and bit. Almost immediately, he let the man go and reached in for the passenger.

The driver fled, and I drew my sword. Leaving the remaining man to the Spectavi on the driver's side of the car, I charged to the passenger side and stabbed straight into the other Spectavi's chest, lodging my sword in the door. The Sanguan swung at me. I ducked and, with one hand keeping my katana steady, drew my knife, then slashed across the Sanguan's midsection. He roared and stumbled away, then bolted from the scene.

The Spectavi on the far side of the car pulled his fangs from the man and ran off. His unfulfilling prey ran the other way, leaving me alone with the Spectavi I had pinned to the car.

I asked him, "What did they say to do for blood?"

He struggled. I pushed my blade in deeper.

He said, "Wha… what do you mean?"

"The thirst. Surely you weren't instructed to attack humans in their cars. How did they tell you to survive?"

"I don't know what you're talking about."

I twisted my sword. Blood ran from him.

"Aghh…" He grimaced, his chest heaving.

I kept turning.

"Aaaghh…"

"You'll bleed to death soon."

"I'm not supposed to attack people." His struggles subsided. "I'm supposed to find someone willing. Otherwise, I'm not to drink."

"Ever?"

"Sanguans, sure, but not people." He shook his head. "I hear the voice in my mind. It won't go away. It told me not to stop that car. I knew it would have been wrong, so we waited for the Sanguan to do it." His eyes unfocused. "But there's another voice telling me to feed, to survive, whatever it takes. Once the car *was* stopped…" He gulped. "There are hardly any people around, yet I need a reliable source of blood." He licked his lips. "That voice, I cannot stop, either."

I pulled out my sword.

The Spectavi slumped to the road. "How do you feed?"

"I'm lucky."

"You know one whose blood remains nourishing?"

"Yes."

"You *must* let me have a drink," he implored me. "I *beg* you. A small sip is all."

"No."

He grabbed my hand. "Please, just a sip!"

I shook him away and brought my sword to his neck. "No."

He growled, then dropped his head. "I'm sorry."

I put out my hand. He took it, and I pulled him up.

"What should I do?" he asked.

Not attack people, I thought. "Keep trying." What would I have done? My lips had grown dry, and emptiness filled me, but if truly desperate, what *wouldn't* I have done to survive? How could I expect him to do any less?

He nodded and, after waiting a moment, perhaps to see if I had additional advice, departed down a diagonal street.

Carrying my sword, I resumed my walk south, among a mixture of small shops and offices, modest houses, and an occasional tall apartment building. All had to die. All were mortal. We "immortals" were only so in one sense of the word. More accurately, vampires possessed the opportunity for immortality. We could burn in the sun, be poisoned by silver, and die in battle, which I had always assumed was why, as Vera, I had chosen my sword's name, Tomori, for *memento mori*. The weapon was to be an instrument with which I hastened my victims to that inevitable finality.

We also withered and wasted away without blood. Death by other means could be avoided by staying passive or better, hidden. But blood, even for the ancients eventually, was a necessity. And blood was running out. Perhaps young Vera had been spectacularly prescient when naming my sword.

I sheathed the cold steel. Or perhaps I had simply chosen a cool name for a weapon I couldn't wait to use to hack apart my enemies. *My* immortal heart continued to pump blood through *my* immortal veins.

But I was thirsty, and at that moment, found myself without any way to remedy it. I couldn't blame that Spectavi—he had to live somehow. And drinking *from him* felt surprisingly wrong. Out on that street, starved for blood, he seemed far more a poor, suffering brother than a sworn, eternal enemy. And the men he had been after...

In the long run, in the hell of a world, what hope did they have? Those who could feed vampires were scarce and clearly getting scarcer. An unwelcome sense of failure accompanied my vision of the unthinkable future that came to mind: one filled with worse pain, deeper darkness, and greater despair.

An email arrived from Victoria.

Erin, Todd had relocated from our headquarters already.

With our reduced forces spread out around D.C., the twins attacked. Using the cameras, they likely also knew exactly who was away in Washington at the time, including Reinald and me.

We suffered heavy casualties. William was killed, as was Reinald. Eventually, Caterine and Ariane fled.

I'm on my way to a meeting with the president and his National Security Council advisors.

I responded, *How will Todd survive without synthetic blood? With the cameras, do you know where the twins went?*

Horns of what sounded like a fire truck blared in the distance. Victoria answered, *The twins appear to have spent the day outside Washington, beyond the view of the camera system. I am searching for their base of operations, though it is possible they have not settled on one and remain constantly on the move. I pray that time will tell.*

We have reserve synthetic for Todd and others who are vital to our cause. For the rest, there is no more we can do. Some have

remained loyal, many have not. If you still have human friends
around, I suggest you get them somewhere safe, away from here.

Where? Nowhere was safe. And while synthetic for Todd
meant he wouldn't go hungry, was it poisoning his mind
further? I sent, *Thanks for the information. Good luck.*

Good luck to you. I may need your help before long.

I couldn't wait until she asked.

Caleb would be safest in South Carolina, and that would
probably have been the best place for Luke, as well. But Luke
would never hole up with Caleb. Fort Washington with my
friends could work, but he had already turned his back on
there once. I texted Luke to check on him, then continued
my walk south.

The Spectavi were losing control. Or they had already
lost it. Victoria could fight Caterine and Ariane, but
uncertain where they rose from each night, she seemed to be
constantly reacting, instead of aggressively hunting.

Once more, I considered that both Caleb and Luke
preferred the possibility of starving as immortals over
continuing their tenuous human existences and that I had
the ability to grant one of them that escape.

But would I just be damning them to a different awful
fate? My fledgling would be powerful, like me, but the world
showed no signs of improving. What if there *was* no hope,
and without blood to drink, the end *had* come for
immortals?

And *one of them*… How could I give one the gift they
begged me for when it meant denying the other?

I imagined picking Luke. As an immortal, he could be

the greatest vampire rock star ever. He would be legendary, and I would be with him every step of the way.

I imagined picking Caleb. As a vampire, he could learn the secrets of history he yearned to know. Together, we would explore the world of fascinating people and breathtaking places.

Either choice meant a companion who would save me from ever having to be alone. Either choice meant having to find a new source of blood because I couldn't keep drinking from the one I hadn't picked. With the stakes so high, the hurt for the one not chosen would run deep. Even if he let me, it would be torture for me to taste that pain with each sip.

If the world continued on its decent into hell, would I meet an excruciating, thirst-filled end with Caleb a vampire at my side? Would I wither away having chosen Luke?

No! Surely we'd find blood. I would refuse to let myself starve, and so would Luke or Caleb. Luke's fans would become *our* fans and flock to us with their blood, as he predicted. Caleb, with me and all of his company's resources, would be too clever not to find a way. Even if the world never changed back to how it was before the red rain, we *would* survive.

And if God wanted vampires dead, He'd have done it swiftly. It wasn't the end. It *couldn't* be the end.

But Luke or Caleb? I could only make one an immortal, and I loved them both.

My path brought me to the desolate streets of Old Town, Alexandria. The bars and restaurants were all closed, their patrons nowhere to be seen. As I had a few times before, I crossed a narrow strip of a park on the Potomac to a dock with a couple sailboats tied at the end. Up the river, a fire burned on the D.C. waterfront. My phone rang.

With *Blocked* on the screen, I answered, "Hello."

"Erin, this is General Sharpe." Snippets of conversations in the background grew louder, then a door shut, quieting things considerably. The general asked, "How are you?"

"Fine." I made it to the end of the dock and instead of sitting as planned, spun around. "How are you?"

"Fine. Things aren't, though."

"What do you mean?"

"There are a lot of worried people around here," he explained. "Things have gotten pretty bad, in Washington especially."

"I agree."

"Those twins are out of control."

"I know." I pivoted halfway down the dock and paced toward the water and the flickering orange glow coming from west of the Capitol building.

"So what do we do?" the general asked. "The president won't leave Washington. He should. No question. But other than that, what should we do? That's what everyone wants to know."

"You're asking me?"

"Not officially, of course. Heh, I hardly know you. But we've heard from the Spectavi—a lot. And I've listened to endless proposals from scared and angry military men and women. I wanted to hear the Sanguan take, or the 'good'

Sanguan take, to satisfy my own curiosity, if for no other reason."

I stopped and looked toward Washington. "There is no 'good' Sanguan take. And *I* may not be as good as you suppose."

"You're better than the rest, I think. And if you aren't, you've convinced me that you are, and you're the one I'm on the phone with. What would you do, if you were us?"

The fire on the waterfront was spreading. "I'd fight."

"We are."

"Fight harder." A small explosion flashed near the Capitol. "This is war, General. I shouldn't need to tell you to fight."

A door opened on his end, letting in the noise of the commotion beyond it. "I have to go. Thank you, Erin." He hung up.

15

Late that night, I tried to distract myself from my thirst. First, I practiced with Tomori in my backyard, then I sat in my basement and scoured the internet anew for old stories or legends that seemed related to the world's current situation. I had given up and was watching the news, trying to think of a productive next move, when an email from Caleb arrived. I settled into my couch to read it.

Erin, I'm in Virginia. I couldn't stay away any longer.

I need to be with you. Every day since I've met you, while the sun shined overhead, I've missed you. That we couldn't be together in the bright, warm light of day always seemed unfair. But without you, I started sleeping away those days, as much as I could. And I made it through one day, then the next, knowing that each night would bring you back to me, or at least some night soon would. I was determined to be awake for every second we could share.

But now, you put four hundred miles between us. There was no chance I'd see you while I slept my days away and wasted my nights alone. I hated it. I hated being apart.

I want you to make me a vampire, so we won't ever have to

be apart. I've never asked anyone for anything that big, yet I ask you because I've never wanted anything more. But I can't force you to give me eternal life. I can't make you let me drink your immortal blood.

What I could do is come to Virginia. I'll settle for mortal nights with you, but as long as I can help it, I won't settle for being apart. I'm staying at our office in McLean. I love you, and I can't wait to see you.

He shouldn't have returned, and that office wasn't far outside the city. But it would be safer than his apartment downtown. I lay down on the sofa. No one had ever written me anything like that.

A text—Luke. *We're playing later, after a few other bands. At RFK. People are already showing up. The buzz online is pretty crazy. I think it's going to be really big.*

I smiled, picturing Luke smiling. I imagined biting him, tasting his absolute, unbridled excitement for the upcoming show. My next instinct told me to drag him away from RFK Stadium, far from Washington, where he would be safe. Or safer, anyway. Maybe. I responded, *What time do you think you'll go on?*

He answered, *5 or 5:30. We're gonna play until after sunrise.*

At least I wouldn't have to worry about him at that point. *I'll meet you at RFK before you play.*

I wrote Caleb, *I'll come by first thing tomorrow. I can't wait.*

Downstairs, in my closet, I took a long look at the leather pants I had worn to Luke's show the first time I bit him. It really sounded as though it was going to be a big night for him, and I figured he'd get a kick out of me wearing them.

I pulled a medium-length black skirt off a hanger. My knife could be hidden under it, and that trumped evoking a fun memory—but I did find the same black tank top I had worn. My tall boots were the obvious choice.

Looking in my mirror, I considered makeup. Why make the effort to appear tanned by the sun's rays, when in the crowd at the concert, light skin and dark eye shadow would work just as well? To any vampires, my scent would reveal my nature regardless of my appearance. To the humans, I'd be another Goth at the rock show. And to any who discovered or guessed I was an immortal, the cross on my neck might suggest Spectavi, rather than Sanguan.

When I finished there, I grabbed my sword and headed out.

———————————

The Deep and the Dark's rhythmic progressive rock emanated from RFK Stadium. I stopped to listen. The circular structure with no shortage of exposed concrete had long since been deemed outdated by the Redskins, who had moved their football games to suburban Maryland. But the D.C. United continued to play soccer in RFK, and the setting fit the concert well, especially on that night.

Regularly arriving cars pulled into the expansive parking lots surrounding the stadium. A reasonably steady stream of people walked passed me on their way inside. Others ran. Dark clothes and torn jeans were prominent, pierced faces, brightly colored hair and chain jewelry less so, but not especially rare.

The metro had shut down, and few cabs still operated, meaning almost all without cars had walked varying distances across the city to get there. In addition to the hardy souls from Washington, lots were also arriving from Virginia, Maryland, and considerably farther. The music grew louder as I got closer.

Twenty blocks to the west—too distant for even me to see—was the U.S. Capitol building. Red and blue lights flashed in the sky in that direction. Some appeared closer and others fainter and farther away, no doubt among federal offices and the monuments. But while I saw the emergency vehicle lights, I couldn't hear any sirens, horns, or megaphones. With the singing and pulsing beats from RFK overpowering all, I certainly understood the allure of the concert.

A young man stopped beside me. "Can I see your sword?"

I turned to hide my fangs. "Sorry." I jogged to the parking lot at mortal speed. A few others glanced at me on my way down the stairs, through the tunnel, and out to quickly filling Lot 8. I spotted Luke's friend's beat-up green-and-tan cargo van, and headed for it. I slowed to a walk when close.

Joe, the lead guitar player, pulled his case out of the van and noticed me. "Erin."

"Joe."

Jonathan, the shortest of the group, came from the far side, twirling a drum stick. "Hey, Erin." I nodded, guessing his drums had been dropped off closer to the stadium and already brought inside.

Gwen, the bassist, opened the front passenger door and slid out. Gwen didn't like me. She was Luke's ex-girlfriend.

"Hi, Gwen," I called.

"Erin…" Shaking her head, she glanced skyward. "I'm glad you're here. I think these guys are insane."

I flashed Luke a smile when he rounded the van. "So do I."

Jonathan threw up his arms. "Come *on*, Gwen. We already—"

"Ayp!" She shot out her hand. "I *see* everyone rushing into the concert. I *feel* the energy. Hell, when's the last time so many people were even *out* after four in this city? And I hear The Deep and the Dark playing in there." She smiled. "We're gonna be better. We're gonna kick ass. This *is* insane, but count me among the crazies."

"Hell yeah!" Luke's was the loudest of the bandmates' cheers.

Joe pulled another guitar case out of the van and handed it to me. "Empty, as requested."

I set it down, flicked opened the latches, and lay my sword on the plush red lining.

"Heh. All that extra space," Jonathan said. "We should fill it with guns or somethin'."

"Guns, grenades, bazookas—fill it with whatever trinkets you want." I shut the lid, closed both latches, and gave the case to him. "In my hands, that sword is death. The knife on my leg, destruction. More suitable weapons for a demon, don't you think?"

"Yeah," Jonathan agreed. "Luke, Erin's awesome."

"I know," he said.

Luke slid the van door closed. The other three headed off. Joe peeked back at us and announced to those with him, "They'll catch up."

I went to Luke. "Big night."

He grinned. "I can't wait."

"You nervous?"

"Nope."

I glanced at the massive football stadium. "How many people, you think?"

"Someone said it holds forty-five thousand. It looked maybe a quarter full twenty minutes ago."

"That's a lot of people."

He grabbed me around the waist and pulled me to him. "I'm *not* nervous."

I kissed him. His tongue met mine and then nicked one of my fangs.

I swallowed his blood and lied. "Neither am I." I sank my fangs into their customary spot near the back of his neck.

Luke, on the other hand, had not lied. I tightened my grip on him and sucked. He had been eager for that bite— those moments together before his big moment onstage. But more, he wanted my drink to be done so he could get into the stadium and prepare.

I released him. "You'd better be going."

His grin returned, and he jogged after his band, while I walked behind them, scanning side to side for other vampires.

The Deep and the Dark was finishing their last song. Inside the stadium, I stood at the far left of the field. Getting a headcount based on the official seating capacity proved challenging because most people stood, and so many were packed close to the stage. But by my estimate, Luke had been about right earlier. The place seemed roughly a third full, and fifteen thousand and growing was a great crowd.

For a good view of the whole area, I positioned myself far from the front. Row after row of spectators, whose presence was turning the grass field to dirt, separated me from my sword in Joe's guitar case backstage. No one would have stopped me from carrying it in, but I didn't want the attention or to suggest I intended to use it, and as it was, I could grab it in a matter of seconds. I had spotted nine vampires, who might have noticed me before quickly returning to watching the show, bobbing along and sometimes singing with everyone else. There had to be more around, and under other circumstances, I might have introduced myself to one or two.

The song culminated in a long, fading electronic note.

"Thank you!" the lead singer called.

A rumbling of drumbeats ended in a loud bang. The crowd cheered.

"You guys rock!" the lead singer shouted. "It's after four, and we're still out rocking!"

Louder cheers.

"Are you ready for Shattered Nights?"

A roar!

"Well, give it a minute," the lead singer said. "Luke needs to bring out his *piano.*"

A mixture of laughter and approving screams came in response while the stage went dark.

I checked my phone—nothing. Over the top of the stadium in the direction of the Capitol, the faint red and blue lights I had seen earlier continued to flash. Thankfully, despite the absence of music, the crowd noise drowned out the accompanying sirens.

Inside RFK, most chatted happily with those nearby. Others yelled across the field or pushed their way through the sea of people to meet friends or find the perfect spot. I couldn't remember ever being as carefree as those at the concert, even during times with Luke and Caleb. I worried about them constantly. As I had worried about Zack and June.

But not enough to keep June alive. She was dead. June was *dead.*

Steady, slow drum beats from the unlit stage brought me and the crowd shuffling to attention—thank you, Jonathan. Hidden in the darkness, he played faster, and the last conversations died as the crowd bobbed along. A lone light atop the stage shone brightly outward. Another light on each side lit. The crowd cheered, and from the still dark stage, drums beat quicker.

I folded my arms. Luke couldn't have planned the introduction because I'd had no idea it was coming.

In the line, two new lights lit. Faster drums. Four more lights. A slower beat. Another light, and another. All of them lit. Gwen's and Joe's guitars joined in. Lights shifted downward to illuminate the stage.

The roaring crowd drowned out Luke's first words. My smile grew. Luke had craved that moment for far longer than I had even known him.

The music was harder than I had liked as a mortal. The drums beat too loudly for that girl, the guitar squealed too high, and the bass resonated too deeply. I danced with the crowd to the sound I had grown to adore, and to Luke.

Shattered Nights was made to be a headlining band, ready to come on when the crowd had been primed to give it their all. And on the nights Luke's band didn't play last, they brought drastically more energy than any opening act I had ever seen. Confidence went a long way, and Luke had no shortage.

He sang from in front of his piano for the first song and was already sweating like crazy. Without a break, he screamed at the start of the second song and strode to the left side of the stage to sing to those over there.

I liked the song, of course. I liked them all. I understood their genesis in Luke's mind. I could replay in my own how he had evolved each—the edits that helped, those that hurt, and the last-minute changes that scrapped good lines for the sake of great ones. To be sure, plenty of songs never worked out, and tons of prospective lyrics stunk, a lot, but I didn't dwell on those failures.

"Cheer up!" a big man with a big mustache called to me as he headed for the stage.

I realized I had drifted into the crowd. I was moving to the music, but my stoic face must have returned. I kept my mouth closed and smiled. He grinned, then resumed pushing his way toward the front. The woman behind me stumbled into me, sending me crashing forward into another group. A few of them looked appetizing, but they probably weren't.

Interrupting the third song's deep bass, a commotion of yelling and arguing escalated to my right. I pushed that way, only briefly exerting force beyond what a mortal could have.

"Leave her be!" a guy shouted.

"Yeah! Leave her!" came from others.

I stood at the edge of the circle surrounding a frightened girl, who was held by a Sanguan I hadn't seen earlier.

"She's mine!" he yelled.

A bunch of humans rushed the vampire, who spun, and with outstretched arms, succeeded in repelling most of them—but not all. Two dove into the Sanguan, knocking him and the girl to the ground. The Sanguan threw his attackers off him, and the girl disappeared into the crowd.

I reached under my skirt for my knife. The Sanguan spun halfway around, twice, and didn't make eye contact with me, but might have spotted the two other vampires staring intently. The surrounded vampire snarled, then raced in the opposite direction the girl had gone. I snapped my knife into its holster.

Everyone cheered. I joined in for the tail end of it and noticed a lighter sky to the west. Not red or blue from police cars or ambulances, but a brighter glow.

Notes from Luke's piano demanded that my attention return to the stage—to him.

His hope still burns.

I closed my eyes and bobbed with everyone else.

His need still burns.

That voice.

He walked away.

The drums remained silent. Gwen's and Joe's guitars provided the backdrop for Luke's incredible voice—for "Ember," my favorite song.

She cried away.

Then, all piano.

The calm crowd focused on Luke hitting his keys. Slow and steady—soft, growing louder.

She walked back in.

Luke played a little higher, then a little lower—he took his time.

"Whooo!" a scream broke the quiet.

Luke sped up.

More stray screams: "Yeeaah!", "Whooo!"

He played faster. Faster.

Her hope still burns.

He stood, slamming the keys.

Her love still burns!

The crowd roared.

Their hope won't die! Their need won't die! Their love won't die!

Most quieted.

Their love still burns.

I exhaled slowly.

Three solid beats from Jonathan began the next song.

Luke wiped his forehead with his arm and moved to his standing microphone.

Boom! The ground rumbled, I stopped dancing, and most around me stumbled off balance. The band kept playing.

Boom—BOOM! Bright yellow and orange filled the sky in the direction of the Capitol—fire. I checked my phone—no service.

Shrieks and cries filled the air. Everyone ran in all directions—to the main entrance and away from it. The sky downtown burned brighter. Directly overhead, four fighter planes screamed that way. At the rear of the crowd opposite the stage, light reflected off a sword held aloft, until the blade swung down. Another sword slashed through the crowd. People pushed toward the stadium exits. The music stopped.

I ran to the stage, weaving past terrified men and women and squeezing between others, then leapt to Luke's side.

The Sanguan with the pink mohawk jumped up to the far end of the stage, carrying a long silver chain.

"Get back!" I yelled to the rest of the band.

Jonathan hopped off his stool. Gwen and Joe carried their guitars and followed Luke to the side of the stage behind me. The Sanguan rapidly twirled his weapon.

I pulled out my knife and flipped open the blade. "What do you want?"

"The *rock and roll* man. Luke." The Sanguan snapped his chain at my face, ripping open a gash in my chin. He snapped again and scraped the other side.

"Erin!" Luke called.

I darted at the Sanguan, then stopped, arching my back low to avoid a high swing of the chain. Catching it seemed risky, lest it tear apart my fingers. I continued my advance until—"Ahh!"—the chain whipped across my back, and I dropped to a knee.

The Sanguan backed up. "Ms. Rose, how nice to meet you!" He whipped his weapon.

I threw my knife—*fswht*—severing the arm that held the chain. "Nice to meet *you*."

He took a horrified look at his cleanly sliced limb, picked it up, and darted away.

I started to stretch my wounded back, but shooting pain made it clear that was a terrible idea. To the touch, my chin felt partially healed. My back would certainly get there. Four Sanguans with swords hacked through the fleeing, screaming crowd. I didn't immediately see any of the vampires who had been watching the show. I raced to retrieve my knife from the other end of the stage.

Luke ran to me. "Are you all right?"

"I'm fine."

Jonathan handed me the guitar case. I put away my knife, undid the latches, and grabbed Tomori.

I threw the scabbard strap over my shoulder and pulled it tight. "We need to get out of here."

"What's going on?" Joe asked.

I checked my phone—still no service. "I don't know."

The orange-and-yellow glow above downtown had widened. To the east, the night sky gave way to shades of ominous blue spanning the horizon. From the main entrance, people parted in a column to the stage. Red ran from hacked bodies and limbs in the line. Ariane emerged, walking calmly with blood dripping from her katana.

I looked behind me. I could carry Luke, and all of them, but would surely be slower than Ariane with the cumbersome burden.

"What will you do, Vera?" the fiend called. "Will you stand and fight? Or will you flee and give me the pleasure of chasing you down before I cut you to pieces?"

Sanguans followed the humans pushing their way out of the stadium, chopping up all they could. I drew my sword, exactly as I had so often in my imagined battles with the ancient twins.

"Brave." Ariane cleaned her katana on her leather pant leg. "Though I have made short work of many brave vampires." She jumped to the far side of the stage.

I blocked her path to the others. "Let them go. It's me you want."

Ariane spun her sword. "Wrong. It is Luke that we *really* want."

"You can't have him."

"I can, and I will." She attacked.

Tyn! I blocked high—*tyn!*—then low, shuffling my feet, focusing to keep pace. I heard the band backing up behind me. *Tyn-tyn—tyn-tyn!*

"Better!" Ariane stopped. "You've gotten better, but not enough."

I raised my blade above my head. Luke's survival had never hinged on the outcome of my imagined battles, but the only safe escape from that bloody stadium bowl—for him and for me—was to finally defeat her.

Ariane smirked. "Caleb wishes for me to tell you that he misses you." She tilted her head. "Oh, no. It was his blood that told me. My apologies."

The strength in my arms evaporated, and my sword fell low.

Ariane went on, "We were not surprised to find Caleb absent from his home this evening. But we *were* surprised to find him out in McLean. My sister argued against bothering to check. She said you'd realize that we know *all* of Caleb's hiding places because I had that little drink in Switzerland. She expected you'd have stashed Caleb somewhere new, far from this city."

I screamed and cut down at her.

She blocked, and I cut harder and harder. Her smile faded as she dealt with my barrage of heavy blows.

I sliced into her forearm, and she dropped that hand from her sword.

Tyn-tyn-swoosh. She dodged a blow. *Tyn-swoosh*. Her arm healed—*thud*—she uppercut my chin, launching me far off the stage.

I got to my feet and—*swoosh*—avoided the swing of a longsword. "Gavin!"

"Erin," he said. Past him, Ariane fought newly arrived Konrad, while Luke and the others ran for the entrance.

"Not me!" I screamed. "Her!" I started past Gavin.

He darted in front of me. "You're all Sanguans. You will *all* pay for what happened tonight."

"What happened?"

Ariane slashed open Konrad's side. He kept fighting.

"D.C. burns." Gavin glanced downtown, where the destructive fire appeared less dramatic against a sky lightened by daytime's relentless approach. "The Capitol, the White House—the Washington Monument's ruined. You *will* pay."

"It wasn't me!"

"It doesn't matter."

"Where's Victoria?"

"Getting the president out of the city." Gavin came at me.

Tyn! I blocked. *Tyn!* I blocked and cut hard—*TYN!*—sending his sword flying from his hands. I slashed up—*fswht!*—through his neck, while his blade clattered to the ground. Victoria's fledgling was headless.

Konrad stumbled to a knee, and Ariane chopped diagonally from his shoulder. Pieces of his body slid apart. She raced toward my friends, and I followed.

"Ugh!" I flew to the ground, driven by Caterine's shoulder. She pinned my arms to the dirt.

"No!" I pushed up at her, but she was just so strong.

"Verraa." The snake above me looked at her cursed sister, who held Luke. Ariane sank her fangs into his neck.

"No!" I twisted my wrist to try to use my sword, but the effort was pointless.

The immovable creature atop me turned her face skyward. "We're cutting it close tonight."

I growled and showed my fangs. Caterine growled back.

I tried again to move my arms. "I'll kill you. Hurt either of them, and I swear to God, I'll *kill* you!"

Ariane sped out of sight with Luke.

"*God?*" Caterine said. "Psht. *God* has abandoned him. God has abandoned you. I don't know what took so long, but as He abandoned us, He has *finally* abandoned all of His pathetic humans."

Luke was gone. I couldn't see him. Ariane had Luke, and they already had Caleb. Their blood was lost to me. I felt the sky turning loathsome blue, the same as I saw.

Caterine smiled down at me. "Luke's hotter. He's a hunk. But Caleb's fine, too, and there's more upstairs, you know? I bet you like that." She leaned close and whispered into my ear. "I'll savor Luke's blood—every sip." She moved her mouth to the other side of my head. "And then really take my time with Caleb."

I shot my head up, smacking into hers.

Blood dripped from her gashed forehead. The wound closed. "But I'll taste you, first." Her fangs sliced into the right side of my neck.

As if from a pair of sudden holes in a massive dam, my blood gushed out of me, into her. My resistance lessened, and from a lone point at my core, nothingness burst outward. My eyes closed, and I could see the void exploding, the shadow expanding. Caterine sucked. The empty hollow deepened and thickened, crushing me. I stared into the too-blue sky, longing for the violent red-orange hellfire I had drunk from Ariane in Switzerland. The chaos, the heat— and then I could imagine nothing except what actually filled me on that trampled soccer field—the perfect black. Just… perfect.

Caterine pulled out her fangs, and my blood ran from both sides of her mouth. "We will talk to you soon, Vera." She leaned back. "No! We will text! What marvelous technology fills this world you let us loose into." She got off me and raced away.

With my sword in hand, I leapt to my feet, and through a mess of bloodied corpses and hacked-off limbs, I ran after her. But I couldn't keep up. Not without all the blood she had taken. Dizzy, I dropped to a knee. My head throbbed, my bone-dry lips cracked, and my fingertips stung. My insides hated me.

Roarr! The famished lion within me pleaded for blood. It wasn't fair!

My skin warmed—the bluing sky. The sun drew near. Caterine was nowhere to be seen. Ariane was gone—so were Luke and Caleb.

Damn light! I sheathed my sword and felt the unhealed holes at my neck. Damn lost blood! Damn everything!

I burst out the stadium exit and headed southwest. Block after city block, each step was agony. But the blinding daytime approached and that pain would be far worse—and far briefer until I was reduced to a pile of ash.

I crashed into trees and garbage cans, but kept running, aching for blood. My eyes burned where tears should have watered. Caleb! Luke! I had failed them. I needed them. I needed their blood.

My eastward-facing back tingled. Curse you, rising sun!

I *hate* you. I hate your rays, as I hate those damn twins.

Fires raged to the north, but it didn't matter. Nothing mattered, except getting to my coffin. My eyelids grew heavy, then my whole head did. I slowed. Luke... Caleb... blood... sweet blood. I stopped and leaned on a mailbox. I was a creature of the night, defeated, famished, and with no place in the day that broke upon me.

I spotted Virginia across the river and raced onto the nearby bridge. Caterine! Ariane! I growled. They had to *die*! Home was close. My coffin first, and then the twins would die.

My tingling back erupted. No! Faster, faster. Light be gone! Night! Darkness, you have abandoned me.

Twelve blocks to go. I slid my scabbard off my shoulder and carried it. Ten blocks. Where are you, fair moon? Return to me. Eight blocks. My entire back sizzled. If an ounce of the perfect black tormenting my insides could have escaped my body, it would have blanketed me in its sweet darkness.

Four blocks. Cursed sun! Two blocks. *Blood! I need you. Blood!* I leapt over my backyard fence and crashed through my sliding glass door. I yanked open the basement door, jumped downstairs, pulled open my coffin lid, dropped in, and slammed it shut.

16

Sun! White-hot light flashed in my mind and stuck. *Flaming, fiery sun!* No!

Cursed sun, go away… *Damn you*, daytime!

But my skin didn't burn.

I felt the soft mattress I lay on, then my fingers found the sides of my coffin. My eyes focused on the underside of the wooden lid. The blinding light of day receded into the corner of my mind. I glimpsed, in that awful, shining sun, men in fatigues approaching my front door—Army soldiers, and they were carrying a box.

I felt heavy. Beyond heavy. My insides cried for blood. Yet there was none—none nearby and hardly any anywhere at all. Luke and Caleb had been kidnapped!

Gasping, I opened my mouth wide to scream. The pressure crushing me from all sides was the first I had experienced the full weight of being a vampire awakened by a threat during the day. I shut my mouth, pushed my palm into the lid, and cringed when a shard of glass dug deep into my hand. My sliding door, I remembered.

My coffin shook gently. The security system Zhilan had

installed was likely picking up the soldiers destroying my front door lock.

Glass crinkled, and a few pieces cut me while I opened my coffin. It stopped shaking, and I climbed out. The lights in my basement had automatically come on. I heard the men upstairs, and with a few keystrokes on my laptop, hidden cameras in the walls showed two of them in my living room, each carrying a side of a large silver box.

One pointed at my basement door. "Here."

If it was a bomb… I closed the computer, rushed into my coffin, and shut the lid. The door upstairs opened.

"There it is," one of the soldiers said.

What was going on? Their plan in my basement seemed pretty clear, but why me?

My burned back burst into pain. Why today of all days, when my drained body couldn't heal? Why today, when Luke and Caleb needed me, wherever they had been taken? Throbbing on the side of my neck meant Caterine's fang marks remained.

One of the soldiers asked, "Why not just shoot her through the lid?"

"Because she might wake up and rip your head off," the other explained.

"Oh."

"With the bomb, she'll never know we were here."

"That sounds better."

My eyes stung horribly, but instead of rubbing them, I recalled my nights as Alexander's prisoner, bound and captive in that lonely steel coffin. At the end, after the torment, after the days of his slow sucking of my blood, I had been in worse shape, I reminded myself. I had survived.

"Two minutes."

"Where's the next house?" the other soldier asked.

"Like a mile down Mount Vernon Ave. You guys go ahead. Once this goes off, I'll catch up."

"Yes, sir."

Two sets of footsteps ascended the stairs. The door closed, and I counted in my head, *one one-thousand, two one-thousand, three one-thousand.*

I got out of my coffin with my sword scabbard in hand and checked the bomb.

1:33... 1:32...

I confirmed that my knife was strapped tightly to my thigh. Standing hurt. The weight of being awake pressed on every inch of me. Crouching didn't help. I certainly couldn't go outside. At the thought, my back burned more. I took another look at the bomb.

1:16... 1:15...

I scanned around the basement, and a plan came to me. I examined my glass-cut skin, shirt, and skirt. Splattered blood had dried everywhere, including where it ran down into my boots. How much worse could I get?

On my laptop, I went to cnn.com.

"WAR," the huge headline read, with a smaller sub-headline, "U.S., Allies Declare War on All Vampires."

Whoa.

I slammed the computer shut and threw it in my backpack, then rushed to my closet. Rifling through hangers, I ripped off my favorite things and stuffed them into my backpack. I quickly rummaged through each dresser drawer, then put on my leather jacket and looked over my desk. My phone, wallet, and keys were already on me. I had laptop and phone chargers in my backpack's front pocket. The Suburban was parked out front.

0:32... 0:31...

On my wall hung the platinum cross necklace Edmond had given me—a reminder of how blind I had been to his lies. Nah. I flung my pack over my shoulder.

0:28... 0:27...

War on *all* vampires? At the wall to the right of my desk, I ran my hand along the paneling, then tapped with my knuckle until finding a spot with no stud blocking the concrete.

0:21... 0:20...

Blood! I winced. But there wasn't any.

0:18... 0:17...

The twins had Caleb and Luke!

0:15... 0:14...

I backed away from the wall and counted in my head, *11... 10...* I took a deep breath. *7... 6...*

Oh the damn necklace! I raced over, tore it off the wall, and shoved it in my jacket pocket. I had lost count.

I darted at the wall, lowered my shoulder, and burst through wood, concrete, earth... earth... earth...

BOOM! Heat surged behind me.

I hit foundation and crashed onto the cement floor in my neighbor's basement. I rolled onto my back. Dirt and dust covered me, and earth filled in the hole where I had entered. The explosion or its aftermath sounded in my basement, but crumbled wall and dirt kept the blast's heat from reaching me.

Caleb. Luke. Blood!

I grabbed my cell, but my fingers slipped off it. I forgot why I had reached for it. Or what I had reached for.

I slid into darkness.

After sundown, still in agony, but with most of the broken glass picked out of my skin and hair, I peeked between the curtains in my neighbor's living room. I didn't see any police or military. I checked my phone—no response to my texts and calls to Caleb and Luke.

I sat down on the couch, hunched over, and reread the line from the article:

Sorting through the carnage at RFK Stadium continues, but officials estimate more than a thousand concertgoers lost their lives in the bloody minutes before sunrise.

I answered Grant's text. *Yeah, I'm okay.* So was he and the others. I wrote Zhilan, *Yes, I'm fine. Are you at Fort Washington?*

I carefully leaned against the cushions. My skin hurt; each cell cried out for the tiniest sip of blood. My quads burned as if they had been skinned raw. The sensation traveled to my calves and to my feet. It hurt to touch anything with my fingers. It hurt to move my wrists and shoulders. My back felt like one big open wound, and having seen burns on Renshu that lingered night after night, I dreaded how long mine might persist.

I stretched out, raised my hands above me, then let them fall and gave up. Nothing helped. Hunched over again, I loaded cnn.com, and the big headline couldn't be missed:

WAR

I gently tapped the link for the article.

At sunrise this morning, the United States Congress declared the nation at war with all vampires, Sanguan and Spectavi, regardless of any other affiliations. Most allies of the United States quickly followed suit.

President Hughes spoke firmly of his decision to end the country's decades-long alliance with the Spectavi. "If the Spectavi cannot protect our capital or their headquarters, we can no longer rely on them. It has been a long while since we have fought our own battles in this war against evil, but it is time. I am calling on our allies and peoples all over the world. It is time for humanity to fight."

Zhilan responded, *Yes, I am at the fort.*

I got up and checked outside again. If anyone was watching for me, they'd be human, and I could outrun them—in spite of my wretched state. For a moment, I wished there *were* soldiers out there, until resigning myself to how useless their blood would almost certainly have been to me. And what if it always would be? I had been so sure things would change back. But what if they didn't, and Luke and Caleb's blood had become lost to me, as well?

I slowly opened the front door—nothing. I stuck my head out—all quiet. Ruins lay where my house had stood.

That Zhilan actually owned it did little to comfort me. I had felt more at home there than anywhere, ever. But it was done. It was gone.

I drove to Fort Washington.

———————————

I walked in, and at the long table, Houjin stopped typing on his laptop to look at me. Hayden and Max spun in their chairs. Alice and Grant turned away from the television. Zhilan stood.

"They took them," I said, struggling, but determined to keep from breaking down.

"Who?" Max asked.

"Luke." It wasn't time to weep; it was time to fight. The wasteland at my core could be ignored. So could my seared skin. "Caleb." It was time to find them. I needed them. Thirsty… I needed their blood.

"The twins?" Grant asked.

"Yes."

"When?"

"The concert."

"I'm sorry," Grant said.

I gulped. "I need to—"

"Come with me." Zhilan headed for the sparring room.

I tripped, following her, but managed to keep from falling.

She shut the door behind me and pointed to a stone bench at the wall. "Sit."

I fell hard onto it. "Ah!" I should have gone slower.

Zhilan sat next to me and adjusted her pink kimono.

My pain didn't matter. "We need to go after them."

"Calm, Erin."

My eyes found no moisture to water. "I need them."

"I know."

Caterine had left me so empty in such a miserable, barren world.

"Do you know where they are?" Zhilan asked.

I was a powerful vampire, yet I had lost those I loved, and without them, had lost my way to live. "No."

Zhilan put out her arms.

I fell onto her shoulder. "I lost them."

"Shh…"

"I love them."

"It'll be all right." Zhilan took a hand off me, and her kimono collar slid down, exposing additional inches of pale neck.

I leaned away.

She pulled my head tight to her firm skin and prominent collarbone. "It'll be all right."

I closed my eyes. Her two-hundred-seventy-year-old blood pulsed loud and strong. *Ba-dup—ba-dup.*

I opened my mouth. Beneath that unblemished white skin, I could taste it. *Ba-dup—ba-dup.* The beats filled my mind. I saw my emptiness rushing away, retreating from the blaze, cowering in the face of her vibrant blood. The razor-sharp points of my fangs rested on Zhilan's neck.

Ba-dup—ba-dup. I could *feel* the pulse. I imagined my pain vanquished. *Ba-dup—ba-dup.* Thick blood oozed out of the delicate creature. I held her tighter, sank my fangs in deeper, and pulled the glorious liquid into the cursed void that fiend had created. *Vwwooosh!* A blazing burst of bloody fire launched through me.

Luke and Caleb had been taken! Somewhere...

I sucked hard.

Damn Caterine!

I sucked harder.

Damn Ariane!

Zhilan gently pushed my shoulders, and I obediently withdrew my fangs. She pulled up her kimono.

I swallowed the last traces of elixir. "Thank you."

"You are welcome. You look much better."

The only pain that persisted was a significantly dulled ache on most of my back. I touched the healed skin at my neck. "Caterine's bite."

"And you do not know where they took them?"

"No."

Zhilan shook her head. "If they wanted them dead, they would have seen to it with Luke at the concert."

"Maybe," I said.

"Maybe," she echoed, depressingly honestly, looking a little weary.

"You'll need blood now."

"Yes, and I will get it," she said.

"What if something happens to those you drink from?" I asked. "How will you live?"

"I will find others," she said.

"What if something happens to them?" I asked. "And there is no one else?"

"I am prepared to go to great lengths to survive. You should be prepared to do the same," she said sternly. "Any word from Victoria?"

"No."

"You saw the declaration of war?"

"Yes, but not much more than the headline."

"While I did not expect the humans to make such a move, Houjin didn't greet it with the same shock as the rest of us." She got up. "Come."

I followed her to the main room and asked a question for anyone. "I heard about the war. But what exactly happened last night?"

Hayden answered, "The twins, of course. Not content to *watch* the world slip into chaos, this 'Hell' they are so eager for, they *pushed*, hard. They went straight for the White House."

"But the president got away," I said.

"Yes," Hayden confirmed. "Once assassinating President Hughes seemed unlikely, the twins tore up a lot of the rest of the city. And they had some help—other Sanguans with more firepower than a pair of katanas. Though, in truth, the twins would have been fine on their own. A burning car hurled as fast they can does quite a bit of damage."

I filled them all in on what had happened with me. "Caleb came back from South Carolina. I didn't know he was going to, but I thought he was safe at his company's office in McLean." I paused. "I was wrong. And then right before sunrise, they took Luke from the concert."

"I am truly sorry, Erin," Hayden said. "And it appears the Army went after you during the day?"

"Yeah. They brought a bomb into my basement. I got away. Zhilan, your house is destroyed."

She shrugged. "It was just another house."

I wondered again why I had been targeted. "Were attacks like that common?"

"Very," Hayden said. "In America and lots of other countries. And in many cases, with most of the younger ones, they were successful. Kidnapped humans were rescued, and a lot of vampires died today."

"A lot of soldiers, too," Grant added, "when the attacks failed."

"This war is going to be bloody," Hayden said. "For lack of a better word."

"Don't 'purges' like this have a history of failure?" I asked.

"That is their history, yes," Houjin said. "But aside from the fact that high-powered explosives are more effective than mallets and stakes, this time, risen vampires cannot learn the names of their attackers by drinking their blood. We've lost our deterrent—the threat of going after the families of those who would slay vampires while they rest."

"Where'd they take Luke and Caleb?" Alice asked.

I shook my head. "I have no idea, but I have to go after them."

"How will you," Houjin questioned, "if you know not where they are?"

"Well..." The surveillance system in Washington came to mind. "Have the twins attacked tonight?"

Alice pointed at the TV. "I think so."

The camera view from the Virginia side of the Potomac showed a fire burning near the severely damaged Capitol. A large chunk of the dome had caved in, and portions of the stone had been burned black. The top third of the Washington Monument obelisk had been broken off.

Grant said, "I hoped the twins would move on, but they haven't. Hardly anyone's left in D.C., mostly just the emergency crews that spent the day putting out last night's fires."

"What do the twins want?" Alice asked.

Besides Luke and Caleb? Besides torturing me? I turned to Zhilan. "What do you think?"

"I think they want the city in ruins," she said. "Vampires are fighting back against the humans. Sanguans and disobedient Spectavi in London, Moscow, Beijing, Rio—all over the world. They are causing tremendous destruction, going after the military wherever they can." She sat down at the table. "But Caterine and Ariane are here. They must imagine a destroyed Washington will be a symbol of their power for humans everywhere to see. Perhaps they even mean to rule from Washington one day."

I struggled to care about those lofty aspirations. "I'm going to find them. I have to get Luke and Caleb back." I asked the group, "Will you help me?"

"Houjin is correct, Erin," Zhilan said. "You don't know where the twins are keeping them."

I shook my head. "Caterine and Ariane are in D.C. right now. I'll *make them* tell me. Whatever it takes."

"I don't doubt your heart," Zhilan said.

"But you cannot do as you say," Houjin added bluntly.

"I have to try."

"You would fail," Houjin said. "And you would perish in the process."

"Zhilan, come with me," I urged. "Grant, Alice, Max, please. Houjin, Hayden—together, we'll have them outnumbered."

Houjin shook his head. "It would be a fool's errand for us all. I've watched those two hack to pieces more skilled and more powerful warriors than myself, Zhilan, or young Hayden. No offense, Alice and Max, but you would not fare well. And Grant, I do not think your bullets would be of use to us at all."

"I have an ax." He brought the weapon from beside him, and it fully unfolded as he slammed it to the table. "It's very sharp."

"Then you are too untrained," Houjin declared. "Too slow and too weak. I've seen Victoria fail to accomplish much beyond grazing those two with her longsword. Many of us have witnessed those battles. She's the best I've ever seen, save perhaps for Caterine, Ariane, and Edmond."

"I'm not bad," I said.

Zhilan nodded.

"You are no Victoria, Erin." Houjin seemed to have had that one ready. "No matter how many of us go after them, the twins will have us outmatched and defeat us one at a time until we are none, or until those surviving have fled. At that point, all we'll be able to do is pray Caterine and Ariane do not chase us."

Hayden spoke up. "They know we're here. Because the guys knew."

"Correct," Houjin said. "And while that means we must be vigilant, I do not envision them attacking this fort immediately. It seems they are intent on using Luke and Caleb to hurt Erin from afar."

I crossed my arms. "So you'll do nothing?"

Houjin folded his hands. "I will continue to watch things develop."

"Why not see what Victoria has to say," Zhilan suggested.

"Fine." I glared at Houjin. "Maybe the *Spectavi* will help."

Zhilan remained calm. "It has been safe for us here—the young and the old. Out there is the opening act of a new war. You do not know where Luke and Caleb are being held, and rushing after the twins poses tremendous risk. Yet I do not advocate doing nothing. Consult Victoria, the one most experienced in dealing with Caterine and Ariane. You do not need us to do that."

I had finally cleaned myself up at the fort, and I was driving to meet Victoria in Reston, Virginia, out the same highway as Eure's destroyed headquarters. There had been disagreement between Zhilan, Grant, and Hayden regarding the best way to travel, but knowing that the military was attacking vampires on sight, we ultimately deemed running at superhuman speed unwise.

The Suburban seemed so empty, so cavernous without Caleb at my side. The big engine roared when I hit the gas. Lampposts slid by faster, and the speedometer turned past ninety-five. I didn't feel particularly inconspicuous, but I didn't care.

Around the country and most of the world, Eure and the businesses it owned had been shut down or were in the process of being shut down, despite all the human jobs the closures cost. Billions of dollars had been seized from Spectavi bank accounts.

Reports continued to come in, confirming increasing numbers of vampire casualties. My friends guessed at the identities of Sanguans when specific locations were mentioned. The Spectavi had also been hit hard. Many were easy targets because, unlike most Sanguans, large groups of the former synthetic drinkers spent daytime in close quarters under the same roofs. Since we knew almost none of their names, that toll was a faceless, growing body count.

The Shattered Nights website had been updated with the news that Luke had been kidnapped. A list of well-wishes extended far down the page, but no one had information about where he had been taken.

My phone buzzed—Caleb! A picture.

Crhssshh—I drove into the guardrail and jerked the wheel left, then stopped on the shoulder.

Caleb lay on a narrow bed atop a white, blood-stained comforter. Chains from cuffs on his outstretched arms extended to the head of the bed. I pinched and spread my fingers to zoom in. Gray tape covered Caleb's mouth. Fang marks littered his neck.

It could have been worse. I forced myself to breathe. There was a lot of red, but he certainly *appeared* to be alive.

Another text—Luke. Poor Luke. One of the twins leaned across him with her fangs in his neck, while he lay bound the same way as Caleb on his own bed. They weren't far from each other—I could see Caleb's arm at the edge of the picture of Luke.

"Ahhh!" With one hand, I ripped the wheel off the steering column.

It could have been worse. They could have been dead. *Breathe.* It could have been worse. *Breathe.*

I threw the wheel into the back and typed, *Damn you! I'll kill you!* But I didn't send it. I deleted one letter after another until none remained. *Where are you? What do you want?* But I knew what they wanted. I had asked them so many times that they mocked me for it. I erased that last question, and hit Send, only asking for their location.

Deep down, I understood Houjin was right about the twins against the others, even Zhilan. And if *he* didn't think he could match them, then presumably, he could not.

I couldn't take both Caterine and Ariane alone, but I hated Houjin's attitude. Surely with our whole group, we could come up with *some* plan to go after the evil sisters.

I got out and ran. To save those I loved and to save the sources of blood my vampire body required to survive, I ran hard. Victoria *had* to be able to help.

———————

I walked around the lowered parking lot gate. The tall office building attached to the garage was home to a large enterprise IT company, which, based on my research, had no affiliation with Eure or the Spectavi. The network-monitoring team worked around the clock, so late arrivals were presumably common, though those on foot might not have been.

Through the garage, outside the doors at the building's entrance, a Spectavi wearing a black dress shirt and gray pants waited with his hands behind his back. I recognized the bald, solidly built software developer who had worked for Todd when we had both been at Snap Safe.

"Gunner," I said, letting Luke and Caleb recede far enough in my mind to conduct a conversation.

He nodded. "Erin."

"You remember me?"

"No, your tattoo. And Victoria's description." He shook his head. "You... *remember* me?"

"Yup, from Snap Safe."

"I talked to Todd," Gunner said. "Is it really true? What you told him about how they messed with our heads?"

"It is. While you don't remember me, I remember that AC/DC's your favorite band, and you sometimes daydream about being a Navy Seal, but for all your running and biking prowess, swimming always kills your triathlon times."

"Wow," he said.

"They messed with my head, too," I offered.

"That's what Todd said."

I nodded past Gunner. "He in there?"

"Yes, sorry." Gunner pulled open the glass door.

I went into a room with three elevators. Todd might be helpful, but Victoria was vital. She would know how to find

Luke and Caleb. Gunner hit the down arrow, and the elevator on the left arrived. Inside, he pulled a key from his pocket for the control panel and hit the button for the B3 level.

He shook his head. "Kinda makes you wonder about the people working here. They've always been loyal to the Spectavi and kept that loyalty a secret, even since the declaration of war."

We stopped, and I said, "It does make you wonder." The doors opened.

Two Spectavi typed at computers in an otherwise-empty bullpen of cubicles. We headed for the glass wall of a dark room, where Victoria stood and Todd sat at a long desk before an array of three rows of nine computer monitors each. Three Spectavi sat to Todd's right, and two to his left, all at laptops.

Victoria pushed open the door. "Erin, I'm glad you made it."

Todd spun in his chair as I entered. I wondered what he was thinking. At least he was safe, with synthetic blood to live on.

Gunner took a seat to Todd's right at a computer playing video of a battle in Johannesburg.

Taking in the size of the monitor array, I asked, "Is this it?"

"Yes." Todd hit a key, and the nine camera shots of the city spread over twenty-seven monitors became twenty-seven distinct scenes. At another key press, four locations showed per screen.

"Where are the twins?" I asked.

Todd looked up. "Nowhere at the moment."

"Nowhere?"

Victoria motioned to the monitors. "We know with near certainty that they are not in Washington."

"Then where are they?"

"We don't know," Todd said.

"So what are they up to?"

"It appears they are intent on keeping the city devoid of people," Victoria said. "Anytime the military or the police attempt to move into the city, the twins or those with them show up to rout the humans. It usually doesn't take very long."

"And they aren't spending their days in the city?"

"No."

I turned to Victoria. "They sent me pictures. I'm pretty sure Luke and Caleb are alive. I asked where they are, but they haven't responded."

"I'm sorry," Todd said. "Victoria told me about your friends."

I nodded, appreciating that the polite sentiment hadn't felt as though it came from a stranger.

"You are fortunate that Caterine and Ariane have kept them alive," Victoria said. "It is a pretty good bet Luke and Caleb are not in Washington. We would have seen something."

"Then what do we do?" I asked. "How do we find Luke and Caleb?"

"Patience," Victoria said.

"No." I shook my head. "I can't handle patience. I can't wait. I need to find them now."

My phone buzzed with an email from Luke's phone: *He's afraid this is how things will end. That he'll have come so close to making it big and becoming a real rock star, but will fail because of the tragic time he lives in. Because you couldn't protect him.*

"Is it them?" Victoria asked.

"Yes."

An email from Caleb's: *He remembers when you rescued him in Switzerland. He thinks about it all the time. He feared he'd meet his end so young, with so many questions unanswered. But you saved him from that fate, and he knows you will save him again.*

I explained, "They're torturing me with what they've read in Luke and Caleb's blood." I asked Todd, "You can't locate their phones, can you?"

He shook his head. "I doubt it. What are their numbers?"

I told him, and Todd typed them into a laptop on the desk to his left.

I responded, *Where are you?* And added the pointless question, *What do you want?*

"No," Todd announced. "The location tracking's blocked."

"I don't know what to do," I said.

Victoria grasped my shoulder. "Endure. You are correct. They aim to torture you. But be strong. They will send images and feelings to hurt you. Don't let them cause that pain."

"How?"

"Refuse to think about Luke or Caleb at all. Or think only of rescuing them."

I pictured myself rushing to save them. Then I saw them both in chains, being bitten by Caterine and Ariane. "I can't stop thinking about what the twins are doing to them."

"Well, you surely have many memories of your nights with Luke and Caleb," Victoria said. "Focus on those better times."

Positive emotions mixed in with the dreadful. I urged myself to replay the good ones and not the others, but a mish-mash cycled through me.

Victoria went on, "I predict you will see Luke and Caleb again. I cannot say when, or the circumstances surrounding it, but an opportunity will present itself. When it does, be prepared to take it."

I nodded. "I killed Gavin." I felt bad telling her, but didn't regret having done it. "When the twins came for Luke, Gavin got between me and him and wouldn't get out of my way."

"Exactly!" Victoria lit up. "Against Caterine and Ariane especially, you *must* be so decisive. They rarely offer time to hesitate."

My cell buzzed—Caleb's phone. *We know the agony of three years confined to bed, our bodies failed, our pain so persistent, so pervasive that we could not recall life without it. We know the total loneliness of three hundred eleven years imprisoned by our bastard brother.*

Luke's phone, *Unfortunately, since Edmond's pathetic neck*

proved too fragile to hold his gigantic head to his body, we cannot share our pain with him. But you? You… his lost love. His vile blood courses through you. I'm sure you believe your life has been hard, VERA. But you are young. You've never truly suffered. You've not experienced pure agony or acute, utter misery cutting into your heart and into your mind. We intend to show you all of this.

I handed the phone to Victoria and drew my sword.

She read the messages. "I do miss Edmond. And while his presence would disappointingly keep me from ending his wretched sisters' lives, his sword and his cunning would be exceedingly helpful in dealing with them." She gave my phone back and motioned to a leather office chair on Todd's left. "Your rage can be a powerful weapon, but it needs to be directed at something."

I cut down, and the halves of chair fell to the floor.

"Put the sword away." Victoria grabbed another chair. "Have a seat." She rolled it my way. "Let's see what we can learn from the twins' ongoing attacks in Washington."

Unable to think of anything more productive to do, I sheathed my sword, sat, and stared at the array of screens. In a top row monitor, a disheveled man with a huge backpack ran with terrible form on the sidewalk, out of the camera's view, onto the next screen down.

"Who's that?" I asked.

"No idea," Todd answered. "Just some guy."

"What's he doing there?"

Todd's eyes followed the guy to the monitor to the right. "When his neighbor's house was attacked, that guy and another guy made a run for it. They went separate ways. The other one's already dead."

The sprinting man stopped, gasped for a few breaths, then slid off his pack and let it drop. He resumed running without it.

"Why were they still in that house?" I asked.

"They probably didn't have anywhere else to go," Todd said. "By the looks of them, the place might not actually have been theirs."

A woman peddled a bicycle furiously on another screen.

"This isn't the whole city," I commented.

"No," Todd confirmed. "We would need way more monitors. But if there's a lot of action somewhere, or the twins appear, it'll automatically show on one of these."

On a different screen, a Sanguan tackled the woman off the bike, driving her to the road. The vampire bit briefly before twisting his victim's neck.

"Is he with the twins?" I asked, impressed by the power of the camera system in action.

"Pretty sure," Todd said. "We've seen him a few times. Once with them."

"Why'd they let you move this out of Annapolis?" I asked.

"We took it because they could not stop us," Victoria said. "At the time, their war had not yet begun, so they could hardly even try."

"Got it," I said. "So, my friends aside, what's your plan for the twins? Now that the humans have declared war on you, and all of us, you're still going to fight them, right?"

She nodded. "I will fight Caterine and Ariane. This war was a long time coming, but as you can see, we were not completely unprepared. It will be harder for Spectavi to play an active role assisting humanity, or perhaps impossible, for a time. But one thing that has not changed is why *I* fight.

"People have plenty of faults, and I've seen them all. Men and women can be truly abhorrent–but most are not. Most strive to live good lives, which I have seen, as well. Yet the world is hard and made harder by the overwhelming evil the twins bring into it with each setting sun. I believe humanity deserves to be free of that evil." She motioned to the monitors. "And it seems humanity has awoken. For a long time, their weapons were no match for our kind. Fifty-nine years ago, when they formally allied with us, those weapons had become formidable, but not formidable enough. The gap has closed further, and they realize this." She looked at a laptop showing a news report with the night-vision enhanced aftermath of a small battle in Houston. "Unfortunately for them, I do not know of any weapon the humans possess that will reliably enable them to deal with the most powerful of our kind."

"I think I know what you mean," I said. "They brought a bomb down to my basement. I got away. Pretty easily, actually."

"Precisely," Victoria said. "And so it would be with Caterine and Ariane. If they use a bomb, the twins will flee. If they use a bigger bomb, the twins will know of it sooner and get away just the same."

"You caught them once," I reminded her.

"Yes, but it required careful planning, and ultimately, great sacrifice to lure them deep into that cave. And attempting to fully understand how we accomplished what we did has proven impossible. We cannot know for certain if our success came because our cannons did not aim directly at them and blasting rock didn't seem threatening, or if the twins merely ignored their warning in pursuit of their prize."

I shrugged. "Either way, what about something like that?"

"Perhaps." She crossed her arms. "I have considered what might work every night since the twins awakened. But they will be cautious, I have no doubt. And if *I* have yet to arrive at a promising plan, I fail to see humans coming up with anything soon. So I continue to fight for humanity and will oppose others like the twins, even while men and women are at war with me."

My phone chimed. Caleb's phone, *He loves you, Vera.*

Victoria glanced over.

Luke's phone, *He loves you, Vera.*

Victoria pointed to a side monitor. "Look."

Forty soldiers marched from Virginia across Memorial Bridge to Washington, behind two tanks. Three attack helicopters appeared overhead on a zoomed-out side-camera view. Except for where a top corner had been blunted, perhaps by a hurled object, the Lincoln Memorial appeared unscathed.

The twins and ten other Sanguans rushed across twelve different screens.

"All of them are at the city border," Todd noted.

The high-speed cameras captured the Sanguans' movements clearly as they ran from one monitor to the next, through empty neighborhood after empty neighborhood, then past museums and monuments. The vampires converged at the steps of the Lincoln Memorial. With a few keystrokes from Todd, the impending battle spread large on half the monitors.

The Sanguans raced to the rear of the memorial, toward the advancing military force. I cringed as the humans reacted in comparatively slow motion. They prepared to fire while their attackers neared. A lone rocket came from a helicopter. One of the twins leapt up to the chopper. Bullets hit a few Sanguans, but not enough to matter.

The other twin jumped, and two helicopters veered downward—their pilots likely dead. In a bloody flurry, the soldiers behind the tanks were hacked to pieces. The third helicopter fell as the first crashed into the bridge and the second into the water. The twins sliced the treads of the tanks, disabling them. Other Sanguans jumped to the vehicles' top hatches, pulled them open, then disappeared inside and climbed out seconds later, covered in blood. The battle finished, all the vampires split up and fled in the same manner they had come, streaking across monitors that flashed to new views to keep up.

"There. And there." I pointed at the two monitors showing where the twins had exited the city.

Todd spun his chair to me. "We'll note the locations, but they're nowhere near each other, and they haven't arrived from or left at the same part of the city twice."

I slumped in my seat. "Meaning this is pointless."

"It may prove otherwise in time," Victoria said.

Time I couldn't bear waiting.

"The humans don't stand a chance," Todd remarked. "Not like this."

"That they'll learn," Victoria said. "What may take longer is learning not to bother returning during the day, as long as the twins have their sights set on the city each night."

An hour passed before another military force attempted to enter D.C. When they did, a larger contingent came than the last, which didn't help. The one after was smaller and moved faster, but the twins and their gang decimated them all. We watched on the monitors, trying to make sense of where the Sanguans arrived from and departed to.

We didn't come up with much, and in between their attacks, Caterine and Ariane continued taunting me with pictures of Luke and Caleb and messages describing their fear-filled, love-filled, desperate, and hopeful emotions. I read them all quickly, then tried to do as Victoria had suggested and focus on pleasant times. As before, I suffered through a painful mixture.

I spent the day in Victoria's room. A raised silver cross covered her ornate black coffin's lid from end to end. On the box's long side, a carving depicted a crowded, dramatic battle in Heaven. Immediately, I picked out the Archangel Michael, sword in hand, poised to strike the defeated Devil at his feet.

The coffin Victoria had brought in for me and placed beside hers was the same color with a large cross on its lid and a smaller one on the front face. My last thoughts before sunrise were of Zhilan's words and what survival might be like without Luke and Caleb.

17

Luke! Caleb! My eyes opened. I closed them. *Blood! I tasted it, I cherished it, I held them and savored each sip—and then I was gone. Caterine drank from Caleb.* I clutched my sword scabbard tighter. *Her damned sister drank from Luke!*

I flung up the lid and climbed out of my coffin. Victoria stood in the doorway.

"Did you find the twins?" I asked.

"Not yet. Do you always spend daytime with your sword?"

"Yes. Did you ever?"

She walked to her coffin and opened it. Her longsword rested on hooks on the underside of the lid. She pulled out the weapon.

I managed a small smile. "Does it have a name?"

"It has many names." She swung the sword slowly. "In English, it is Doom. An inevitable end for those I fight."

"Like Tomori," I said. "Doom means death for vampires who call themselves immortal. Did I get my sword's name from yours?"

"In part." She set hers back on the hooks in her coffin

and closed the lid. "But you were full of your own ideas."

"Like what?" I asked.

"Edmond and I discussed everything with you. You never stopped with the questions, especially when you first came to us. We answered most in one way or another, and you benefitted from answers drawing upon our centuries roaming the earth. But we were careful not to tell you what to think. We pushed you to make up your own mind, and when I gave you the sword on your thirteenth birthday, you named it based on your understanding of life to that point."

Victoria held out her hand, and I gave her my katana.

She half pulled out the blade and inspected its edge. "We discussed immortality—the word and its different meanings—how incomprehensible it would be to live forever, and how you didn't want that for yourself."

"Why didn't I?"

Her gaze shifted to me. "Because you missed your parents and didn't want to spend forever missing them. And having tasted the bitterness of their deaths and lived with the pain of their continued absence, you feared a long list of mortals left behind over an endless vampire life."

"Sounds like I knew what I was talking about. There's Luke, Caleb, and another friend, June, who was killed recently. My list has begun."

Victoria sheathed my sword. "You were indeed wise for your age, but you were also very scared. The pain of your parents' deaths weighed on you. You didn't dwell on it constantly. That hurt didn't consume you, and most of the time, it hardly affected you at all. But fear of fresh, lingering pain was the ultimate reason you refused to become a vampire."

"Until you wiped that person away." I couldn't help saying it.

"Yes, but look at you now."

I took Tomori back. "I didn't have much of a choice. Death was my other option, which was also your fault."

"You had the *same* choice. After two years of life full of pain and hardship, surely death seemed the easy route. You could have lain on that basement floor and let the end come, yet you chose to fight your way to Edmond's blood, to struggle on. There *will be* pain in your future that you cannot begin to conceive of at this moment. *That* is the nature of our immortality—life, just more of it. Vera was scared of it. Erin was not. You are braver than you were."

I fought off a smile. "But the circumstances were totally different. Vera expected to have a whole human life. I had two years to that point."

"The circumstances were different, but the result is what it is. Vera's life made her scared of it never ending. Your life made you want to fight for it to continue."

"And now I want to fight for Caleb and Luke. I want that more than anything."

"You may get that chance," she said.

"Why do you think this—everything with the rain and what's come after—is happening? I know I've asked you before, so I'll ask it differently. Do you think the Devil's winning?"

"Maybe," Victoria said. "Satan may have the upper hand, but he will not win in the end."

"How can you be so sure? Look at us. *His* evil empowers us."

"I *have* looked at us, as I have looked to the Lord, as I have looked inside myself—far inward, to ever deeper depths as one century turned to another. What I have come to see is Satan's greatest failure. You and I, we feast on mortal blood. We crave it, we love it—we *must* have those drinks. And with them, the furious fires of Hell rage inside us." She nodded. "Some of our kind allow that fire to control them. Those vampires Satan may claim lordship over. But not me, not you, and not any of us who drink those infernal drinks and wield Satan's awesome power without obeying his venomous commands. *We* are proof that Satan's evil does not reign supreme."

"What if things have changed?" I argued. "The twins' evil came into the world so long ago. What if you're right about *that* evil, but now, in this day and age, the red rain means something worse—worse on Earth or worse in Heaven? Or both."

"It is a war, not a single battle. And I have told you who I believe will win the war."

I nodded.

Victoria said, "I liked your hair longer, you know."

"What?"

"It was prettier. I've thought it since it's been short. You have never had it that short, by the way. And while I did not rush to judgment, I have recently become certain."

My cell buzzed.

From Luke's phone, *He knows you'll come, but when you do, what if you can't save him?*

From Caleb's, *He's upset. He can't be mad at you. It's sweet, but he's so upset you didn't make him a vampire weeks ago.*

"From the twins?" Victoria asked.

"Yeah." I put aside my past and questions about the divine and returned to my present failure to protect Luke and Caleb. But they were alive, and if I saved them, they wouldn't be added to the list I carried into my future. I *had* to save them.

My phone buzzed again. I could hardly look.

It was Grant. *We can't stand not helping anymore. What can we do?*

I smiled. "Grant and the others want to help." I texted, *Thank you. Let me think. I'll get back to you soon.*

"Cherish friends like that, Erin."

"I know. I do." I walked out to chaos on the computer monitors—hacked-up bodies, fire, and wreckage on most. Todd sat, half-watching a report from Atlanta on a side laptop.

I pointed at the screens of D.C. "The army tried to reoccupy the city?"

"Yup," he said. "And the Marines."

"Jeez." I couldn't understand why they expected it to go well, but their persistence was admirable. "You think they'll keep trying?"

"Yes," Victoria answered. "Certainly for a while. Appearances, if nothing else, will not allow them to give up the city lightly. This night will play out much like the last."

I glanced at the chair where I had sat to watch for hours

the day before, then at a screen of motionless, bloody soldiers. "I hope you're right. I have a plan."

"Can you all hear me?" I asked, optimistic the microphone from the tiny earpiece would pick up my voice well on the calm, cloudless night.

"Loud and clear," Grant answered.

"Yes," said Alice.

"Yes," and "Yup," confirmed Hayden and Max. Both had positioned themselves to the northeast.

"I hear you fine," Zhilan added last, from the southeast.

All of them were in Maryland, while I waited to the southwest in Virginia, west of the large military presence in Rosslyn. D.C. was shaped like a diamond on three sides, and the Potomac River served as its border near me. We had it surrounded.

"Good," I said. "Todd?"

"Yup," he answered from in front of the monitors at the Spectavi command center in Reston. "I'll let you know."

The plan was to wait for Caterine, Ariane, and their gang to respond to a military advance into D.C., and then for us to follow the twins, unseen, after they finished wiping out the attacking forces. The pictures of Luke and Caleb they had sent throughout the night before, while not conclusive, indicated the twins likely returned to that location repeatedly. My hope, awful as it was to think about, was that they intended to stick to the same strategy.

Victoria, with responsibilities that extended beyond Caterine and Ariane, would be staying at the command center to start, then would meet us when we closed in on the twins' ultimate location. Houjin had chosen not to join us. According to Zhilan, he had no interest in risking his life to save two of my mortal friends.

I tapped on my earpiece. "Todd?"

"Yes."

"Only us on this channel?" I asked.

"Yes, what's up?"

"Did you ever get in touch with Sagar, that computer programmer?"

"I did," he said. "It didn't take long for him to convince me he had worked on our team and then had been erased from our memories—hard as it still is for me to accept. And then, uh, we talked for a while about the cameras, privacy concerns, what could happen with the system in the wrong hands—like the twins' hands."

"You're starting to sound like your old self again," I said.

"Good." He paused. "That's good. So then I was talking to a few of the others around here. A few I really trust, and—oh, soldiers. Erin, switch back."

I did, and to the whole group Todd announced, "Near the Palisades. Erin, Grant, Alice, that's you."

I ran northwest at full speed, planning to take Chain Bridge, two miles away, over the Potomac.

Todd finished, "MacArthur Boulevard. I'll send a cross street on the likely route."

I was already on the D.C. side of the river when the text arrived, *Newark and MacArthur*. I stopped, plotted a short course, and took it.

In a residential neighborhood, I leapt to the roof of a two-story house that I judged to be empty, two blocks from the intersection. From there, I heard vehicles advancing on four-lane MacArthur before I saw them.

"Route 50," Todd said. "To the east. Zhilan, Hayden, Max. Just over the line."

"Got it," Max said.

Two attacks at a time *was* a wrinkle. Between houses and trees, I made out a tank leading two canvas-sided troop carriers. How far would the twins let the column get? For a better view, I leapt from rooftop to rooftop, heading toward MacArthur.

A twin streaked down the street and slashed a troop carrier's thick tires. The vehicle stopped, tilted to the damaged side. I stood and reached for my sword, but held it half drawn. That wasn't the plan. Caterine had to lead me to Luke and Caleb. I slid the blade back in and crouched low. Four other Sanguans appeared with her.

"Grant, Alice, you make it?" I asked.

"Yeah, we're—"

BOOM! Massive explosions rocked the line of military vehicles.

Two Sanguans who hadn't been caught in the blast fled west. Caterine sped south. I raced after her.

"Grant?" I whispered.

"We lost the twin, but we're on the other two."

"It's Caterine. I've got her."

She ran through trees to the river, and in a matter of seconds, racing over rocks and dirt on the bank, she had

251

entered Maryland. I kept my distance and struggled to stay silent on the jagged, uneven terrain that was totally new to me, though likely nothing to the seasoned immortal.

She *would* lead me to Caleb.

Caterine continued west.

She *would* lead me to Luke.

I could taste their blood—each sip saving me from starvation.

I slipped off a rock, and my foot splashed into the water. I leapt into the trees as Caterine glanced back. She went up from the river onto the highway that ran parallel to the woods. I did the same.

She turned northeast onto a less busy road, running through one deserted neighborhood after another. The houses started getting closer together. The road widened at a T-intersection and a dump truck passed on the cross street. Caterine disappeared.

I spun and couldn't find her. *Damn!* I darted left and then far to the right, but didn't see her. I ran back where I had been, then returned to the intersection. I checked the GPS on my phone. I was a mile and a half west of D.C.

"Grant? Alice?"

"We lost 'em," Grant said.

"Where?"

"Vienna, Virginia," Alice announced.

"Interesting move back there," Grant remarked.

"What do you mean?"

"The weapons I noticed shouldn't have caused the tank and troop carriers to blow up," he explained. "And they all detonated simultaneously. I think they were empty, except for the explosives."

"Ah." I got it. "Clever."

"Not enough," Grant said. "I bet the vampires who escaped noticed a lack of heartbeats when they got close. Where are you?"

"I don't know. Northeast of the river. Near Glen Echo?" I asked, "Zhilan? Hayden? Max?"

Zhilan responded, "Ariane went north."

Hayden chimed in, "The others went south."

"Guys," Todd interrupted. "Friendship Heights to the west, Anacostia Park to the east, and Hillcrest in southeast. You're going to have to split up a little more."

"No problem," I said. "Zhilan—Hillcrest. Max and Hayden, go to the park." Two there seemed logical. "Grant, Alice, and I will take Friendship Heights."

Grant said, "Erin, if one of the twins shows, you stay on her, and we'll follow the others out like last time."

I wouldn't have had it any other way. "Sounds good."

With specific directions from Todd, I raced into D.C. and caught up with three jeeps speeding for downtown, each with a soldier manning a huge machine gun in the back. I followed the humans a mile into the city before Caterine arrived with two other vampires.

A spray of bullets spit from the three machine guns, but mostly missed their marks. The vampires slashed apart the soldiers and threw the vehicles into houses and offices lining the street.

Streams of fire from massive cannons of two low-flying

A-10 Warthog jets rained down. Car windshields shattered, roofs tore open, and tree limbs, leaves, and trunks burst. A direct hit exploded the head of one of the Sanguans.

While the other with her split off to go his own way, Caterine fled west. I pursued from a distance, glad to be nowhere near the rocky riverside. Hiding behind trees, rushing between houses and ducking behind rare cars that remained on the street, I chased her out of the city and then north again into Bethesda, Maryland, before losing her.

My friends had a similar experience—east, then northwest for Ariane, and east for the vampires fighting alongside her.

While waiting for the next waves of attacks to decimate, the twins texted.

Luke's phone, *He remembers the first time he spotted you at one of his shows, standing in the back, and each of the shows you've been at since. He couldn't believe how lucky he was— that of all the music in the world, you loved his.*

Caleb's phone, *He remembers your peck on his cheek after your first bite at the basketball game. He remembers his heart swelling when you called him from England to discuss his poor brother, David. Joy filled him at the sound of your voice, and hope followed after the call, hope that you felt the same for him as he did for you.*

I reread the messages. I adored Luke's music. I remembered that call from Caleb. My focus had been elsewhere, but I had felt something, too. For the first time in a while, I couldn't ignore the dull burning the rising sun had left on my back. I read the messages a third time.

Finally, I switched to the map. In both rounds of attacks, those with the twins had gone east, west, or south, while the twins had ultimately gone north. Ariane, from the east, had gone northwest. Caterine had gone west out of the city and then turned northeast. If they both were headed to the same place, and that place was not far beyond the northern tip of D.C.—which sounded like reasonable assumptions—we had narrowed it down considerably.

Todd announced two new military advances.

A pair of white office towers at a big intersection ahead gave me an idea. I responded to the group. "I'm going to stay where I am. I wanna see if Caterine takes the same route, and if she does, I'll start tracking her from here."

Between the towers, I jumped to a recessed window on the western building, then leapt to another higher on the eastern tower. I jumped to the other tower, a few floors higher, then back and finally to the western, landing on the lowest of three rooftop levels. I easily leapt up to the highest, smallest roof, where I lay on my stomach at the edge, overlooking an intersection of roads to the northwest, north, and northeast.

A steady breeze blew. Streetlights blinked yellow. A car drove north, then there was no traffic. The first I had noticed my improved vampire eyesight was when opening the front door of Edmond's house during my escape from Eure. To my continued amazement, memories from when I was mortal, before I could see so far, often included details at such great distances that my transformed mind must have been making them up.

A drop of water hit my head. A line of thick clouds advanced rapidly across the sky. The wind picked up. A heavy drop hit the back of my neck. I put out my arm, and a drop fell into my palm. *Blue.*

Howling wind and steady rain intensified, and when the line of clouds reached my position, a torrential downpour overtook me.

A puddle collected in my hand. The color reminded me of the near-perfect blue water surrounding Ahmose's island, Seorsum, that I had seen in the memories of the boy who had escaped from there to Rome. The blue in my palm was that pure. I licked my hand—nothing special.

A fork of lightning lit the sky. Caterine darted northeast. Pushing off the roof's edge, I launched myself out and down to the drenched street. I pursued her in a dead sprint. We left the city, and around bends and curves, we went east. I kept closer than before.

She cut onto a small side street, and I followed. Through sheets of rain, we turned a corner. Thunder boomed, and she was gone. Running around, I found the road circled back to where I had been. It could have been one of the houses—Luke and Caleb could have been in any of them—but I didn't see Caterine.

I stood in the middle of the street, soaking wet, watching for movement. Branches of lightning spanned the clouds. Rumbling thunder ended with a burst.

I asked my friends as quietly as I could, "Anyone near Washington Avenue and Ellingson Drive?"

Hayden answered, "Yes. I'm at Ashboro and Grubb. I chased Ariane here."

A quick check of my phone indicated he was less than a quarter mile away. "Wait there," I said. "Grant, Alice, come to me. Max, Zhilan, meet up with Hayden. He and I are close. Try and spot the twins on the way out next time, and if we miss them, on the way in."

I hid among a clump of trees for cover and refuge from the pouring rain. My phone buzzed. Windblown drops combined with those penetrating the treetop canopy to pelt my screen while I read.

Luke's phone, *He remembers the night, full of excitement, when he first asked you to make him a vampire. He remembers when you said no. And he remembers his faint, fading hope each time since, when he's asked you the same desperate question.*

Caleb's phone, *He's afraid you don't love him. If you did, he knows you would make him a vampire. But his hope that you will change your mind and pick him has not died.*

I couldn't pick Caleb, and I couldn't pick Luke. I loved them both so much. And I was so close to them. I wiped my phone as dry as possible and put it away. So close...

Todd announced three new advances into D.C.

I responded, "Tell Victoria to meet me at Washington and Ellingson."

"You found them?" Todd asked.

"Just tell her. And everyone else, be ready."

"Be careful, Erin," Zhilan warned.

"I will." I didn't intend to be. We might never find them, I worried. We could be that close and not track them to the precise house. "Tell Victoria to hurry," I urged.

And what if the humans stopped trying to reenter D.C.?

What if their latest attempts had been their last? I couldn't miss the opportunity.

"Victoria's on her way," Todd said.

From another clump of trees, exploding a blue wall of rain, a vampire burst down the street toward me. I opened my mouth to scream Caterine's name, to goad her to fight, but stopped myself from making the sounds. That wasn't the plan. She sped by. It was safest for us all if we stuck to the plan. I took a slow breath, then another.

Hayden said, "They came from a driveway on Ashboro. It's... I'm there."

I checked that Caterine was out of sight and darted to the trees she had come from. A path led to another street. I ran and spotted Hayden.

"There." Hayden pointed at a pair of two-story houses, one oddly positioned in a lot past the other.

Alice and Grant arrived. He asked, "Which house is it?"

Zhilan and Max showed up. A faint heartbeat came from the direction of the houses.

"Don't know," Hayden said. "But they exited this driveway."

I focused to separate sounds from the rain, and softer than my friends' powerfully beating immortal hearts... a quiet one, distinct from the first. I stepped toward it.

Zhilan grabbed my arm. "Where's Victoria?"

Lightning bolted far behind Hayden, who nodded in the direction I had come from. From out of the same woods, water flying off her, Victoria raced our way.

Dressed for battle in her leather top and loose skirt, with

her longsword, Doom, across her back, she slowed to a walk. "Zhilan, Hayden. Hello, all." Victoria looked at the pair of houses. "One of these?"

"We think so," I said.

"I'll check the first." She headed to it.

I ran to the far one, followed by Zhilan, Grant, and Alice, and found a side door locked.

"Careful," Zhilan said.

I pushed near the doorknob, sending the deadbolt ripping through the wooden frame.

"Could be booby traps," Zhilan finished.

We went inside. The modern furniture in the living room screamed suburbia, not booby trap.

"You hear the heartbeats?" I asked as we slowly spread out.

"Yup," Grant said.

Alice peered up a staircase.

"Downstairs, I think," Zhilan added.

"Yeah." I dried my face with my sleeve and in the kitchen, inspected the edges of a white door. "Here." I didn't see any wires or anything around the frame that I might trip.

Zhilan joined me. "Let's—"

I opened the door. A staircase with a wooden banister led down into to a brightly lit, finished basement. On the third step, I crouched low to see. Luke and Caleb! I raced down the stairs, to their tape-muffled screams.

Tyn!—from above. *Crsh—tyn!*

"Grant!" Alice screamed.

I ripped the tape off Caleb's mouth.

"Erin—" he started, before I turned away.

From upstairs—*tyn-tyn! Tyn-tyn!*

"Agh!" It sounded like Grant.

I tore the tape from Luke's mouth.

"Erin—" he began, as I watched Hayden tumble down the staircase, katana in hand, grappling with Ariane.

Caterine dove down after her sister, and Zhilan followed. I broke open the cuffs around Luke's wrists and then Caleb's. Hayden got to his feet and positioned his back to Zhilan's. *Tyn-tyn!*

"Vera!" Ariane yelled, repelling a blow from Hayden. I drew my sword.

Fshwt! Ariane sliced across Hayden's nose.

Tyn—Tyn—Tyn. Caterine thundered blows at smaller Zhilan.

Victoria leapt downstairs. Zhilan ducked under her sword swing as the larger warrior engaged Caterine. Chains still held Luke and Caleb's ankles to the beds. I stepped forward, ready to defend them.

Grant jumped into the crowded basement, ax in hand. Grimacing from a pair of huge gashes in his side, he got to helping Hayden. Max followed from upstairs, driving both feet into Ariane.

Alice rushed to me. "Let's get them out of here."

Caterine threw Victoria crashing into the far wall. Ariane launched herself off the carpet, dodged a gunshot, and got Max in headlock. She dragged him toward me. Caterine grabbed Alice.

"Stay where you are!" Ariane commanded.

Victoria pushed herself off the wall.

Ariane only needed her left arm to hold struggling Max. "Don't move." She pointed her blade at Victoria. "Especially *you*."

Victoria appeared unscathed. Red-splattered Hayden and Zhilan exhibited remnants of healing cuts and bruises. Grant clutched his bleeding wounds. Caterine held Alice in front of her in a one-arm headlock and brought her to the far side of Luke's bed. Ariane dragged Max to near Caleb.

"You're outnumbered," I said. "Let us go, and we'll let you go."

"We are outnumbered," Caterine agreed. "But we expected to be outnumbered, and *you* are in no position to dictate terms." She held her katana against Alice's abdomen.

Ariane brought her sword in front of Max the same way. "Shall we kill one first?"

"Let them go," I said, catching glimpses of terrified looks on Luke and Caleb's faces. Their hearts beat fast, but weakly. "Fight *me*. It's *me* you want."

Victoria stepped forward.

"Stop!" Ariane called. "Sheathe your sword, Victoria. You too, Vera."

Victoria didn't, so I didn't.

"Do it!" Caterine pushed her blade into Alice's abdomen until red trickled into her sliced shirt.

Grant rushed toward her. Victoria shot out her arm and stopped him. Victoria put away her sword, then I did.

"Now," Caterine said, "Vera will choose."

"What?" I glanced from Luke to Caleb, then to Alice and Max.

"This one"—Caterine tightened her arm around Alice's neck—"plus the one my sister holds, Luke, and Caleb—that makes four. Two of them may leave with you, and Vera is to choose."

"You are to learn the nature of pain, Vera," Ariane said. "We told you this."

Zhilan raised her sword.

"No!" Ariane called. "Any of that and our charity—our mercy—will be revoked. I assure you, more than two of this pathetic band will die this night."

I looked at each of the four prisoners again. "I can't choose."

"Sure you can!" Caterine said. "Leave the men to die, or leave the vampires. Do as you please."

All eyes in the room focused on me. Grant's begged for his Alice. Alice's pleaded that her wondrous immortal life wouldn't be cut so terribly short. Hayden's appeared sickened—whether with the twins or with himself for failing in battle, I did not know. Max's said sorry and that they yet hid the tale of his and Grant's history. Caterine and Ariane's eyes burned red with rage, venom, and amusement—utter amusement. Zhilan's were heavy, full of more of the sorrow that had darkened her youthful face of late. Victoria's stare was stone focus with no room for sadness or surrender.

I said to the carpet, "I can't choose."

Fswht! Ariane pulled her blade through Max's midsection.

"No!" I yelled, while the halves of Max's body fell bleeding to the floor. "Stop!"

"You can have Luke, and you can have Caleb," Caterine said.

Luke scooted toward me on the bed. "Erin, please!"

"I love you Erin," Caleb pleaded. "I want to love you forever."

"*I* love you," Luke added.

"We will not bother them after tonight." Caterine pressed her blade into struggling Alice. "But you cannot also save this pretty little fawn."

"Wait," I said, watching Grant.

Caleb started, "Erin—"

"Pick," Ariane said.

I couldn't let Alice die. I looked to Zhilan. We *had* to be able to fight our way out of that basement.

"Pick," Caterine echoed.

I *couldn't* choose Luke over Caleb.

"Pick!" Ariane commanded.

I *couldn't* choose Caleb over Luke.

"*Please*, Erin," Luke begged.

I met Victoria's gaze and found ancient resolve, but nothing fresher to guide me.

Caterine yelled, "Now, Vera!"

I darted to Caleb and sank my fangs into his neck. *Vwoosh*. I pulled a little of his blood into me—*love…* everywhere. All he wanted, all he yearned for, was to be with me.

I sucked harder—*vwoosh!*

He loved my smile, my emerald eyes, my long legs and arms, and every inch of my body.

I burned with Caleb's blood, and I hated it. I drank and saw his dreams of our endless life together—what the decades and the centuries would have brought. He loved our adventures and all he had seen with me and learned from me. Caleb loved my sharp fangs.

And I loved him—God, I loved him.

But not enough. I loved Luke, too, and *that* was why I drank Caleb's blood and didn't stop drinking. I tasted the depth of Caleb's love—both the naked, overwhelming emotion and his anguish at my unwillingness to choose him over Luke. For the first time, I understood just how much my feelings for him, blunted by my feelings for another, paled in comparison. I prepared for assurances to sprout up, that I could eventually love Caleb as he loved me and that I could find some way out of that house with both he and Luke, but guilt took root instead.

I opened my eyes—the damn light! The fluorescent white blurred by my tears, seared the moment into my mind. I shut my eyes and pressed on.

Vwoosh! The cursed, cruel, agonizing fire roared!

Caleb loved my bites, his precious moments without a care in the world. He cherished that time with me that freed him of his nagging fear that any night, for whatever reason, I'd pick Luke over him. When Caterine had ordered me to choose, Caleb's heart had assured him, while a quiet voice in his mind asked if his life had reached its end. Would his love for me go unreturned, he wondered.

I stopped and half withdrew my fangs. It would kill him to know for certain that I didn't feel the same for him as he did for me. It would leave a void that he could never fill.

Why hadn't I chosen long before? Why had I let it come to being forced into a choice? I had been such a child! But I couldn't scream. I sucked. Caleb's pulse weakened, and I failed to fight the furious blaze within.

Caleb ached at the thought of a future without me. I had ached at the thought of failing to protect him.

Caleb's body burned while fire from his blood touched every part of me. He savored being in my arms, safe from the twins' hellacious bites. One by one, his worries about me and his future slipped away. His fear of imminent death went last, when his ecstasy left no room for a single iota of thought.

Caleb's blood cooled, and I stared at his sweaty skin inches from my face. I drank on because I couldn't bear to do it again. I gulped cold, lifeless blood. I swallowed more and more.

"He's gone, Erin," Zhilan said softly.

I lay Caleb down, wiped my face, and looked at stunned Luke. I tore open the cuffs around Caleb's ankles, then did the same to Luke's. "Come on."

Ariane flashed her fangs. Caterine smiled and released Alice, who rushed to Grant's side.

Luke got up. My friends parted so I could carry Caleb to the stairs.

"Bye, bye," Caterine called.

I turned to them. "I'm going to kill you both. Not tonight. But tomorrow, I will find you, and I will kill you."

Caterine nodded. "We shall look forward to it." The

twins burst through the ceiling and headed for the rear of the house.

Victoria drew her sword.

"No," I said. "I need to get Luke somewhere safe, and I can't ask you all to fight them without me."

Victoria lowered her blade.

"Are you okay?" I asked Luke.

"Yeah," he said quietly.

We climbed the stairs.

"Are you?" Grant asked Alice.

"I'm fine." She called up to me, "Erin, I'm sorry."

"No," I said. "I'm sorry. About Max and about so much."

18

Victoria suggested leaving Caleb's body with his family, for their sake, and I probably should have. But I couldn't. I imagined a gravestone above his decomposing skeleton that my guilt constantly compelled me to visit—a monument to my failure that would weather and age, even as I did not. Keeping Caleb from his family was one more selfish way I wronged him.

Luke had come with us to Fort Washington, but we hadn't said another word to each other. While Caleb's drained body rested on a long table in the crematory, the halves of Max's corpse were slid into the chamber. Hayden closed the thick metal door, and Grant started the gas. Fire burst inside. Half a minute later, Hayden opened the door, and nothing but a thin layer of ash covered the tray that slid out.

I laid Caleb on the tray. His body slid in, the door closed, and Grant looked to me. I nodded.

Grant ignited the flames, and the burst sounded and didn't shut off. The others sat, while I stayed standing. For an hour and a half, while the fire reduced Caleb's mortal remains to ash, I stood, about to cry. The skin on my back had healed, but no amount of blood could cure the deepening pit in my stomach.

The flames consuming Caleb's body evoked memories of the small fire outside the chapel in Blatten, Switzerland, where we had burned the True Cross. Visions and sensations of a different blaze—that of me sucking his blood on other nights—returned, as well. Oh, how we had burned in each other's arms!

But it hurt thinking of those times, so I kept replaying Blatten and Caleb holding my hand, because that memory hurt a little less. If only I could have returned to that night, or any night after, and made a damn choice.

I shed a single tear when finally, Grant shut off the gas, and the fire died. I'd figure out what to do with Caleb's ashes later.

I took Luke to a friend's house south of Alexandria. I didn't kiss Luke, and I didn't bite him.

He went inside, and I sat out on the front porch to keep watch. And I cried. I cried and cried because Caleb was gone. I wanted to curl into a ball on the concrete or lie on my back with my eyes firmly shut and never move again, but I didn't. I just cried and watched for vampires.

Twice, Luke came out to talk, and both times, I sent him back inside. No one else came near, threatening or otherwise.

Max, I apologized to in my mind, over and over, while I struggled to make sense of Caleb's death. Was Caleb's all my fault? Or only mostly? I should have done so many things differently. But would Caleb have let me?

At the first sign of twilight, I returned to Fort Washington to spend the day with the others. I didn't say a word before lowering my coffin lid.

I awoke and entered the main room, relieved that my immortal friends appeared healed of their wounds from the prior night's basement battle. Luke, still riddled with the twins' fang marks, waited among them.

I gestured at him and motioned toward the entrance. "Let's go outside."

He followed me up and across the lawn, out to the front of the fort, where I stopped near the small lighthouse at the river.

"How'd you get here?" I asked.

"My friend's car. How are you?" He shook his head. "That was stupid. I'm sorry."

I smiled gently. "I'm fine, but you have to go."

"Where?"

"Anywhere," I said, despite what I'd say next, meaning I'd have to find another way to survive. "Just not with me."

"I don't understand." He reached for my hand.

I moved it away. "We're done, Luke."

"But I love you."

"And I love you."

"Then how can we be done?"

"Because I don't love you enough. And I didn't love Caleb enough."

"How can you say that? It's not your fault they made you pick. Those twins are evil. They're sick. Don't let—"

"That's not it," I said. "Our love is real, believe me. My heart knows it, and I feel it in your blood each time I drink."

"Then what's the problem?"

"I shouldn't have loved you both. Or I shouldn't have been *able* to love you both." I shook my head and gazed out at the dark river. A slosh of water gently hit the shore.

At another slosh, my heart beat strong.

From the clutches of that awful moment, on that awful night, my heart pounded with a force I didn't recognize and leapt to a place it had never known existed. "I should have been so overcome by love, so struck by it, that I couldn't have been with you both. I… I shouldn't have even wanted to. Long before we wound up in that basement, my choice between you two would have been easy." My heart sank, those fresh, potent beats done, me left missing them.

"And I shouldn't have settled for half your time," Luke said.

"Maybe not." I looked back at him. "But we're all to blame. I've glimpsed love in some form in most I've drunk from, and I thought I understood it, but I didn't. I really didn't."

"How could you have?" Luke argued. "The way your life's gone."

"Well, after this, I think I finally do understand what our love is and what it isn't. I adore seeing you on stage and just being with you—at a show or not. But ours is still a child's emotion. It's an infatuation that grew into more, but stopped growing when all three of us settled for love that was… good enough."

He sighed. "I guess."

"The world being a mess certainly didn't help," I added.

"It's back to normal, you know."

"What is?"

"The world," he said. "Or people's blood, anyway. They say it was the rain last night. They're calling it the 'blue rain.'"

Blood! I smiled as my body warmed. Blood for me again filled the world, and we would survive. *I* would survive. "Humans finally fight for themselves, and God's happy… So much for the grand test of my lifetime."

"What do you mean?"

My smile faded. "I thought I'd have more to do with changing the world back. I told the general that he needed to fight, but that was all. I guess it really was time for humanity to stand up to us vampires. That and turning their backs on the immoral Spectavi…"

Luke nodded. "Why'd you pick me?"

"Because I didn't love Caleb the way he loved me, and that would have meant a different kind of death for him. I love you for all you want to accomplish, Luke. I love that you're willing to do anything to be a rock star." Caleb's aspirations had seemed limited to becoming a vampire and being with me.

Luke's face brightened. "I'm on my way."

"Seems like it."

He inched closer. "I'll miss you." He leaned to kiss my cheek.

I leaned away.

"All right." He looked at the ground, then up at me. "Good luck, Erin."

"You, too, Luke."

He started to the parking lot, and I called, "I'll miss you so much."

He nodded, then continued toward his car. I headed up the hill to the fort, across the lawn and down the stairs, then tapped on the wall to close the sliding slab at the entrance above me. I sat on the concrete steps in the dark hallway.

Was it so bad that Caleb had just wanted to be safe, in love with me and together forever? Could that eventually have been enough for me? Could I have felt as strongly about him as he did about me? From that hidden, subterranean tunnel, the life he had dreamed of sounded pretty good— better than losing him. And far better than losing them both.

That life had *tasted* good each time I had drunk in glimpses as they had blossomed within Caleb. Years would pass, the world would change, but our feelings for each other would endure. And then I had sucked those dreams out of Caleb entirely. The peacefulness, the contentedness... the companionship of such a life. So simple. So beautiful.

Yet the world was so harsh. Was there room in it for such a peaceful existence? For one so passive?

And who knew where Caleb's next years, or even next months or days, would have led him? I knew his mind and his past as well as his heart at present, but I could only guess at his future. *He* could only guess at his future. Who knew what he might have eventually aspired to do?

Who knew if such aspirations even mattered?

But I knew what my heart told me about Caleb. And Caleb's heart had told me that if I had just said goodbye to him outside the fort and Luke had been burned in the crematory, two men would have been dead, instead of one. Certainly, Alice didn't deserve to pay for my weakness—my inability to choose. Hell, I didn't know if *I* deserved to suffer for that indecision, either. Another time, in a world without the twins or in a world where it hadn't rained red, I might have learned my lesson in a far more bearable way. Or maybe the world was simply that hard, and nothing could have saved me from learning my grim lesson, my gruesome way.

I had made the best decision I could. I didn't doubt that scars from my failure to choose, and then from my ultimate choice, would always be with me, but at least reason had guided me. I got up and made my way down the hall. Those scars would come, that couldn't be helped. But they would form over time—time that had yet to begin.

My wounds were so fresh—so raw.

Entering the main room, I called to the group, "We have to kill them."

Houjin said, "Erin—"

"Are you going to help?" I asked him.

"No."

"Then leave." I approached the table, clearing him a path out. "This isn't a debate subject to the rules of logic. This isn't philosophy or politics, and this isn't about nations rising and falling or systems of government changing or being invented. This isn't *just another night* in a saga spanning the millennia. *This* is the night after Caterine and Ariane made me kill my friend—and killed one of your friends! This is the night they are going to die!"

Houjin looked at the others, then made eye contact with me. "Best of luck to you all." He left, and his footsteps grew quieter in the hallway.

"Good speech," Grant remarked.

"We could have used him with us," Zhilan said. "But he would never have come."

Hayden crossed his arms. "What do you have in mind?"

———————

For two hours, we took turns sitting and pacing around the table, planning.

Hayden zoomed in the map on his laptop. "I don't see how we do it without her."

"Victoria will fight with us," I assured him and the group.

———————

Grant got up from the table, did a lap around it, then stopped. "They still have access to the camera system?"

"They should," I said. "Victoria told me her Spectavi scoured those houses and the ones nearby, but they didn't find the control and monitoring computers."

———————

I finished an abbreviated version of the story of Caterine and Ariane's seventeenth-century capture. "With blasted rocks at the entrance trapping them, they spent nine years in the cave, withering away to almost nothing."

"I don't think they will fall for that a second time," Hayden said.

"What if we split them up?" Alice suggested.

"Yes," Zhilan agreed. "We need to stop thinking of them as one unit. Defeating such ancient *individuals* is a daunting enough task."

Grant said, "As much I dis—"

"The King of Spain is dead." Hayden looked up from his phone. "Vampires assassinated him. Word is just getting out."

Standing, I leaned harder on a chair back. "Wow."

"Sorry." Hayden put down his phone. "You were saying?"

Grant started over. "As much as I dislike admitting it, I know I can't stand toe to toe with either of the twins."

"Nor I," Hayden said. "Not accomplishing anything. Surviving is a more realistic goal."

"They're bigger than I am," Zhilan added. "With a longer reach, though the difference is not drastic. But they are stronger than all of us."

Is there anything inside the memorial?" I asked. "Aside from the big statue of Lincoln."

"Speeches carved in the side walls," Alice said. "Gettysburg and his inaugural address."

"Second inaugural," Hayden corrected. "And there are murals above the speeches to freedom, justice, and other principles he embodied."

"Were you at the inauguration?" I asked, looking at Zhilan.

"No," she said.

"No," Hayden echoed. "Nor was I at Gettysburg, which I regret to this day."

———————

Zhilan said, "Our best two, without question, are Erin and Victoria."

"Wow," Grant said. "I never imagined you'd admit it. A few of us thought Erin was better than you, but—"

"Grant!" Zhilan stopped him. "It is not the time. But if you must know, I trained her, hopeful she would surpass me. And she has." She glared at him. "And if you want me to continue to train *you*, watch it."

Grant shrugged. "I was just saying…"

I smiled, and Zhilan shook her head.

———————

I got off the phone with Victoria and returned to the group. "She's in. She thinks it's a good plan."

Grant slammed his fist on the table. "All right then."

"It's dangerous," I said. "I know what I said earlier, but if any of you don't want to be a part of this, I understand."

"I'm in." Grant looked me in the eye. "When I saw you for the first time, when you were a stranger, mortal and petrified of me at that bus stop in the rain, I knew there was something about you. I didn't know what, and I sure as hell didn't know it would lead to this." He gently pulled Alice close and kissed the side of her head. "Any of this. But now, you're practically family, and such an affront against my family demands a response. I'm with you."

"The twins are evil." Alice gave a weak smile. "And you need me. I'm excited. I'm kinda scared." She shrugged. "Let's do it."

"They killed Max," Hayden said. "Then what they made you do, Erin…" He shook his head. "They have to pay. And I refuse to sit idle while Caterine and Ariane effectively control Washington, D.C. and it is in my power to do anything about it. We have a good plan, though it is significantly less good if any of us do not participate. I'm in." He turned to Zhilan.

"Renshu would do it," she said. "He would race into battle with you all." She formed a small smile. "And then those twins would slice him to bits. As they may all of us." She grew serious. "I understand the humans' decision to wage their war, but I do not like it. A world at war is no place for anyone to live, and I do not see how the conflict could end while Caterine and Ariane are at large."

She looked at me. "Before last night, I feared you would not find peace from your guilt over freeing the twins until they were stopped. After last night, I see that guilt has grown to rage—a powerful rage like the one I watched consume you before. But it is hard to blame you. I hate that Tao is gone, I hate that Renshu was cut down by the Spectavi, and

I hate how the twins have hurt you, Erin. Battling them will be dangerous, and we may not all return from it, but I hate this war most of all. While patience has long served me well, in this case, it seems *the world* would be best served by a quick conclusion to its conflict. I will fight tonight in hope of helping my dear friend find peace, along with countless others."

"Aye, Zhilan," Hayden said. "It is a noble goal for the world, and I see it the same. I'm no stranger to revenge, but this is that, justice for the twins, and something far greater. We *mustn't* waste this chance."

I pictured Ariane carrying Luke from the concert and the photographs she and her sister had sent of him and Caleb, the emotions they had spelled out, and the fang-made holes in their necks. And my fangs in Caleb's neck, his blood turning cold…

I imagined myself with memories of how we had extinguished the evil that was Caterine and Ariane, thoroughly and for all time. I *had* to make those memories real. I *had* to become that vision of myself. It *was* dangerous, but we had to try. I said, "Thank you, all of you."

My phone rang. It said *Blocked*, so I announced, "It's probably the general." I answered the call. "Hello."

"Erin, it's General Sharpe. I heard about your house after the fact and that you had likely escaped. Are you all right?"

"I'm fine."

"I'm relieved to hear that. Uh, any chance you're with your friends? I have a question that I think is best asked to you all."

"Yes, I'm with them," I said. "Zhilan, Grant, Alice, another friend, Hayden. I'll put you on speaker." I placed the phone on the table and hit the icon. "General?"

"Hello, this is General Sharpe."

Zhilan responded, "Yes, General, we can hear you. What is this about?"

"The French twins."

"What of them?" Zhilan asked.

"We're not having any luck against the pair," Sharpe said. "We've taken out all the others fighting with them, we think, but we haven't gotten those two. And we've lost a lot of good men and women trying. I hoped you might have a suggestion or two about how to go after them."

Grant spoke up. "You declare war on us, you blow up Erin's house, and you want *our* advice?"

"I didn't know about Erin's until the next day," the general said. "And I'm sorry. Her house was just one of many on a long list."

"We're going after the twins tonight," I said.

"Oh," General Sharpe replied. "Where?"

"D.C."

"Good, good. Uh, in that case, is there anything we can do to help?"

"No," I said. "Our plan is set."

"Well then, I suppose I should leave you to it. Good luck—"

"Wait," I said. "Stay out of our way. Stay out of D.C. tonight, and don't interfere at all. Can you make that happen?"

Silence for a second, and another, and then, "Yes. If

you're going after the twins, then yes. I believe I can arrange for our troops to stay out of your way."

"Thank you."

"Good luck," the general said.

I hit End.

19

Near the Pentagon, I stood under an overpass, collecting myself. Illuminated windows lined the massive government office, but traffic to and from the building was almost non-existent. A lone helicopter had departed the far side, headed west, minutes before. Todd had confirmed my spot was hidden from any cameras across the river in D.C.

I double-checked the strap on my sword scabbard. I pulled tight the straps holding my knife around my left thigh, over my black pants. Above the rounded neckline of my long-sleeved shirt, the cross on my neck was right where it should have been. I brushed strands of my short hair out of my face.

"I can do this." I took a deep breath and ran up to the Fourteenth Street Bridge. At that point, cameras in the empty city *could* see me.

I sprinted across the bridge, then north through yellow blinking streetlights, and before I knew it, I stood on the National Mall—the long, tree-lined lawn with the Lincoln Memorial on the west end, the burned-out Capitol building to the east, and the broken Washington Monument on a mound near the middle. Down the lawn, I raced for the Capitol, with occasional parked cars, disabled military vehicles, and one burned, blown-up museum after another on both sides.

I stopped before the Capitol steps and repeated, "I can do this."

I drew my sword and screamed, "Caterine! Ariane!" I slowly spun to the desolation. Surely they'd be watching such a prominent location. "Caterine! Ariane! Show yourselves, demons! I'll kill you!" How long it would take for them to arrive, we couldn't know, but we were confident they would not shy from the opportunity. "Cowards, fight me!"

They came from the north and stopped with their katanas drawn. I darted back.

"Vera," the one on the left said—I couldn't tell which it was. "How's Luke?"

I retreated farther, half-turned away from them.

Slowly approaching, the other twin asked, "This is how it will end for you? You test yourself against us both?"

I kept retreating.

The one on the left squinted. "What's this? Second thoughts?"

I peered down the Mall.

"Young fool," the twin on the right said.

I sped toward the Washington Monument and heard behind me, "Or perhaps not so foolish."

While I ran, I looked back to find the twins in pursuit.

"Veeeerrrraaaaaa…" one called.

The other yelled, "And where is Victoria?"

I passed the broken obelisk, then the long reflecting pool at the center of the Mall, and as I neared the Lincoln Memorial, Victoria raced out from behind it.

Tyn! The ancient combatants clashed blades.

"Ariane!" Victoria called. "Are you finally ready to die?"

I ran to the rear of the monument, suddenly knowing that Caterine was the one still after me.

Tyn! Ariane yelled, "I'll kill you while my sister kills your precious Vera!"

I crossed Memorial Bridge to Virginia, their sword strikes growing ever quieter.

Tyn-tyn-tyn.

"Fight me!" Caterine called.

Tyn—tyn———tyn…

I veered south onto the GW Parkway and sheathed my sword in stride.

"Stop!" Caterine yelled. "Stand and fight!"

I ran faster than I had ever run, while Caterine slowly closed the gap. My breathing became harder. I raced onto a smaller highway. My legs grew heavier.

"Yesss…" Caterine hissed. "You cannot run forever, young one." She drew closer.

I didn't have the air in my lungs to respond. I reached Interstate 395 and battled my tiring body to continue south. A semi-truck with a long white trailer barreled down the right lane. I needed to stop, so I leapt for the front cab and held on to the door handle, huffing and puffing.

With a thud, Caterine landed on the top of the white

trailer. The driver stuck his head out the window and gave me a worried look. Gasping for air, I couldn't spare any to speak to him, nor the focus to form an explanation. With my head half turned away from Caterine, I watched for her out of the corner of my eye.

From the trailer, near enough not to have to yell loudly, she leaned her head down the side. "And where are your friends?"

I gasped, gradually managing deeper breaths.

"It matters not," Caterine said. "They will be dealt with. But first…" She disappeared above the trailer, then flew at me. "You die!"

I ducked as she sliced the cab's side. The driver groaned. I pulled myself forward for a boost and resumed my southward sprint, with Caterine following and the truck drifting to the highway's shoulder.

Faster, faster, I pleaded with my legs, recalling the night it had all started—all the running, block after block. Caterine gained more quickly. A sword strike might mean I would never again be held in that warm embrace I treasured.

Swoosh! Caterine missed me.

Car! I dodged.

Caterine slowed, avoiding the same obstacle, but I was tiring, and she resumed gaining fast.

An exit on the right. Breathe. I was getting close. Another exit. Breathe—just a little farther.

Swoosh! Air from her katana brushed my neck.

Everything had worked out. I loved my immortal life, and *damn* if that bitch was going to take it from me!

Fshwt! Her blade sliced across my back. Blood streamed.

Run! Dammit. Run! You're close. He promised he'd be waiting. Breathe and run!

"Die!" Caterine called. "And know that your friends die next."

Down the highway in the distance, Zhilan raced toward us.

Fshwt. Caterine cut open my leg.

I limped, but didn't slow. I was a vampire! I could keep going. Hayden followed Zhilan. Breathe! Keep going!

"Die!" Caterine screamed.

There he was, past Hayden, coming for me. He was always there for me.

Fshwt! Caterine slashed my neck. My eyes grew heavy, but my legs kept pumping. No more air… but there was Grant, running, reaching for me.

Zhilan swung her blade on the way past me—*tyn!* Caterine must have met it. I passed Hayden—*tyn-tyn*—and collapsed into my maker's arms.

20

From behind Robert E. Lee's mansion in Arlington Cemetery, I watched the blue dot representing Alice speed south on my cell phone map. Not long before, I had seen Alice pass by on the highway down the hill, disguised as me, with freshly cut short hair, an airbrushed cross tattoo on her neck, and Caterine on her tail. It appeared our trick was working—Caterine thought Alice was me, and Alice was successfully drawing Caterine south on the highway to Zhilan, Hayden, and Grant. I judged she had made it far enough.

I bounded down the hill to Memorial Bridge. I raced across, straight for the column-lined rear of the Lincoln Memorial and toward the loudest sounds in the deserted city—the sharp clanging of Victoria's longsword against Ariane's katana.

I leapt over a line of trees, up to the side of the monument. On the closed-off street down the steps Lincoln watched over, Ariane faced away from me. Victoria appeared unhurt.

One quick strike before Ariane noticed me would do it.

I pulled Tomori from my back and couldn't stop from picturing Caleb's sweaty, drained neck.

At the steps, I raised my weapon. I could taste Caleb's neck. I closed in.

I had *loved* Caleb's neck.

Ariane's blade struck Victoria's. The twin spun, and—*tyn!*—her katana met mine.

Her eyes widened. "Where is my sister?" She blocked Victoria.

I swung my sword hard. No answers for Ariane.

"Caterine!" Ariane's cry soared.

I cut—*tyn!* Let her die wondering.

Victoria swung—*tyn!* The clash of metal echoed.

My thunderous blow—*tyn!*—echoed longer.

Ariane met each of our attacks, spinning when one came from her other adversary. Sounds of our steps, our shifting, and our effort filled the quiet air. I cut, cut, and cut—*tyn—tyn—tyn*—with the precise power I had learned to unleash. Victoria had long been so skillful.

Ariane hit hard and sent Victoria off balance, then swung at me. I avoided it, and Ariane barely managed to repel her old Spectavi enemy.

Ariane darted for the grass Mall. I blocked her path, and—*tyn!*—she blocked my strike. We exchanged rapid attacks, trading a series of lightning-quick cuts, until Ariane faked, I flinched, and she started down the Mall.

Tyn! Victoria arrived to block her path.

Ariane went left, and I got in her way. She tried right, and Victoria kept her from going farther.

Ariane screamed, "Where is my sister?"

Victoria must have had the same idea I did, because as we battled back to the Lincoln Memorial, we didn't answer.

"Caterine!" Ariane called from the staircase.

But no one could help the lonely twin.

Tyn—tyn!

Not her sister.

Tyn—tyn!

No other Sanguans.

Tyn—tyn!

Just Ariane and us, until she fell, at long last, and bled at our feet.

Swoosh! Ariane avoided my cut and darted right. Victoria caught her and threw her up into a Memorial column. I raced to Ariane and swung down—*shww!*—slicing stone when she rolled out of the way. She stood and ducked. Victoria's blade slashed column.

Ariane ran to another pillar. Trading blows, weaving in and out of the line of columns, I saw Luke and Caleb chained to those beds... but couldn't spare the focus.

I cut. Ariane blocked and spun to Victoria. The hellborn fiend was so fast! I met her next strike. My footwork had to be perfect. I cut, and the demon blocked. My form had to be perfect.

Emily, my mother, came to mind in a memory I had read from my grandfather. She was long gone, killed by the Sanguan she had sold her blood to, so I could attend a better school. My father, Ryan, had been beaten to death by the men whose drunken bar fight he tried to break up. Vera had been wiped away by a Spectavi monster.

Shww! I sliced stone.

Fshwt! Ariane cut deep into my side. I stumbled backward into a column and held the bleeding wound. Ariane met Victoria's strike behind her, then lunged at me—*fshwt*—slashing my thigh. *Fshwt.* She caught my shoulder, and—*smack*—her elbow sent me and my head crashing into the wall, south of Lincoln's statue.

Ariane dodged and kicked Victoria, sending her flying out to the street. The twin came at me.

Tyn. I blocked and got my other hand on Tomori.

Tyn. My wounds were healing.

Tyn! She made me kill Caleb!

Ty-ty-ty. We cut faster—*t-t-t!*

Swoosh! I missed.

Ariane raced to the entrance—*tyn!* Victoria met her halfway down the stairs. From steps above, I cut high while Victoria began a mighty swing at our foe's midsection. Ariane repelled us both.

I reached my katana far behind me and hammered at Ariane's neck. She blocked me and parried Victoria's strike at her stomach.

I thundered down another cut. Victoria swung longer.

Harder, I cut. Victoria went to her body.

Harder, I hammered down. Victoria struck strong.

I cut harder. Victoria—*fscht!*—*fscht!*

"No!" I screamed as the two halves of Victoria's sliced body fell, and Ariane's head rolled off her neck to the stairs. Blood poured.

"Victoria!" I rushed to her. "No!"

Focus filled her face—pure focus—but she could not answer me.

I glanced at Ariane. Her head remained severed. It and her stump of a neck continued to bleed.

I pushed the two halves of Victoria's body together, but noticed no sign of her mending. I squeezed her body together—no change.

I bit a gash in my left wrist and let my blood run onto where the pieces of Victoria met. I moved my arm along the cut line to cover it all, but by the time my healing wound slowed to a drip, it still hadn't helped. I bit through my wrist again and let my blood run onto her lips—nothing.

"Victoria..." I grabbed her shoulder. "Why?"

Down on a landing between sets of steps, Ariane's fifteen-hundred-year-old head lay in a pool of blood. I went to it and swung fast—*fscht*—cleaving the skull in two. I crouched low to an upturned half and found no raging inferno in her eyeball, which had turned a paler red.

I stood, readied my blade, and swung low. *Fsht—fst-fst-fst-fst-fst.* Ariane's head was cut into more pieces than I cared to count.

"No!" Caterine screamed, rounding the memorial. She held her katana lazily at her side and stopped beyond my reach, staring at her sister's unmoving body. "Ariane!"

I gripped my sword tight. Where were my friends? Caterine's blazing red eyes shifted from her sister to me. I'd fight the demon myself.

She snarled at me, her fangs in full sight.

I roared, the lion within me hungry for more. "How many of you do I get to kill tonight?"

She shook her head. I raised my sword and stepped toward her.

"You won't kill me." She backed away. "I made a promise, but not you."

From behind the memorial, Hayden darted to us, bloodied and favoring his right leg, but holding his katana steady. Caterine readied her blade, again stepping backward on the landing.

"Where are the others?" I asked Hayden.

"Alice was hurt bad." He looked over the fallen combatants. "Zhilan and Grant are getting her help."

"What promise?" I called to Caterine.

"To my sister," she said.

Remembering from Ahmose's story, the vow exchanged near the end of their bedridden illness, I relaxed and took a hand off my sword.

Caterine followed suit. "To be with her always, in life or in death."

"Death then," I said.

"Yes." She glanced at Hayden. "Once more, I will suffer the same fate as my sister, but not by your hand, Vera." She dropped to one knee and, staring down, forced herself into kneeling on both.

It was going to be over. The twins were about to be over.

I hazarded a question, "Why *so much hatred*, for so long?"

"I've told you," Caterine said to the steps.

"But fifteen hundred years, with the gifts you were given?"

She looked up at me. "Because of the gift that was stolen." Her eyes flared. "I was in love—with a man and a future with him. It was the life I had always dreamed of, and I had found it." She clenched her fist. "Then that life was ripped away from me."

"But you killed him," I said. "Michel."

"He died to me when he abandoned me to rot in that miserable bed in the corner of that godforsaken house. But before that, for as long as I had known him, I had imagined a lifetime with him and, for the first few days after falling ill, confidence that my good future would indeed come to pass gave me strength. And while my love went with the man when he rode away on his horse, the visions of my stolen future *never* faded. I couldn't forget. I *couldn't* keep from replaying scenes of my life that never had a chance to be. It was the same for my sister and Fabian." Caterine spun her katana and held it with both hands, pointed inward at her abdomen. "Though, Ariane seemed to take her loss even harder than I."

Hayden stepped toward Caterine with his blade high.

"I return to you, sister." Her arms tensed.

"And brothers," I said. "Where you're headed."

Caterine stared at me. "Perhaps." She stabbed herself.

Hayden chopped down. Her head fell forward off her neck. Blood streamed from her head, neck, and stomach as her body crumpled. Through expanding, steaming-hot puddles, I went to her skull and hacked it apart like her sister's.

"So that's what happened to Ariane's head," Hayden said.

"Yup." I examined bits of Caterine on my katana, then wiped both sides of the blade on my leg before putting it away. "Will Alice be okay?"

"Caterine hurt her pretty bad—deep cuts into her back, leg, and neck just before Alice got to Grant." Hayden sheathed his sword. "But with Zhilan seeing to it, she should survive."

"Good," I said. "Let's burn the twins right here. Right now. I don't want to look at them anymore. I don't want to think about them anymore. I just want to watch them turn to ash."

Hayden gazed down the Mall toward the Washington Monument. "Move Victoria." He darted to an Army jeep and rummaged through it.

I carried the halves of Victoria's body down to the bottom of the stairs, one at a time, and carefully set them on the ground. Hayden checked two other jeeps before returning with a gas can and a silver lighter.

He picked up the twins' swords, then poured gasoline onto Caterine's decapitated body. He doused the pieces of her and her sister's heads. Up the stairs, he covered Ariane, then made sure not to miss any of the puddles of their blood. When the can ran empty, he set it down and met me at the base of the staircase.

Hayden handed me the lighter and darted back. "Just in case."

I flicked open the top and lit the flame.

They would be gone. The nightmare that stretched into a past—a life—I couldn't remember, would be over.

I threw the lighter to the landing where most of Caterine lay. Fire rose skyward and spread up the steps to Ariane. They burned. The twins burned!

The burden of having set them free melted away as those flames grew. Mountains of stress and worry vanished. Lightness and freedom overcame me.

Only I couldn't celebrate that freedom with Caleb, and I wouldn't celebrate it with Luke. The blaze flared, but no ghostly likenesses rose from Caterine's and Ariane's bodies. No screams or terrible last gasps came from the most ancient vampires. The twins and their blood turned to ash.

A new weight touched me. The more the blaze diminished, the more the force pressed down on me. Caleb was dead. He had been avenged, but *I* had drunk the last drops of his life from him.

Smaller, the fire burned. Lower, the weight of Caleb's passing crushed me.

The flames flickered out.

So low.

A gust of wind swept Caterine and Ariane's ashes into the air.

21

Alone in the crematory, I looked over Victoria's body. She lay on a table in an unzipped black body bag, dressed as she had been and splattered with blood from the battle. Her longsword lay on the table behind me.

Alice had been in pretty grim shape, but drinking from Grant and Zhilan kept her going long enough for them to get her to nearby humans, whose blood brought her all the way back. Her hair remained short, from how we had it cut to look like mine, but the airbrushed cross tattoo was gone from her neck. Despite our good plan, in my heart, amazement and shock vastly outweighed pride, satisfaction, or jubilation over the defeat of Caterine and Ariane. Most of all, numbness reigned at the loss of one so dear to me.

"Quite a price," Zhilan began, coming into the crematory and standing on the opposite side of the table. "To say the twins are no more."

"Quite a price." I pulled the red cross hanging off Victoria's necklace out from her top.

"You could keep it," Zhilan suggested.

"All right." I pointed at her sword. "And that?"

"Do you want it?" Zhilan asked.

"I don't know." I walked to the table and picked up the huge weapon, then got both hands on the handle and examined the blade from the guard to the tip. I set down the sword. "What would I do with it?"

"I could hold on to it," Zhilan offered. "It would be safe."

"Okay." I returned to Victoria's body and glanced at the crematory chamber. "Should we burn her?"

"It is up to you."

"I don't want to." I shook my head. "I know she's gone, but I just don't want to."

"We could bury her," Zhilan said.

"What do you think *she* would want?"

Zhilan brought a finger to her chin. "To guide you. To continue to be there for you in some way, however you deemed best. In that way, a piece of her spirit will endure."

I watched for Victoria's lips to form the words to the right answer, but they did not move.

"We should bury her." I would visit the grave often. It would be unmarked to protect it from vandals, but I would know which immortal warrior rested there.

Zhilan nodded. "Saint Chéron Cemetery in France has a beautiful view of Chartres Cathedral. I believe Victoria would like that."

"I believe she would."

My phone buzzed—a text message. "Todd," I told Zhilan. "He wants to meet me out by the beltway."

"Will you go?"

"I'd rather collapse here and… be done." I read the message again. "But I'll go."

———————————

I stepped out of Zhilan's Mercedes two spots from Todd's car at the otherwise-empty park and joined him at a table in a small pavilion.

He said, "I'm sorry about Caleb. It's such a shame."

"It is." I tried to put it out of mind. "So they fired you?"

"Yup. They're a mess. Whole factions of Spectavi are splintering off, and lots of individuals are going their own way entirely. Some of them have been able to adapt to drinking real blood, but others aren't handling it well at all. I was given word that my services would no longer be required."

I smiled. "I'm sorry to hear that."

"*Right*. I don't count myself among them anymore. I couldn't… knowing what I know."

"Yeah."

"Besides," he said, "the camera system's been rendered inoperable."

"The control centers? You destroyed them?"

"Well, we wiped out the software and smashed the hardware in our control center. We still don't know where the other one is, but it doesn't matter anymore. While you guys had the twins occupied, and afterward, with the city nearly completely empty, my team and I destroyed almost all the cameras."

"Wow," I said. "There were a lot."

"It helps to be as fast as we are."

"True."

"Plus, you should have seen how excited they were. For a bunch of software developers that sit behind computers every night, this was like their big secret mission."

"Gunner loved it, I bet."

"Yeah, totally. We figure that without the Spectavi leading the push, the government won't be able to muster the support to rebuild the system. And even if they do, they'll design it so it won't work with that other control center."

"I suspect Vice President Turner will be quite vocal about *not* rebuilding it."

"Exactly," Todd agreed. "And you know what's interesting? That's not what got me fired."

"No?"

"No. My termination letter was waiting for me in Reston and didn't mention anything about all that. Victoria signed it. You wouldn't know anything about that, would you?"

I smiled again. "Maybe."

"Well, thank you."

"You're welcome. Although in retrospect, I don't know how much it matters with the Spectavi falling apart."

"It matters," he said. "It's reassuring to have someone I can trust, someone who knew my mind before they messed with it."

"You can always trust me." I pulled out my phone and opened the *Photos* app. "I was going to show you this, if I had to, to convince you that we had really been together." I tapped the thumbnail and handed it to him. "Us, during the day, in the sun on the blue water."

He shook his head. "I believed you, but this... well, it's us."

"Yup. It's better, I think, that you believed me before seeing it. But that is us." I asked, "What will you do now?"

He handed me the phone. "I thought I'd see what it's like out west. Word is, I was headed that way once before, looking for a fresh start, and didn't quite make it. This time, I will."

"That sounds great, but the war's out there, too," I said.

"A few of my friends have a little setup that's been safe so far. We don't think the humans know it exists. I'll stay with them for a while."

"Nice," I said. "Wait. What are you going to do for blood? Do you have a supply of synthetic?"

"I'll run out in a few days. It's a little scary, to tell you the truth. I've never drunk human blood."

"But you want it?" I asked.

"Why not? I need to drink something."

Thank you, William. "It's nothing to be scared of," I assured Todd. "It's wonderful."

"How do you know when to stop? So you don't kill the person?"

"You'll know." I recalled the flame, the heat, and the pulse the moment before Caleb's blood cooled and the moment after. "And knowing that you *should* figure out when to stop is the most important thing. It seems you've already taken that step."

He nodded.

"Find a great teacher," I added. "Someone you trust to

guide you to the right path. Or at least a reasonably good path. Don't try to do it alone."

"Okay," he said. "And how 'bout you? How are you doing? Any chance you're in the mood for a change of scenery?"

"A change of scenery sounds amazing. But not yet for me. I don't think I've really processed everything that's happened, except that I feel like I should be here to see how things go in Washington."

"Got it." Todd tapped his knuckles on the table, then stood. "I'm sad to be leaving you, again. But I'm very glad to have met you, again."

"Me, too." I got up. "And I'm so glad you know the truth. The way you acted on it, I really do feel like I'm standing across from the same person as before."

"Vampire," he corrected.

"Right, vampire."

We headed for the parking lot.

"Gimme a call if you're ever out west," he suggested.

"Likewise if you're back east."

"Well…" He opened his car door and got in. "Goodbye, Erin Rose, for now."

"Bye, Todd."

He shut the door and drove off.

The last of my energy slipped from my mind, then my body, during my return to Fort Washington to spend the day.

At nightfall, I lay in my coffin, wondering what the hell had happened. I had *killed* Caleb. As I had in that basement, I attempted to fully grasp the way his feelings for me had consumed him. I searched inside myself for love that matched his, and like before, it wasn't there. I hated it, but it just wasn't.

General Sharpe texted, *Did you get them?*

I responded, *Yes.*

When I went out to the main room, Grant, with Alice at his side, asked, "We're going for a drink. You guys wanna come?"

"No thanks," I said.

Hayden got up. "I will."

"Not me." Zhilan sat down at the table and pulled a laptop toward her.

Houjin had left for California. Max and Renshu were gone. Gone like Tao and June, and gone like Caleb.

After Grant left with Hayden and Alice, I sat on the couch to read the news on my phone. While no reports mentioned Caterine and Ariane's deaths, that the twins had abandoned their constant watch of Washington was becoming apparent. The military had begun reentering the city on a large scale.

I shifted to lying with my head on a side pillow and kept reading while Zhilan's typing at the table produced short, precise clicks.

Around the world, humans had suffered significant casualties at the war's outset, but the death toll sharply declined when, aside from D.C., they stuck to doing most of their attacking during the daytime and opted for a defensive approach after sundown. Considering that strategy, I figured Grant, Alice, and Hayden would be safe out getting their drinks.

Shattered Nights had already scheduled new shows in prominent venues. Between the concert at RFK and Luke's return from his abduction, the band was garnering more attention than ever.

I put down my phone and used my arm to block what light my eyelids couldn't. Hopefully, Luke could take care of himself. With humanity's blood returned to normal, I supposed he stood as good a chance as anyone did. And his not being with me anymore meant I wouldn't anchor him down and drag him to some new, terrible fate. He had lost a love, and that was bad enough.

I had lost two, and I had *killed* one. I had reduced Caleb to nothing but lifeless ash. I rolled to bury my face into the couch.

The strangers I had drained on the street as a new immortal didn't compare. Louis had been shoved down my throat in Switzerland for the sake of my arm. There was a reason for all the vampires I had sliced apart, some better than others. But I hadn't loved any of those victims. I hadn't promised them or myself that I would protect them. I hadn't failed them so spectacularly.

I heard Zhilan get up and go into one of the back rooms.

And Victoria was gone. My immortal mother. My teacher had battled the twins for eight hundred years, and just like that, dead.

Zhilan came to the rear of the couch with a folded wool blanket.

"I'm not cold," I said.

She let it unfold and spread it over me. "Of course not." She returned to the table.

Trying to recall the last moment my body had felt cold, before I left that mortal sensation behind, I pulled the blanket close under my chin. At least Zhilan was still around, along with Grant, Alice, and Hayden. At least I wasn't alone.

I awoke the next night, thirsty and seething at visions of Caterine and Ariane.

Grant, Alice, and Hayden went out again while I stayed in the fort with Zhilan. Back on the couch, I wrapped the blanket around me, closed my eyes, and shoved Edmond's wicked sisters from my mind. Then I couldn't stop thinking about my last sip from Caleb, the fire that had come with it, the sips that came moments before, and all we had shared since his first, soul-warming kiss.

That fire turned dark as coal. Instead of the brilliant flames of Caleb's blood that had fueled the demon me while they burned his life away, an empty black blaze hollowed out an abyss of ever-growing thirst.

Luke's blood would have been incredible—backstage of a show, onstage in between songs, or ripping him away from his microphone and having my drink mid-song.

Caleb's would have been better still—out on his rooftop balcony, under the moonlight in Paris on a trip we surely would have taken, or in the back of the Suburban after he had watched over me all day—after *he* had protected *me*! Ahh! I had *failed* him. Failed. Failed. Failed.

I didn't deserve any blood.

———————————

The third night, Grant, Alice, and Hayden prepared to go to the same hidden club as they had the two previous nights. Horizontal on the couch, staring at the muted television, I declined, at which point, Zhilan also declined.

Grant walked into my view. "Are you sure? It's safe."

"No," I said, aching for blood and angry with my stubborn self for refusing to go with them.

Alice bit her fang into her lip. "It's really fun."

I hated that look. And I hated that she had Grant. She wasn't clinging to him or clutching at him, like she had so often, but she couldn't hide that *damn* look.

"No," I confirmed, and they left.

"You need to feed," Zhilan said.

"I know."

I didn't hate Alice. And I didn't hate Grant. Neither of them, even a little. I was just so jealous. She had him, and he had been smart enough to protect her—to hold on to who he loved.

I raised the volume on the television, where a reporter stood outside the Pentagon.

The anchorwoman said, "That's a lot less than yesterday."

"Yes, significantly less," the reporter agreed. "The generals are cautioning against celebration, but they seem pleased with how many vampires they've been able to eliminate during the day. They're running out of targets, and that's a good thing."

"A very good thing," the anchor said. "What's the mood like out there, aside from the military?"

"Optimistic." The reporter motioned past the camera. "I spoke to people headed in and out of the shopping mall earlier, and the sense I got was of real optimism. There are far fewer vampires around, and like before, blood for them isn't scarce."

"Good to hear," the anchor said. Video from the New York Stock Exchange played with the loud closing bell. "After the break, we'll check on how the financial markets are reacting to the war's progress." The scene faded out to a commercial.

I hit Power, and the television went blank. I closed my eyes—black. I opened them and stared into the blank screen. Nothing. Yet I saw a depth to darkness, like the famished chasm at my core. From that pit, outward, the darkness enveloped me, and it was everywhere. I was surrounded by the black, as I had been lying on Edmond's basement floor—human, nearly drained of blood, and close to dead.

Then it wasn't me. Caleb stood all alone in the void. When my love for him fell short, had I sent him there? Did he dwell in that place, or had he passed through it? Maybe there was no black, and it was and had always been all in my mind. A bright light flickered in the distance. Would I ever know? Or would I merely worry about it forever?

But *forever* didn't mean as much to me as years and

decades and centuries. Centuries! Would I live for *centuries* haunted by the fact that I had loved two deeply, instead of one with all my heart?

Zhilan came over and sat on the other couch. "You look terrible."

"Thanks," I said. "Why didn't you warn me?"

"Hm?"

I sat up. "About Luke and Caleb."

"What would I have said?"

"That I was being stupid."

"You were in love."

"But with both. It was so dumb."

She shrugged. "Love is complicated. I am old and have been in love, and I have met many older than me who have shared stories of their great loves—both brief accounts and enthralling tales of relationships that spanned centuries. Yet I have never met one I considered an *expert* in love. I do not believe that such a thing exists." She folded her hands in her lap. "I did not know how your situation would work out."

"I just thought... I don't know what I thought."

"It could have ended many different ways," she said. "Worse than this, or better."

"They could both be dead." I hated saying the word "dead," but the assessment was true. I could have killed them both.

What I had figured out I wanted, I didn't know if I deserved. But I *really* wanted it, and it wasn't in that fort. It also wasn't the blood I would finally let myself taste, but satisfying my immortal thirst was the first step on the path. I stood. "I'm going to find a drink."

Zhilan nodded. "Good."

———————————

The following evening, near the little lighthouse at the fort where I had said goodbye to Luke, I scattered Caleb's ashes into the Potomac. I didn't know if it was the right thing to do with them. I hadn't fully thought it through when opting not to bury his body. Maybe the ashes should have made their way to his family. Or maybe I should have spread them somewhere else. Switzerland came to mind.

Scattering the ashes meant choosing a place I would always remember, like the gravesite I had sought to avoid by not burying him. But his family might make a gravestone for him in any case, I realized. And the alternative to me dealing with the ashes was asking someone else to, which would have been heartless. I already associated the lighthouse with saying goodbye to Luke, and picking it offered an easy way to feel a small measure of closure—one less thing to worry about.

In the middle of the fort, I met Hayden as he came up the stairs to the lawn, carrying an old brown travel bag and his sword.

I asked, "Looking forward to Texas?"

"I am," he said. "And it'll be interesting to see how things go. This war's winding down already, and the Spectavi that are left are a fractured and weakened group. I hear they can produce synthetic blood again, but since their old factories were shut down, they can't make a lot. And some Spectavi have no interest in the stuff, anyway. They've got problems."

"Good," I said. "It's crazy that *this* is what it took to end their efforts to wipe us out, but—"

"For now," Hayden said. "At least for a while, you're correct that the Spectavi won't hunt Sanguans on as large a scale and with as grand aims as they had been of late. And it *was* a shocking way to 'win' this round, but there will be another round against them. There always is."

I nodded.

"How are you holding up?" he asked.

"I'm all right," I said. "But it's a lot to deal with. I mean, Caleb's really *dead*. I just scattered his ashes, and I don't think everything's totally sunk in."

"It will."

"And my guilt?"

"Will fade," he assured me. "It wasn't all your fault. You must see that."

"I do," I said. "I really do."

"Good."

"But no matter how I look at things, how I rearrange or judge the facts in my head, part of what happened *was* my fault. And no matter how small or large a part, that it led to the disaster of Caleb's life being cut short… being over… it hurts so much."

"In time, you will feel better," Hayden said. "I promise. But you will not forget, that promise I offer with regret. Time is our gift, as it is our curse. In this new world, free of Caterine and Ariane, I implore you to focus on the gift—the opportunity—and to look to the future."

"Yeah," I said with a sigh.

"Until next we meet, best of luck to you, and be safe."

"Same to you, Hayden."

———————————

Late that night, the hardware store parking lot outside D.C. ended up being as empty as we had expected. I stepped out of Zhilan's car and waited with my hands in my jacket pockets as General Sharpe's Impala pulled in next to me. He got out and joined me between the vehicles.

"I saw they promoted you," I said. "Congratulations, Lieutenant General."

"Thank you. It seems my persuasive argument to stay out of your way and *do nothing*, while you took care of the twins, has been the defining moment of my career."

"And you're on the National Security Council now," I said. "Is that why you asked me here?"

He had been appointed assistant to the president for Vampire Policy after the last one resigned, or as everyone assumed, had been forced to resign. The war had been almost universally accepted as a good idea, but years of staunch support for the Spectavi were not judged in as kind a light.

"Something like that," General Sharpe began, then shook his head. "Actually, yes, I'm *not* here to be evasive."

"It wouldn't really matter, would it?" I considered biting him to discover the exact purpose of our meeting—and to understand every last detail of the man who had called it.

"No," he said. "It would not matter. But that's unnecessary. Hear me out."

"Sure."

"The busiest days of the war are already behind us. We've retaken Washington and restored order in all our major cities. For most of your kind—Sanguan and Spectavi—vulnerability at daytime proved impossible to overcome."

I leaned back on the car door. "So I've heard."

"And yet plenty of vampires remain."

"I've heard that, as well."

"We don't know how many, and it's the oldest ones and the smartest that we couldn't get."

"Indeed," I said. "What are you going to do about it?"

"See how it goes."

"See how it goes?"

"The vampire bars and clubs will stay closed," he explained. "The hotels and *all* the businesses will, too. Attacking humans from four to six in the morning—or at any time—will remain illegal. We won't stand for any crimes."

"Are you saying we're supposed to move? Surely a few countries, somewhere in the world, will become havens for our kind."

"Probably," he said. "And move if you want. *Or* stay here and stay out of sight. Don't leave a trail of bodies."

"I don't kill when I drink."

"Exactly," he said. "Plus, I don't want to come after *you*—just as an example—because I don't think I would succeed. And *if* I could, it might take me leveling a city block, or a whole city. Look at Washington. It's a mess."

"Then we're to stay in the shadows…"

"Whatever works. You look human enough—except for

the fangs. And your eyes, when I really look close... but whatever works. Tell the others not to terrorize people. Vampires who do, we will track down, and we will punish severely. But stay out of our way, and you are likely to find that we stay out of yours."

"That's why I'm here? To pass along your message?"

"No," he said. "It would be helpful, but that's not why. I asked you here because I want you to assist me in dealing with those we can't."

I folded my arms. "Why do you think *I'd* be interested in hunting vampires of *your* choosing?"

"Because I need someone I can trust, and I think you'll agree that it needs to be done."

"It sounds very Spectavi."

He shook his head. "We don't want an army of immortals on our side. We don't want another alliance with half of them. Hell, we don't want *anything* on the record, in the news, or in the public eye. We could just use a little help from time to time."

Caterine and Ariane were gone, but there were other ruthless vampires. Some simply enjoyed being cruel to men, women, and even fellow immortals in a variety of ways. I could fight those savages to help maintain a manageable situation for vampires. Or I could fight them because it was right, and the worst of us were very wrong. I could fight them for Victoria's memory, to honor the principle she had been willing to die for—that humanity deserved freedom from the evil of our kind. Or I could fight them because lying on the couch in the fort, huddled under a blanket that offered warmth from cold I would never again feel, would not lead me where I hoped to go.

I stood straight. "You really have the authority for this?"

"Yes. The twins are defeated. On the National Security Council, it's no secret that vampires made that happen, but I'm still getting a lot of credit. I may exercise a certain amount of discretion when discussing specific tactics, but I find myself with all the authority I want."

I took a last moment to think. "I don't go after anyone I don't agree to."

He nodded. "Fine."

"You'll be *asking* me, not *ordering* me to do anything."

"Understood."

"And I may need to bring a few friends along on some missions."

"By all means."

"And this truce, if you can call it that, between your kind and ours—how long does it last?"

"Who can know? I'm fifty-one, and I'm not pushing for early retirement. *I* trust you, and I trust your friends. And *I* would much prefer this arrangement over an effort to wipe every last vampire from the earth. That campaign seems unimaginatively destructive, and likely an impossible task, regardless." He shrugged. "But that's just me. It's a big world, full of people who've recently seen vampires vulnerable like never before. There'll be a new president in a few years. You have my word, and you can trust it, but who knows what the future holds?"

While I was confident that humans posed no threat to

me, and the general had echoed the sentiment, they could be a nuisance, constantly hunting me and my kind. The truce seemed better.

And he had said, "Who knows?" "Who knows?" was uncertainty. For the first time in days, uncertainty had me wanting to be out, off the couch. Uncertainty sounded wonderful. Uncertainty was not certain pain and despair while recounting all my failures or being damned by them. Uncertainty was hope, and surprising and perhaps undeserved as it felt, hope for a future brighter than any life I had ever known.

"General Sharpe." I extended my hand, and we shook. "Give me a call when you've got a target in mind."

"You got it."

I opened my door.

"Thank you," he added.

"And thank you." I shut the door, started the car, and drove off.

22

A month later, in a barn at a farm an hour southwest of D.C., Zhilan wore a short, tight yellow dress with an embroidered red dragon down the front left. She moved rhythmically, gracefully, and purposefully to pounding music, surrounded by sweaty, scantily clad men and women.

With my arms crossed, I stood against the wooden side wall, impressed with the clarity of the songs and the dramatic effect of the occasionally flashing lights. One guy dancing near Zhilan and two girls chatting and laughing on the other side of the room had steel collars adorned with satanic symbols around their necks. Without fear of being drank from by any except those who had locked the collars on them, the three of them appeared not to have a care in the world.

To my right, I overheard the sweet things a devilishly attractive vampire told a gorgeous young woman. She was making him work for the consent to bite he seemed committed to waiting for. A huge male vampire walked past me and nodded to a guy, who froze, then smiled. The immortal grabbed him, sank his fangs in, and when he was done with his drink, added a gentle kiss on the guy's forehead. The mortal man glowed as he resumed dancing.

The barn had been transformed for the night. Rumor was the owner drove a harder bargain to rent the place than the police, who accepted a pittance to look the other way. To explain the limousines and streams of cars driving onto the farm to the locals, their story said that a Russian oil baron had rented out the place to throw a party for his rich friends. Word of the event's true nature had spread to the people and vampires who needed to know, and the place had filled up.

Down the wall to my left, men and women danced around Grant and Alice, who leaned against the weathered wood, sucking from each other's necks. Many stopped and gawked.

Caleb would have gotten a kick out of the barn—before he met me for sure, when he went to clubs all the time. With the war calming and the specters of Caterine and Ariane no longer burdening us, I bet we could have had fun together in a place like that.

That the twins had been reduced to ash was truly a weight lifted, and with it came the appealing expectation that Edmond would also be far less on my mind. William had given me a fresh, if painful, glimpse into my lost life, and it might have been nice to hear less dreadful stories of my time as a scientist from him. Victoria, I would miss dearly.

Yet a certain excitement came with all those vampires from my past being more permanently behind me. Also comforting was that Grant, Alice, and Zhilan's immediate plans had them remaining near D.C. I'd put an end to one immortal in New Orleans, whom General Sharpe and I had agreed needed to be dealt with, and I looked forward to future missions taking me to new places for the first time.

In the United States and all over the world, most of the vampires who continued to be killed by the military were targeted because they had recklessly attacked humans out in the open. My kind was quickly learning the consequences of such behavior. A world that demanded we lead inconspicuous lives was very different, but we could get by. I hadn't spent recent nights hunted by police, soldiers, or other immortals, and while I took my knife, I didn't carry my sword everywhere I went. There were far fewer vampires, but what I watched in the barn proved that our way of life would survive.

A guy with a tribal tattoo covering his arm stopped in front of me and tilted his head to peer at my neck. "Why the cross?"

"Because there's a war going on," I said over the pounding beats.

He straightened his head.

My eyes shifted to the ceiling. "Good." To the ground. "Evil." Then back to the man. "And us in the middle."

He put his arm on the wall beside my head. "Well, which are you?" He licked his lips. "Good or evil?"

I shrugged. "I do the best I can."

A vampire in a latex top and matching skirt grabbed the man from behind. He didn't resist, and she spoke into his ear, "I'm evil, baby. You *need* evil." She chomped into his neck and sucked down a gulp before withdrawing her fangs. She led the man into the dancing crowd.

A clean-cut, athletic guy came by. "Hey."

"Hey."

"You should be dancing," the guy said.

I knew what I wanted, and it wasn't dancing. In the wake of Caleb's death, my low had been lower than any I had ever known. When I had awakened alone in that apartment bedroom for the first time as Erin, fear dominated a multitude of bleak emotions, but drinking Caleb's life away had driven me to a pure low—lower than when I held my murdered friend Kristi's bite-riddled body, lower than when Todd had come home and hadn't remembered me, and lower than when my recklessness had made me a prisoner, locked in a coffin, unable to save Todd before the Spectavi permanently altered his memory. I had found myself lower than when Caterine and Ariane killed Nate in the battle on the rooftop in Paris and lower than when learning of poor June's death, tragically not long before the world became significantly safer for humans.

I would never forget my many decisions that had directly contributed to Caleb's doom. Those memories would always hurt.

"Come on." The guy smiled, and it was a nice smile. "Let's go."

I missed Caleb and Luke, all the time some nights. Every night, I missed them some of the time. But from my low, I could see a new high, one imperceptible to me before, one my wildest dreams had been incapable of dreaming. That high was a love deeper than I had ever felt—one where my previously hard decisions would be no decisions at all. I yearned for a love so powerful it made me ache and so precious that its loss would destroy me. I wanted a love that soared above all else in my life.

I shook my head at the guy in front of me, who likely wasn't that intoxicating high. "No."

"No?"

"No dancing." I rested my arms on his shoulders, around his neck, and focused on the music over the clamor of the crowd.

He pulled me close, hesitantly, and tilted his head.

That high probably wasn't in that barn, but it was out there, somewhere, for me to find one night. I brought my lips to his tensed neck. I had so much life to live, so much more to do.

He kissed my cheek, then my chin. My fangs touched his soft flesh. The hard world had changed, but it still lay before me, a world of opportunity.

I sliced in, and vibrant blood hit my tongue and the back of my throat.

I swallowed it down—*vwoosh!* The furnace within roared to life. A swirling blaze launched out.

I held that man tight and drank. Flames whipped through my vampire body—up and down, then again, softer.

I sipped, and a sphere of fire built at my core. I sucked, and the sphere expanded. From its center, a deepening heat radiated. Molten, pulsating lava washed over the globe.

Fresh blood fueled the fireball, and the pulses became low waves of liquid flame rising from its surface. I sucked, and the waves rose higher… before they crested and fell.

I hurt, yet I burned.

I had scars, yet I had hope.

I would do more than survive, and I would do more than get by. I intended to thrive.

THE END OF BOOK V

CONNECT ONLINE

Thanks for reading. If you enjoyed the story, please leave a review at your favorite online retailer.

Get the latest updates about S.M. Perlow's works by signing up for his newsletter:

smperlow.com/newsletter

Find him online at:

smperlow.com

twitter.com/smperlow

facebook.com/smperlow

Works by S.M. Perlow

Vampires and the Life of Erin Rose

Novels
Choosing a Master
Alone
Lion
Hope
War

Short Stories
Alice Stood Up

—

The Grand Crucible

Novels
Golden Dragons, Gilded Age

—

Other Works

Short Stories
The Girl Who Was Always Single

www.ingramcontent.com/pod-product-compliance
Lightning Source LLC
Chambersburg PA
CBHW031017120726
47905CB00007B/1953